Fiorina

A Woman in the Wind

Pietro Vitelli

Translated from the Italian and Corese by Cinzia Barba

LONGBRIDGE BOOKS

Legal Deposit
National Library of Canada

Library and Archives Canada Cataloguing in Publication

Vitelli, Pietro, 1937-
[Fiorina. English]
    Fiorina : a woman in the wind / Pietro Vitelli ; translated from the
Italian and Corese by Cinzia Barba.

Translation of: Fiorina, storia di una donna nel vento.
ISBN 978-1-928065-06-7 (paperback)

    I. Barba, Cinzia, translator II. Title. III. Title: Fiorina. English.

PQ4922.I84F5513 2016   853'.92   C2016-901991-8

Published by Longbridge Books
PO Box 91510, RPO Robert
Montreal (QC), Canada H1R 3X2
longbridgebooks.com

Cover image: Gioia Miccio
Printed in Canada

To children, grandchildren and great-grandchildren, so that the memory of this story may never die

Note to the Reader

This work is translated from the Corese dialect as spoken in the ancient city of Cori, located 60 kilometres south of Rome. The foreword below, translated from the Italian, makes references to the original work.

This is a work of fiction. The characters in this book are creations of the author's imagination. The character of Fiorina and the events in her life are true accounts compiled from the real-life experiences of women the author has known.

Table of Contents

Foreword

The Language of Life and the Life of Language

"We are only what we remember to be." Within these words, which the protagonist Fiorina addresses to her interviewer-inquisitor-interlocutor – the narrator-author – towards the end of the novel, is enclosed the deep meaning of Pietro Vitelli's fictional account. But very little else in the work's structure is rendered so linearly. Rather, from the outset, the work is complex, layered and even proudly artistically constructed.

Language is at the core of Vitelli's original work. The author refuses to acquiesce to the "neo-dialectal" tendency of recent years, especially as it is manifested in Italian poetry. On the contrary, respectfully mindful of the work of his fellow townsman, Elio Filippo Accrocca (also alluded to in the novel), Vitelli includes poetry in Italian, rather in the Corese dialect. Meanwhile, he uses Corese as the language of narration, thereby building on the current tradition significantly.

Dialect or vernacular language, in the definition given by Dante, is a tool to reveal sounds and meanings not readily accessible otherwise, as if "sucked from the breast of the wet nurse," and gain access to deeper and more expressive emotions. It is not up to Vitelli to create poetic text; instead, he uses his prose to show the disempowered and stereotyped status of contemporary Italian. The author, man of both culture and letters, invents the dialect as a structural vehicle to tell the story – both his own and that of others. And obviously, once such a tool is used, it becomes difficult to ignore its own characteristics.

This is the first innovative aspect in *Fiorina*. Its compositional process is not dissimilar from that of the Italian literary tradition, ranging from Petrarca to Verga, all the way to the late-twentieth century writers. Often, that which is closest can only be recounted once it has gotten further away. Thus, Vitelli places his characters across the Atlantic Ocean in order to recreate his native land and have them speak his native tongue, which, over the decades, has become the language of life.

From the first pages of the novel, the switch from the Italian language to the Corese dialect is abrupt: "Would you like to continue our conversation in Corese" and "Isn't it better if we speak in Corese?" And the story, as alluded to above, emerges in Corese dialect, deeply and constantly, full of the sounds and sensations of the village of Cori, over time and space.

Vitelli is a great novelist and, in as much, he is able to reveal aspects of himself, in some passages epically deep, by telling Fiorina's peculiar and typical story. Her character seems to stand between Alberto Moravia and Elsa Morante's heroines and shows aspects and levels of unknown and disturbing modernity.

Vitelli succeeds in rendering his personal attachment to his native town objectively by extending the narrative to include national and international relationships; one might be tempted to call him "glo-cal," if we could employ such a foreign expression.

The story unfolding between Cori and Toronto, one of the most Italian of cities outside Italy, is characterized by a close relationship with the province of Lazio, and in particular, with the several communities of the Lepini Mountains. Toronto, Montreal and Canada represent either an "elsewhere" or the chosen shelter for the dialect and the literary and human heritage from Cori. Through the transition to a life of exile, the uncultivated dialect acquires a portentous power, writing the script of true life and thus thickening and crystallizing the emotionally charged instants evoked in memory.

The "returns" – which in several chapters highlight the pivotal moments of the different characters as they waver between North America and Italy, Canada and Rome, and finally Cori – cannot but confirm the deep structure of the narrative and substantiate Pirandello's words that "life cannot be lived if it isn't written about."

The events depicted, Fiorina's story – her personal and family episodes, her passion, though unusual, and even extreme in its respectful and timid expression – remains lively, intense, and certainly beyond the reader's expectation.

Finally, the novel also tells the author's story. His search for himself is woven through his narration of another person's story, which becomes his own only when meaning merges with sound. Thus, Fiorina's story becomes the story of the Coresean Vitelli, purposely written in the Corese dialect.

We have come full circle and, perhaps, from the mother tongue of life can emerge a new life for language.

Rino Caputo, Professor of Italian Literature
Department of Literature and Philosophy, University of Rome Tor Vergata

I

First Encounter

Her hair was long, black as coal, and beautiful. She was certainly dyeing it. Her eyes had a penetrating look, even when she merely glanced at you. At seventy, she was still trim and fit, and she carried herself with style and self-possession. She wore tight white pants and a flowery pink blouse, the low-cut neckline almost revealing her full breasts. She was simply stunning, and still able to drive a man crazy. She came to pick me up at the Strathcona Hotel. Looking at her, I felt a bit lightheaded. I had never met her, and no one had ever told me about Fiorina.

The only Fiorina I knew was an old lady who owned an olive grove next to my father's farm. My parents and I used to gather hay there when I was a child. That Fiorina, as well, must have been about seventy years old at the time, but what a difference – night and day! I remembered her as looking older than she was, with a wrinkly face and short, coiled hair – a mix of ash and grey – held up with bobby pins. She used to shoo the chickens back into the coop with a squeaky voice that you would have recognized among a million people. Her grove consisted of about fifty olive trees and a garden. She worked the land herself and raised chickens and hogs. My parents were fond of her. I kind of liked her too. But what a sight!

The Fiorina before my eyes was as straight as the branch of a hazelnut tree – slim, with long, shiny hair. Seeing her walking up to the hotel reception desk you could tell she was a beautiful and elegant woman, full of confidence. She was asking the concierge for a Mr. Vitelli. Then, almost as if she could read my mind – oh, my head was spinning as I contemplated her beautiful walk! – there she stood. And before the receptionist was able to reply, flattering her with my hawk-like eyes, I called out to her: "Fiorina? It's me, Pietro Vitelli. You speak Italian?

"Sure! I am Italian, actually Corese. Welcome to Canada. Are you ready to go? I have the car in front of the hotel."

"Yes, I'm ready. Let's go.

I knew we were going to her house. Right behind her stood a man, probably in his fifties, carefully watching over the scene. He had a friendly but strange smile on his deeply tanned face. I wondered if he was her husband, a co-worker or simply a friend. "Please, let me take this," he said, grabbing hold of my bag, as we headed out of the hotel. It felt like I never left Rome.

You are probably wondering what on earth I was doing in Canada, and why Fiorina had come to pick me up at the hotel. This wasn't the first time I had been in Canada. I had visited a few years earlier as Councillor of Latina, elected in Cori, and later as Councillor of the Lazio Region. I dealt with people who had left the towns where they were born, their parents, their families and their friends. They had departed to put bread on the table and to make a better future for their children. Others left to seek fame and fortune. But that life made it very hard, if not impossible, for them to return home, especially after they had become established and successful. I was also part of the regional immigration office for a number of years and had visited Canada then. I was able to meet many people from different walks of life, common folk and people who had become "important" for one reason or another.

I was so awed and amazed listening to their stories – what they thought of or hoped for in the world in which they came to live, of the things they said to me about the life of famous Italian immigrants of the past – that I wanted write and publish a book on the history of Canada, as I had done on the life of Father Francesco Giuseppe Bressani. Now, I was in Canada to gather material to write a book about the life of Enrico Tonti.

You know how things work: if you are someone – a politician, an artist, a journalist, or some successful business person – they want you as a guest on radio or television, and they let you to speak. They ask you questions and you tell them what you think. In Toronto, and pretty much all over Canada, there are radio and television stations where they speak mainly in Italian. In interviews they ask different things like what's going on, starting with the more important issues and moving on to minor ones. They listen to everything. They ask you to tell them about things going on in your country.

Like most programs that have special guests, often the people listening call in to ask questions or to participate in some quiz. In the last fifteen years, I have visited Quebec and Ontario many times, appearing on a variety of radio and television shows, but I had never heard anyone speaking Corese call into any of these programs. Nor had I ever met anyone from home, other than Eliseo Sciaretta from Giulianello[1], who lived roughly a hundred kilometres north of Toronto. I have known him since we were kids. We had met on the train that took us to school in Velletri (once there was a train that served both Cori and Giulianello).

---

[1]Giulianello is a township six kilometres from Cori

However this time, during one of these radio programs in Toronto the host asked listeners to guess my place of origin based on my dialect. Fiorina called in. She was able to answer correctly that I was from Cori, and thus won a dinner for two at an Italian restaurant in Mississauga. How could I not be curious? At the end of the quiz, I told her to call back.

And that is how I had arranged this appointment. Now, she stood before me, walking out of the hotel followed by the unidentified man. They seemed to be two wonderful people, and I felt at ease with them.

II

Fiorina's Boutique

Meanwhile, in front of the hotel, Fiorina walked up to a car longer than a truck, white, wide, with tinted windows. She opened the door and said, "Please get in." To the other man who was with us she said, "Flav, get in on the other side."

I got in and, wow, I felt like I was in a house, not a car. The seats seemed more like sofa chairs, and there was a television and a bar with plenty of bottles and glasses. Fiorina picked up some sort of phone apparatus to talk to the driver, who was African American.

"Please, Dick, go up Yonge Street, to the store."

The car moved like a boat. I felt like a pasha. Fiorina sat facing me and smiled. She looked happy, as if she had met an old friend or a close relative whom she hadn't seen in years.

"When did you arrive in Toronto?" she asked.

"Five days ago."

"And you're leaving when?"

"Sunday night. In three days."

"Are you going to be busy all the time?"

I became increasingly curious and amazed, as I looked at her. We hardly knew each other, we had barely said a few words, yet she was already casting her spell on me. There was not a wrinkle etched her face. She wore only a bit of makeup. Her hair was perfectly coiffed, not a strand out of place. Her eyes were so bright, they seemed to emit light. Her mouth was wide and full-lipped, revealing ricotta-white teeth that were perfectly aligned.

Certainly, I did have quite a few things to do, and a lot of friends I wanted to visit, I thought. I also wanted to get to Windsor, where I had more friends to see. But this Fiorina had stunned and intrigued me with her beauty – and Lord knows what she could tell me about her life in Cori.

So, naturally I said, "I should be free on Saturday."

"Why don't you come and spend the weekend with us? Flav and I would love it. Sorry, I forgot to introduce him. Flav… Flavio is my son."

Flavio, who was sitting next to his mother, extended his hand to shake mine. It caught me totally by surprise. I would have never guessed that this big man with skin like a Riace bronze statue was her son.

"It is nice to meet you, Flavio."

"You see, we usually spend the weekend up north, just outside Midland, at our cottage on Georgian Bay. If it's not a problem and you are free, even on Sunday, you can take your luggage with you and we'll accompany you directly to the airport."

I really wanted to go, yet I didn't know what to say. Finally, I answered: "I'll call you tomorrow night, not too late, and I'll let you know."

While we were talking in that huge, soundproof boat of a car, without realizing it, we were on Yonge Street, behind a never-ending line of cars and in the middle of skyscrapers, dwellings, and stores of all kinds. On both sides of the street were cinemas, theatres, dance clubs, concert halls, and billboard ads for strip clubs. Yonge Street is a very long street but, contrary to popular belief, it is not the longest street in the world. Nevertheless, it is often referred to as "Main Street Ontario."

I resumed the conversation. "I didn't think you'd speak Italian so well. I thought you might have retained your dialect, which is what usually happens to many immigrants from Lazio who are living in Canada. What did your parents do for a living? Where did you go to school?"

"I'm from Cori, but my father was the son of a wartime general from Piemonte, under the King. He was born and raised in Rome, where he worked at the Treasury Department. He had an older brother who had immigrated to Canada in 1927. My father first saw my mother during one of his many visits to Cori to visit friends. They had invited him to go thrush hunting. My mother was really young when they met that day in the countryside, but it was love at first sight. My father immediately declared his intentions were serious and asked her parents for her hand in marriage. They told him that she was only sixteen. He replied that it didn't matter, that he would wait. To make a long story short, four years later they were married. They went to live in Rome. I was born a couple of years later, in October of 1929.

"Who was your mother? What was her background and from what area?"

"My mother's name is Flavia P. She had the same name as her mother, my grandmother. She was absolutely beautiful. She was the daughter of the town cooper."

"So, then, if you were born in Rome, you must know very little about Cori."

"The truth is that I was born in Cori. My mother wanted to give birth in her mother's house. Back in those days, even in Rome women gave birth at home."

"Since we are both Coresi, do you mind if we speak informally? None of that Mister and Madam. In English we only use the second person anyway. A formal third person equivalent doesn't exist."

"Of course, for me it's a pleasure, Sir. I mean, Pietro. You are an important person and I like you."

Hearing her say "and I like you" didn't only warm my soul, but every part of me – my face, my arms and my chest.

"Thank you. You are too kind. Since you are Corese but probably didn't go often to Cori, you know and understand little of the Corese dialect."

"No! Despite my father's objections, my mother almost always spoke to me in Corese. Besides, I used to go to my grandparents' house for the holidays, where they only spoke Corese."

"Well, then you must have sweet memories and maybe feel a little bit nostalgic about Cori."

We were still travelling along Yonge Street, looking at the stores and the people passing by. We were talking and relaxing, as if we were sitting in someone's living room. Bay Street, the Eaton Centre, College Street and Bloor Street were behind us.

"I do have some sweet memories of Cori, the paradise of my childhood years; but Cori also left me many scars from hell. It is where I met the devil…"

Suddenly, her face turned ashen, her eyes cold and hard. Her mouth closed and the words came out tightly, slowly and frozen. She looked at me as if from an other universe.

"The last time I spoke about those times feels like a lifetime ago. If you want, and if we have time, I will tell you the story. And you can tell me all about Cori and how it looks nowadays."

"You don't have any contact with Cori? When did you leave Cori and Italy altogether?"

"I left Cori at the end of 1944. I went back for a short visit in 1949, and two more short visits in 1950. The same year, on September 12, I left for Canada. I was twenty-one, and my son was five."

The limousine had long passed Eglinton, Lawrence and Finch, three of Toronto's main arteries. We were now in Richmond Hill. Dick eased the car right, onto a side street where I could see a little square surrounded by three-storey houses and many different shops. The limo came to a halt in front of a two-storey building that was roughly twenty metres long. Dick got out and came around to open our doors.

As we emerged from the limo, Fiorina instructed me to leave my bags. "Come, I'll show you our shop."

She proceeded towards a storefront with huge plate glass windows, gleaming with luxury items. It was a jewellery store! Above the entrance the sign read Fiorina's Boutique. Flav entered first, as the automatic doors parted. On either side of the doors stood two armed security guards.

The store seemed like a parade ground, very wide and deep. The neon lights hanging from the ceiling made the interior extremely bright. All of the glass cases were under lock and key. Behind the glass cases were jewels of every kind – gold, silver, platinum, crystal and many shiny diamonds – not only jewels and gold, but all sorts of items of different shapes and sizes and for different uses.

There was an exceedingly long counter covered with a red velvet cloth. Behind the counter stood twenty or so very attractive young salesmen and women. They were all attired in black pants and a white shirt. The men sported red ties and the women light blue ones. They went about their business, but acknowledged the presence of their boss with smiling eyes and nods.

Fiorina appeared to take in everything at once, as she strode across her store. Flav walked ahead of her and I followed behind. I felt somewhat intimidated. We stood in front of a dark wooden door. Flav opened it and walked in. Fiorina stepped aside.

"Please, sir, enter. I am sorry…I mean, after you, please."

It was quite obviously her office. It was wide, full of heavy dark wooden furniture, including a desk, cupboards and cabinets. There was a dark brown leather sofa with two matching leather armchairs and a crystal chandelier with countless bulbs. A painting hung on the wall behind the main desk. Those who know art would easily recognize it as a Tamara de Lempicka painting, and it certainly did not look like a copy. Goodness only knows how much it was worth. But there were also many other paintings, all studies of the female form. On another wall hung a Frida Kahlo self-portrait, also apparently authentic. Oh, my God! Where am I, I wondered.

Fiorina pointed to one of the leather armchairs. "Please, make yourself comfortable." And then to Flav: "Flav, offer Pietro something to drink."

Flav went over to the cupboard and pulled out a tray. He placed three glasses and a few bottles on it and, turning to me, asked: "What would you like, Mr. Pietro?"

I took a long look at the tray to see what was on offer and said, "Listen, Flav, there is no need to be formal. We can address each other by our first names."

After looking over the bottles again, I nodded at the Martini bottle. "A bit of Martini, thanks."

Meanwhile, Fiorina sat down on the armchair facing me. She also asked for a glass of Martini but told Flav to add some ice. There must have been a fridge in the cupboard because he returned with an ice bucket. He poured himself another Martini and we all took two ice cubes each.

There was a knock on the door.

"Come in," said Fiorina.

24

A fit, dark-featured young woman walked in. Her straight hair was tied up in a ponytail. She had such a pleasant personality and features that she could probably warm even a dead man. She told Fiorina that someone wanted to speak to her. Fiorina told the girl that the client could wait. When the girl left, Flav sat on the sofa, gave his glass a swirl and offered a welcome toast. The three of us clinked our glasses. Then Fiorina asked her son to deal with the client, because she was busy with a really important guest.

Fiorina sipped her Martini slowly. She crossed her legs and smiled at me. She was very beautiful. Not only her face, but everything about her – her hips, long legs and her curves.

Finally, I found my courage and with confidence I said, "Fiorina, my compliments! This 'boutique' seems to be worth millions. You really did find fortune in Canada. It's a pleasure to see a person from Cori, from my hometown, who has achieved so much. I don't know how long it took you to build up this fortune. I'd be interested, if possible, to hear the story of this enviable success. Another thing that makes me a little curious: you said that you left Italy when you were twenty-one and your son five, but you haven't said anything about your husband. I hope to meet him."

Fiorina's face darkened and turned to stone.

"Pietro, my story isn't the shiny glitter that you see. My husband unfortunately died thirty years ago. I met and married him in Canada. Flav is not my husband's child, and Flav has never met his father. I met that bastard in the ugliest and most cruel hour of my life."

My jaw dropped as a heavy silence fell over the room.

"Forgive me. I shouldn't have brought it up."

"Don't worry. You couldn't have known and I understand that you're curious. But I already told you that the time I spent in Cori was full of happy memories and worry-free days, followed by a terrible phase of my life. I still have bleeding scars deep in my soul. To go back there even through my memories is really painful. I never went back to Italy or to Cori and I have no contact with the people there. Yet, Cori is still a living part of me, even if you are the first person from Cori that I've seen in the last fifty years."

"Let's not talk about it anymore; I don't want to bring up painful memories."

"I didn't think you were such an intriguing, curious and good-looking man. Listening to you talk on the radio I knew right away that you are cultured and knowledgeable, with a life full of experiences, and maybe I agreed to meet you because after all this time I needed to talk, to confide in someone, to go back to my homeland, even if it's only through my memories. So don't worry. It's almost noon. Let's go home and get something to eat. We can continue our conversation there. Let me just make a quick call."

She spoke with someone at her house. She told them to make sure that everything was ready in an hour.

When she hung up, I said, "After all this time you've been in Canada, I'm surprised to hear that your Italian is still excellent."

"As you already know, here in Toronto there are many Italians, even if their Italian is often influenced by their dialect. Notwithstanding, many of the people who came here continued their studies. I should also tell you that after a long period of time and with some difficulty, since I had a young son, I was able to go to University, where I studied Italian literature. Let's go!" she said as she stood up.

She looked at me with a smile so electrifying that it could bring back the dead. She walked toward the door. I followed. We made our way back through the big store full of shoppers, yet I didn't see Flav. He must have been in some other office.

"Wait a moment." She told me.

I waited as Fiorina headed towards a glass door. She went in. Maybe that was where her son was talking to the clients. Many of the other clients walked around the shop looking at the glass cases. Some were alone, but many more were in couples. You could tell from the way they behaved that they were sure about what they were doing, and that money was no object. Some whispered closely. Others handed the salesperson their credit card. Others, still, headed toward the exit with satisfied smiles, clutching their luxuries in small boxes or little paper bags with blue cord handles, as if they had just won the lottery.

Fiorina emerged smiling. She seemed even more beautiful.

"We can go. Flav will catch up with us later."

Fiorina said goodbye to a few people and then we left. The big limousine was still at the curb, waiting. Dick opened the doors for us and we slid in. He got in behind the wheel.

"Dick, please drive us home!"

The limo moved away smoothly, as if it were navigating in a calm sea. It manoeuvred back towards Yonge Street. But instead of going up Yonge Street it turned left and headed down the street. We travelled for a few kilometres; then, at a traffic light we turned left again. Eventually, the limousine turned onto John Street.

"Is this your limousine?" I asked Fiorina.

"No, of course not! We rent it for special events or to welcome somebody, in particular when I pick them up at the airport or at the hotel – and for me, you are somebody particularly important."

I looked at Fiorina with admiration and empathy, curious to hear what she has to say, curious about the way she moves. All of a sudden a light bulb went on in my head.

"Fiorina, would you like to continue our conversation in Corese?"

"What a strange request! Converse in Corese? In Canada? It's been half a century since I spoke it. I guess it could be interesting..."

"A strange kind of trust seems to be developing between us, something special is happening. I am taken by this growing friendship. I don't know if you feel it; something that binds the present, the new world, the limousine, the jeweller's store to an ancient world, that of your childhood, that of donkeys and oxen on the streets of Cori, that of adolescence, of youth. The Corese dialect could be the ideal language to remember it in."

"I can try. I have no clue what could come out of my memory, but your proposal seems fun, and maybe it will be less painful to recall my past."

Fiorina looked at me and smiled. From the car window I could see that we were heading toward a residential area. Dick slowed the car down, stopped in the middle of the road, let a couple of cars go by and then turned left. We turned onto a side street. The sign read Deanbank Drive. The houses looked very luxurious, even the semi-detached ones.

"This is a really nice area! It seems to be exclusive, for people who are well off..."

"Yes, this is a very green area, clean, calm, homes for families that are generally well off and upper-middle class. We are in the City of Markham."

We were in an area where there were even more trees and more green spaces, with houses in the middle of huge gardens. Every now and then I glimpsed swimming pools.

"Here we are, we've arrived. Is that how you say it?" Fiorina spoke in dialect.

I was caught off guard, since I had already forgotten that I had proposed that she speak Corese.

"And this is something that I didn't expect at all. It is a pure Corese dialect!"

Dick, in the meantime, had turned the car onto a private street lined with tall trees that must have been a few hundred metres tall. He parked the limo in a square lot in front of a two- storey house with a balcony. He opened the door for Fiorina and she invited me out, reminding me about my bag. She took twenty dollars out of her wallet and gave them to Dick. You could tell that it was just a tip. I knew very well how much taxies cost – imagine a limo. Then Fiorina told him to say hello to some Robert fellow and that in a couple of days she would pass by. I speculated that Robert must be the owner of the limousine company. Dick said goodbye, got back in that boat of a car and left.

III

Fiorina's House, Jadwiga

The limousine drove down the secluded path and away. Fiorina, with the walk of a thirty-year-old and at a relaxed pace, headed towards the door of the house. She took hold of my hand and said, "Come on!"

A warm flush washed over me, and I felt strangely calm as I approached this paradise. Fiorina opened the door and we went in.

We entered the living room, which was wide and long and full of luxurious furniture. I didn't see any chandeliers; however, there were floor lights that shone upwards to the ceiling. Opposite the door, a large window offered the view of a large green field full of trees adorned in the colours of fall. The other walls seemed to be made of a light-coloured wood. Near the wall on the right, a wooden staircase led up to the second floor. The wall on the left had an arched doorway that led to more rooms.

We passed underneath the arch and found ourselves in a smaller room that contained a big rectangular table almost ten metres long. An area of the table had been set. From another door a woman emerged.

She appeared to be in her forties, with red hair, blues eyes and a nice round face. With a pleasant smile she said hello and welcomed me. Even she was wearing pants. A white blouse covered her large breasts. She was also wearing a light blue bandana. She told us that everything was ready. Fiorina thanked her, turned to me and introduced me to Jadwiga, the housemaid, adding that they had spent many years together and that she was more friend than maid. I noted that she was of Polish descent but kept it to myself.

Fiorina pointed to a door. "There's a washroom there if you need it. If not, you can sit on the sofa and wait ten minutes. I'm going to change."

She proceeded up the stairs; in the meantime I went to the washroom. It was quite a nice bathroom for just a guest bathroom. It had everything. When I was done, I returned to the armchair and sat down. In front of the armchair was a cute little square coffee table with various magazines and newspapers piled on top. I grabbed a copy of *The Globe and Mail,* but instead of reading I continued to look around.

One of the dining room walls was all glass. Beyond it, I could see the green field. A bit further away, a forest. The trees were tall, and their leaves were a yellowish-green mixed with some red. It was a beautiful view. A thousand different thoughts came to mind. It really is a luxurious house, I thought to myself. Back home we would call it a *villa.* On the other walls were paintings of landscapes depicting rivers, lakes, woods and country scenes – probably the work of Canadian artists. It seemed that Fiorina had had a tough life in Italy, but here she was making up for it. I was curious to know how she managed to obtain so much. While I sat pondering these questions, every now and then Jadwiga would come in to fix something or to bring something to the table. She seemed to be on mute, only smiling at me.

Fiorina returned. "Come, let's sit at the table and have a welcoming toast. Flav says he's sorry, but he has to stay and work. He doesn't know when he will be able to make it, but he'll join us later."

Jadwiga came flying in as if she had already been summoned, without us having said a word. She handed us two full glasses of Martini.

"Thank you for welcoming me. I never could have imagined anything like this. My happiness is overflowing. To find myself in Canada with a lady who was born in Cori is such an amazing experience that it will stay in my heart for my rest of my life. Tell me, how did you do it?"

"All in good time. I will tell you all about it," Fiorina said with a happy expression on her face.

We sat at the table and Jadwiga served us in silence. Our first dish was vegetable soup, followed by stuffed turkey, as if it were Thanksgiving Day. There was a Canadian red wine from the Niagara Region, salad with avocado, and an apple pie for dessert. Later, while Jadwiga cleared the table, Fiorina led me to a sofa where we sat down to wait for our coffees.

"In 1950, what made you decide to come to Canada?"

"Mostly because there was no one left for me in Rome or in Cori. At the end of October 1949 my grandmother died. My grandfather had already left us at the end of 1947. My mother was an only child. There were some cousins with whom we had lost contact, and others we didn't get along. I never did know why."

"But what about your mother, your father…"

"The Lord took her with Him due to an incurable illness. She was only forty years old, and God only knows how much she suffered, and me along with her. I wouldn't wish what I endured on anyone. If heaven exists, my mother should be there now. After my mother died, my father was never the same. The pain ate away at his soul. He got sick and in February 1950 he died too. All I had was my young son. My heart was like a pillow full of needles. For a couple of years, my father's brother, who lived in Canada, had been writing to me and telling me to come here because I was alone. His house was big and I could find a better future for me and my son."

The skin on Fiorina's face grew taut and seemed to show all the suffering in the world. It was still beautiful but different. A dark shadow came over her green eyes. My heart opened up even more to this intriguing and mysterious stranger. In the meantime, Jadwiga brought the coffee.

"Why don't you get a cup for yourself and sit down with us for a bit, please?" Fiorina implored Jadwiga.

It was then that I noticed how pretty Jadwiga was, too. She had a round face with wide eyes that shone. They were the colour of ash, and her lips were soft.

"Jadwiga is everything to me. Without her I wouldn't know what to do. I first met her during breakfast with a client I was meeting at the Four Season's Hotel. She had arrived in Canada not long before from Poland and was working as a waitress at the hotel bar. She had served me breakfast. A bit of small talk and I found her to be nice, kind and gentle right away. At home I needed someone to give me a hand. I went to see her again and I asked her if she'd like to come stay at my house and work for me. I offered her a room in my house, meals, and the same pay she was getting from the bar. She couldn't believe it. That was it, and now she's one of us."

"I think you made a good decision. She seems well-mannered, respectful and on top of things."

"You should know that she was enrolled at the university in Torun, Poland, studying for a biology degree. I don't know where it is, but she told me that it's a beautiful and important city. I told her to continue her studies here, that I would help her financially. She didn't want to, though she did a course to be a nurse. She would have found a good job without trying, but she preferred to stay with me."

"Wow, Jadwiga studied in Torun. That's nice, I've been to Torun many times myself and I have a bunch of friends there."

Jadwiga returned and sat down as she thanked Fiorina, who told her that I had been to Torun many times. Jadwiga's face lit up. She was incredulous.

"Really? How? I'm from Wadowice, near Krakow, where I lived until I was twelve. Then I went to Kruszwica with my father, who went there to work as an engineer in a sugar factory."

Jadwiga remained speechless and stunned to know that at Kruszwica, not too far from Torun, near Lake Goplo, I had spent some of my best vacations over the years. All the while she had lived there for ten years before her father went back to Wadowice. What a small world after all! Many times I had stayed at the hotel across from the sugar factory in Kruszwica. In Kruszwica I spent some amazing and unforgettable days when I was still a young lad. I will never forget the spectacular trips on the sailboats on Lake Goplo with my friends Jan, an engineer at the sugar factory, Karol, and Roza, who was one of Jan's close friends, even though she used to swarm around me like a bee over honey. I told her all about Mysia Wieza, the tower of the rats, and the story of Prince Popiel, who commanded those places years ago, and about his misfortune when he was swarmed and eaten by an army of rats. I told Jadwiga the little I knew about Poland, as she stared at me with her eyes shining in disbelief. Clearly, she still loved her homeland.

Fiorina's face was relaxed as she followed our conversation in silence, smiling curiously, while listening to what Jadwiga and I discussed. The phone rang. Jadwiga got up to answer it. After a while she came back looking serious.

"Flav said that something came up at the last minute so he'll be late. He should be back just in time to bring Mr. Pietro to the hotel."

"Tell Flav there is no need. I'll bring him myself or have him accompanied."

Jadwiga, who had finished her coffee, was eager to get back to her work. Fiorina asked me if I wanted to rest. Even if the thought of having a nap after eating was really tempting, I didn't come to meet with Fiorina just to fall sleep.

"The thing is, Fiorì[2], the time that I have with you is so short that if I can talk as long as possible with you, I would feel a lot better than sleeping for three days. What you've told me until now has already given my heart a jolt, not to mention that it has piqued my curiosity. I want to know everything; tell me what you remember from when you were a child, of Cori and how it was. Start from the beginning and tell me what happened and how you became who you are."

"You would need to stay at least a year for me to tell you the complicated story of my life, though I think the time has come for me to get everything out. It could just be that the Almighty, who knows everything, sent you here on purpose. Come, let's go out into the garden. It's October, but it's a nice day and we can relax while we talk. Even if I already know that bringing everything that happened to me to the surface will give me some pleasure, it will also be very painful, for there are some terrible scars."

---

[2]In conversation in the Corese dialect, the person's name loses the last syllable and the last vowel becomes accented.

IV

Cori: Days of Youth

We got up and walked across the living room. We passed a big shiny window and entered a garden that was long and wide with a lawn that seemed to have been manicured by a barber. It extended towards the hills, where you could see tall trees of many different kinds, encircled by rosebushes. Approximately ten metres from the house there was a swimming pool, now covered for the season, and around it lots of green grass and a bench. The sky-blue plastic pool cover was almost completely blanketed by leaves, which had turned an ugly shade of brown.

Fiorina turned onto a trail that ran towards the side of the hill. She walked in front of me and my eyes were fixed entirely on her. She really was a fine-looking lady. Her legs were long and straight, and her skin-tight pants revealed strong yet soft curves. We came up to a maple tree that was about twenty metres tall and several metres thick, with a bench under it. The tree was a riot of colours: some leaves were a greenish-yellow, some yellow and some red. It really was stunning.

"Let's stop here for a bit." We sat down.

"Well, here we are. I wonder, where should we start?"

I glanced at her curiously and in silence, anxiously waiting for her to say something.

"You already know that I was born in Cori. My mother used to say that it was a Friday, as the sun was setting, and from the window a yellowy-red light poured in. The room was comfortable, and inside it there was her mother, her grandmother, a certain Tutarella and the midwife. After a few pushes and contractions, all of a sudden I was born. It was a very difficult yet routine birth. She used to say that it seemed as though I was impatient and I couldn't wait to get out, not to mention that I started crying right away, almost as if I was saying, 'Here I am, and now you have to take care of me.' My mother said that the happiness she felt during the first hour when I was born she never felt again.

"The house quickly filled up with people. My grandfather arrived with tears in his eyes. He left a young lad hammering the barrels in his shop. Then my grandfather was dispatched quickly to the post office to send a telegram to my father who was working in Rome. In those days it wasn't easy to travel. My father saw me the day after I was born and my mother used to tell me that as soon as he set foot in the house he started crying.

"I'm sure you realize that I don't remember anything about my first couple of years. One of my first memories, when I think of that world, is when we went to Cori by train. I was so excited during the trip that I found it hard to contain myself, as if I was going to jump out of my skin. The bus took us from the train station and let us off in the valley side of town, in Cori Valley, near a fountain. There we found my grandfather, who tied my mother's luggage to the donkey's saddle. Then he took me and cradled me in his arms. We crossed the entire town. Everyone we met said 'hello,' and to me it seemed like I was sitting on a cloud. My father had remained in Rome. When we got home, my grandmother flew down the stairs and hugged my mother. She threw her arms around her neck as if she never wanted to let go. Then she turned to me. She took me in her arms, showering me with kisses while she went up the stairs and brought me in the house.

"Every year we spent a lot of time in my grandparents' house, not only for the usual feasts and birthdays, but during the entire year. This went on until I was six years old and I started going to school. During the school year I used to be in Rome for eight to nine months. When I went to Cori, it was like being in heaven. My grandparents used to let me do whatever I wanted. Often, my mother would leave me with them for weeks at a time. My grandfather used to work for a cooper. Sometimes I would go visit him there. I would remain hypnotized and enchanted, watching how he would bend and curve the wooden pieces, preparing the rings and slowly, with a lot of patience, make barrels of all shapes and sizes. When he hammered the rings with an organized rhythm, I felt like I was listening to a concert that was just for me.

"My grandfather used to love singing. Often, he sang arias from romantic operas. I never did find out how he learned them. One time, perhaps when I was ten, he brought me to see an opera at the *Olimpo*. If I remember correctly, that was the name of the theatre in Cori. To listen to him sing between the hammer strokes on the steel gave me a pleasure that I can't describe. I would have never left my grandfather's shop while I was watching him work; however, most of my time was spent with my grandmother.

"The kitchen was the heart and soul of that house. It was a large room, somewhere between fifteen and twenty metres square, with a big square table in the middle and a huge cupboard on one side full of plates, glasses, knives, cups, bottles and other things. Against the other wall was my grandmother's kneading-trough, where she used to mix flour to bake bread, and where she used to let it rise before putting it in the oven. She used to store it for days. Beside the knead-ing-trough there was another cupboard full of all of God's goodness: oil, vinegar, wine, lard, sausages, codfish, beans and fava beans, flour, thin flour and bran. The cooked food she stored in the bottom part of the kneading-trough. What I liked best when I was in the kitchen with my grandmother was mixing flour to make homemade pasta, donuts and spiced sponge cake. I used to like getting covered in flour and seeing how flour, water, eggs, with enough mixing, turned into something.

"In the morning I liked to wait behind the door, anxious to hear the knock of the milkwoman. Her name was Lucia. She was a short, puffy woman, approximately forty. Her hair was curly and red, held away from her face with bobby pins. Her face was square and pleasant. She was always smiling and carried a strange container on her head. The cylinder tin, measuring about seventy centimetres in length, was narrow at the top and its lid was tied to the container with a little chain. On the side of the container there was a small receptacle, also tied, and inside there was a tin cup, which was used to measure the milk that Lucia sold. Every cup cost about twenty-five liras. My grandmother used to buy two cups, or about half a litre. When the milkwoman got to our house, we would have breakfast with milk and barley coffee. Grandmother would break up a piece of bread or a cookie in the milk for me and that was my breakfast. It was a few bites' worth of paradise."

As Fiorina continued telling her story, I felt like a child listening to my own grandmother who used to tell me fables. Fiorina's face was really beautiful and at the same time serious as she spoke. Her eyes were lost in the distance. The light in her eyes was a pale green and you could read the words in them before she even pronounced them.

The sun was still up and it was nice sitting there. But Fiorina got up and I got up after her. She placed her arm through mine. She started walking down a little path near the hill. All of a sudden she turned to me and stared into my eyes: "Do you really want to hear all this?"

I stopped in front of her: "Fiorì, the emotions that you are giving me I'll never forget. Go ahead and tell me."

Fiorina smiled, started walking again and continued with her story.

"Those years that I spent in Cori, it was like living in paradise. I was probably seven or maybe eight years old. Some Sundays my grandparents brought me to a shepherd in the countryside. They would make me get up early and get me ready. Whether it was just us or some friends or neighbours, we would cross the whole town. I was amazed when we passed in front of the elementary school. A couple of years before they were excavating the foundations. I was scared when I went by it, and there were a lot of people working there. Now it was a big building that left me in awe. It was the biggest building in all of Cori.

"When we walked by the elementary school, my grandfather would always whine and complain. He didn't like that building. He used to say that it had ruined the town. The school was needed, but they could have built it in San Francesco, or Stozza, Arboreto, or Begliovetè, instead of digging up all the stones in the centre of the town and detracting from the town's ancient beauty."

I felt like a ham listening to her grandfather's judgment. Who knows what the other people of Cori thought while they were doing the work? Who knows how many discussions on the verandas of the townsfolk must have taken place with regard to the location of the school. I also think that with the machines used back then, it must have taken quite a while to finish and, more importantly, it probably created jobs for a lot of people.

"Your grandfather had a really nice character! But I think he was right. Who knows what he would have thought if he saw them building the middle school between the Tempio d'Ercole and le Pietre."[3]

Obviously, the school was needed. The new building became equally famous among the residents as a point of reference. It was in the middle of the town and within easy walking distance, even if a few people already had cars. Today, it would be better if there wasn't a school in the middle of the town, since there are so many.

"My grandfather was quite a character; he didn't keep any of his thoughts to himself. Even though he wasn't a socialist, he was all work and church; however, due to his big mouth he had received a couple of beatings with sticks, and a few bottles of castor oil had been forced down his throat by the fascists."

"It's unbelievable. What absurd times those were. So your grandparents took you often to the shepherd's hut?"

"When I was in Cori, for me those were real feast days. We would pass in front of the medical clinic and climb up the little staircase that brought us to a little alley with a steep slope. Under the Zoppi's garden, we passed by a little tower and we would arrive at Piazza Monte. We went down Regina Elena Street, which brought us to the tiny church of San Nicola. Near an olive grove with a red gate there was the shepherd's hut of Arduina. My grandmother said that in all of Cori she made the best ricotta cheese. It was full of people every time we went. It was a big shepherd's hut made up of three smaller huts. In the largest of the huts there was a big burning fire with a huge pot on it. There were all kinds of people – small, big, rich, poor – shoemakers, tailors and employers. Everyone had their own tin. My grandparents had even brought a tin for me. They would break up a piece of bread in my tin.

"Arduina, once she saw me, would run over to me and, as she said hello, would fill up the special spoon with the hot whey and she'd

---

[3]Tempio d'Ercole and le Pietre are famous monuments in Cori.

fill my tin with it. You could smell the herbs, sheep and peppermint all mixed together. Once the bread was soaked with the whey we would eat all of it and, later, Arduina would come with some hot ricotta cheese. It had such a soft and smooth taste I was never able to find here in Canada. I can still remember how it tastes.

"Some Sundays even my mom came with us. She would dress up fancy, as if she had to go to church, but there was no way of convincing her to go to Arduina's. We all had to follow her because she wanted to go to the Tratticci's shepherd hut, which was near the Madonna of the Soccorso[4]. That's where I went, where we all went, the last time that we went to the shepherd's hut. It was 1943.

"I think that was also the last time that I saw my mother bursting with happiness. We were all together – me, my mother, my grandparents, and even my father. While we climbed up the hill, my grandfather sang 'Figaro qua, Figaro là' under his breathe. My mother would answer with the sound of 'Tango delle capinere.[5]' After Segnina Square, as we were heading to the Soccorso, there was a group of people that had gathered and had started to sing 'faccetta nera, bella abbissina.[6]' I cannot describe my grandfather's face and all the horrible things he said. I was already grown up and I understood well. He rolled his eyes and said that the fascists and their friends would ruin us all.

"But my mother was happy. She was the prettiest of them all, even more than the girls that were younger than her. She was crazy about Tratticci. He was a short, plump man, dressed in ash-coloured velvet pants. He also wore a heavy sheep wool sweater with a black vest over top. There was always a hat on his head, even when he was in the hut fixing the fire or turning the ricotta in the pot. The first ricotta cheese that he made was for my mother. After he finished

---

[4]Famous sanctuary on the hill two kilometres from Cori.
[5]Famous Italian song.
[6]Famous fascist song written in 1935.

43

serving everyone, before making cheese, he would step outside onto the porch where we were gathered together eating, sit down on a wooden stool, smoke his pipe and tell stories. My mother never tired of listening to him."

We got to the top of the hill. Fiorina had stopped walking. We turned around. In the distance you could see the meandering Don River as it disappeared into the yellow-green woods. Even further away, towards the horizon, the trees became a reddish colour, blending with the chocolate-coloured houses scattered along the river bank. On one side, the luxurious green that seemed never-ending was a beautiful golf course.

Fiorina's face was calm and beautiful. The storytelling was making her feel good.

"Fiorì, do you know that all of this is amazing? You are talking about places and people that I know. I knew Arduina the shepherd. Even I as a child have been to the shepherd's hut. What you don't know is that I was born on Regina Elena Street and often Arduina used to come to our house to sell us ricotta. When you used to go to the shepherd's hut I could have been no more than four or five years old. Maybe on some Sunday we might have both been at the same shepherd's hut without knowing it, and without ever expecting that we would meet fifty years later in Toronto.

"I don't ever remember being at Tratticci's; however, I did meet him and I remember him as if it were yesterday, walking across Segnina Square on a donkey with a bundle of hay tied to the side of the saddle, with his black hat on his head and his pipe in his mouth. To me he looked like a king."

Fiorina came closer. She took my arm and put her radiant face close to mine and gave me a kiss on my cheek. My face was on fire and I felt it turn pepper red. "Wow, God must have sent you. What luck that the other day I just happened to be listening to the radio.

Maybe the time has come for me to tell my story, to talk to someone who is really interested. It's a shame that you have to leave so soon."

"I love listening to you tell your story. I hope that I can learn more about you and Cori when you were younger. Today in Cori, Tratticci and Arduina are long gone. Not even Regina Elena Street exists."

"How can that be? There's no Regina Elena Street?"

"The street that is there now is called San Nicola Street. I grew up playing on that street and even now I spend peaceful days there and, sometimes due to the way life is, even the saddest. Even the Church of San Nicola is no longer there. For a long time after the war, it was occupied by refugees and homeless people, and at one point they destroyed it. Now, where the church once was, there is a piece of land that has been turned into a garden. Today, the children don't even know that a church once stood there. When I was young, they used to hold a feast there and everyone would come together – the people from the valley side and those from the mountain side of Cori."

"Most likely, I wouldn't even recognize Cori today," Fiorina sighed.

"Why don't you come and visit some time? You could stay at my house."

"It's impossible. Cori, for me, was the place of my sweet child-hood days, but it was also the place of bitterness and misfortune. I have to tell you the truth, and I feel that I'm very fortunate to be here in Toronto. I found myself and I like it; however, I also like telling you about Cori. It seems that I am reliving a dream. You know better than me that those dreams seem real; but they are only uncontrolled fantasies that come into your mind, Lord knows how. Everything that I'm telling you about Cori is true, but they seem like dreams. Yes, so much time has gone by that it seems all like a big illusion."

As Fiorina was telling me this, we started walking back down the hill. A strange silence came over us. We walked really slowly. Fiorina again offered me her arm. I looked at the Don River in the distance, a meandering silver line that disappeared. We arrived in front of Fiorina's beautiful two-story house and to break the silence I said: "Why don't you tell me more memorable things about Cori when you were young."

"Everything, at least for me, was nice and beautiful in Cori up until the beginning of the war and the fall of Mussolini. There were a lot of poor people and very few aristocrats. The owners behaved like real owners. My grandfather couldn't stand them. He didn't have anything and used to beg to get a few days of work. The decision-makers were on the side of the rich landowners, obviously not for the poor. My grandfather was dying inside. Almost all the people that worked the land had to give the better half of the harvest to the owners. Very few people had inherited something, and to dig and sell what little was needed to live was difficult.

"I often heard discussions in my grandfather's house about the good harvest years and the bad, how many barrels the people ordered or how many were brought in to be fixed, and how many paid and how many didn't. My grandfather was a craftsman so he wasn't that bad off. But when it was a year of hardship and drought, he couldn't put away oil or wine like the tailors, shoemakers, saddle makers, chair makers and blacksmiths. It was difficult to make it through the winter. The people from Cori were connected to one another. In the town there were many shepherds, but their herds of sheep, goats and pigs were diminishing. The shepherds came also from Carpineto, Segni, Gorga, and perhaps also from townships farther away. There was a lot of pain and suffering. There weren't any feasts or parties. Many people weren't treated fairly.

46

"My grandfather couldn't stand those who were in charge because they only took the landlords' side. When someone tried to defend, to criticize, or to demand some rights, often they were abused and punished and forced to drink castor oil. He wasn't against those who were in power; however, he couldn't bear injustices and unfairness. He would talk back. My grandmother used to tell him to mind his own business, yet he couldn't stay quiet when he saw that poor people were treated wrongly or unfairly, because it was as if they were doing it to him. There were unpleasant things that one saw or heard. But for me staying in Cori was like staying in heaven. I could have never guessed what was going to happen and everything that the war would bring."

We had made it back at the house. Jadwiga was approaching, a happy look on her face. She told us that Flav had called to say that he was sorry but he wouldn't be able to make it. Fiorina told her to prepare some tea for all three of us. We sat in the armchairs, facing each other. Fiorina crossed her long, beautiful legs; she smiled at me with a calm, relaxed and sweet expression.

V

The Corese Way of Life and Immigration

Fiorina was sitting in front of me in the living room, which was illuminated by the bright yellow light of an amazing sunset. She enchanted me, appearing to be twenty years younger. Her mouth was like a magnet. Jadwiga brought a tray with three tea cups and a plate containing different kinds of teas, a tea kettle, a sugar bowl and silver teaspoons.

I took a bag of green tea and put it in my cup, Jadwiga smiled as she filled it with boiling water. Then she filled Fiorina's and then her own. We drank in silence, exchanging inquisitive glances. Eventually, Jadwiga returned to the kitchen with the cups. Fiorina smiled. Clearly, she was happy.

"I'm sorry that you have to leave so soon. Why don't you call the hotel and stay at my house tonight? I have a guest room and maybe Flav will join us later on."

"I would love to, that way I can hear more of your story. Getting to know you will help satisfy my curiosity, which is growing stronger by the minute. Unfortunately, it isn't possible because people are waiting for me. If you don't mind, can you call me a taxi? Seeing how the hotel is so far away, I don't want to bother you, and in forty minutes I must be going. Otherwise, I will be late and I don't like making people wait for me. There's still time for you to tell me more from your childhood in Cori."

Fiorina got up and disappeared into the kitchen. I looked at her as if I had known her my whole life. Tall, she moved like a princess and walked like a ballerina. She had made her way into my heart. She came back and sat down.

"I told Jadwiga to call a taxi and to be here in half an hour. I was thinking that Saturday and Sunday you could come spend the weekend at our cottage in Midland."

"I don't want to make any promises that I can't keep, but I will try to come at all costs."

"Please come. I don't want to nag you, but as you can see I like talking to you. I obviously can't talk like this about my hometown Cori, not to mention about my past, with just anybody. I'll be waiting. And don't forget, Flav will come pick you up at the hotel."

"I like listening to you and I will try to fix things in my schedule so that I can come. Even for me, listening to you makes me feel like I'm back in the days when I was just a young boy. What did you like to do while you were in Cori?"

"I really liked the time of the year when we harvested the grapes. I've liked it since I was a young girl. My father and mother knew that, and at the end of September, even if there was school, they used to take me to Cori for a couple of days. I remember that the streets of Cori were full of mules, horses and donkeys that went around the vineyards with buckets full of grapes tied to their saddles. Everyone was busy – the men, the women, and the children big and small. First, we went off to the vineyards to gather the grapes and then to the wine cellars to press the grapes, first with our feet and then with the wine-press. You could see the weariness on the people's faces.

"But there was a lot of happiness too, because once the grapes were turned into wine juice there would be enough wine for personal use and to sell. Not everyone had their own animals. Many worked only as drivers. They taught their animals to move and transport things, and they made a living that way. My grandfather knew many of them because he usually repaired or sold barrels or buckets to them. Sometimes even the mules, horses and donkeys couldn't get to all the cellars because some of them were located in narrow paths or on streets that were either too steep or had many steps. In some cases, the animals were left behind, away from the cellars, and the buckets full of grapes were carried by people on special stretchers.

"The stretchers were made out of two poles held up by crossbars. In the middle there was a square where you could put a cone-shaped bucket halfway in. Once they had put the base in, two men took the ends of the stretchers and lifted. That way, the cone-shaped bucket was blocked halfway and could be easily transported to the cellars. Some drivers and some owners brought the grapes in a handcart. The cart, pulled by mules or horses, could bring up to ten cone-shaped buckets. Wherever you went, all you could smell was the odour of crushed grapes. During wine season when you walked down the streets there was another odour that you'd smell due to all the animals: manure. There were a few designated sweepers; however, the stench remained. The strong smell was not a big problem because it was part of the tradition of grape gathering.

"For me, those were days of feast and celebration. All that coming and going and hustle and bustle seemed to put me under a spell. It was like I was in some fairytale. What I liked most of all was when my grandparents use to take me to crush grapes with my feet. Everyone would take turns crushing the grapes in the butts[7]. They would place the butt upright after they had taken the lid off. Then they would throw a bucket of grapes in and two or three people would go in the butt barefoot to crush the grapes with their feet. Slowly, while they crushed the grapes, someone else would throw more grapes in. When it was almost full, they would let me and some other children in.

"Dancing barefoot on top of the grapes, surrounded by the smell of grapes, rubbing grapes on each other's face – it was one of the best things. I dream about it still. I think the saying 'I'll slap you silly with grapes' in Corese dialect, Te tògno na mustacciata a jo mucco, must come from the action of people throwing crushed grapes in each other's faces during the grape gathering season. When they would pull me out of the butt, happy as can be, slippery and messy with fresh grape juice and almost drunk, I felt as light as a feather. My grandmother, and sometimes my mother when she was in Cori, would come and get me, and as soon as they saw me, they would laugh at how dirty and silly I looked. Once I was home, they would put me into a bathtub full of warm water and brush and wash me as if I were a mule. When I would tell my friends at school what it was like, they couldn't believe what they were hearing. They would make me retell the story over and over again, while they looked on, their mouths and eyes wide open."

I could never tire of listening to Fiorina. While she talked, her face would light up with a smile. Sometimes it was mischievous, or melancholic, or nostalgic, or affectionate, but a smile would appear on her lips and accompany her words. I was bewitched. Suddenly, there was Jadwiga, telling me that my taxi had arrived.

We rose. Jadwiga, a curious glint in her eyes, handed me my jacket and my bag. They accompanied me outside to where the taxi

[7]The butt (from late Latin buttis, from old French and late Middle English bot, from Italian bótte) is a traditional large wooden container (cask) in the shape of a double truncated cone containing 1000 liters of wine.

was waiting. I kissed Jadwiga goodbye and gave Fiorina a kiss on her cheek.

"I'll be waiting. You can't leave the country without coming back to spend some more time with me." She said this in a sweet tone, with hope, like an affectionate threat.

I climbed into the taxi and looked at her caringly. The taxi pulled away. I turned back as the taxi travelled down the path and saw Fiorina and Jadwiga, their arms linked, heading back into the house. They didn't seem at all like employer and employee.

The taxi driver turned right and slowly but decisively got onto Yonge Street. The taxi driver seemed like a nice person; he guessed right away that I was Italian. While we headed downtown, his conversation kept my mind off Fiorina, her story, and all my confused feelings that went along with it. He was an immigrant from Somalia and spoke Italian. He had been living in Canada for the past twelve years. In his country he was an engineer, but in Toronto he worked as a taxi driver. He hadn't found the time or the way to have his degree evaluated and recognized. With a wife and three kids, the only thing he could do was accept any employment. Working as a taxi driver wasn't that bad, he said, even though the taxi did belong to someone else. His wife worked at a hotel, his kids studied, and his voice softened when he said that his kids deserved a better life than his.

We arrived at my hotel. I paid him and wished him good luck in life. My Ciociari friends were already waiting for me – Filomena, Peppino and Leonardo. I dashed up to my room to freshen up, and then we were off to spend an evening in Woodbridge at the Sora Club to eat pasta and goat meat. The majority of people at the club were men. The night flew by, as we talked about many things, including Italy. It was midnight when they got me back to the hotel – just enough time to have a quick shower and get under the sheets. It had been a memorable and somewhat heavy day that would be hard to forget. I fell asleep thinking about Fiorina and Jadwiga, each lovelier and more interesting than the other, the image of them walking back into the house still on my mind.

The following morning I was supposed to meet up with Eliseo Sciaretta from Giulianello. He had immigrated to Canada forty years before. I hadn't seen him since we used to take the train together to go to Velletri. It felt like it was a lifetime ago. That train no longer runs. At the end of the 1950s, the train used to leave from Terracina and pass under the mountains, gathering students and workers from all the different Lepini[8] towns and taking them to Rome. The Cori station was three kilometres out of town, and you had to take a bus that ran on diesel to get there. Many students from Sezze, Norma, Bassiano, Sermoneta, Cori and Giulianello used to take the train to go to school in Velletri. The train ran on coal. There was also a rail-car, *the littorina,* that ran on naphtha that we could take to return home from Velletri.

We all knew each other, and there were groups and cliques that had formed based on which town one was from, which team one cheered for, which political party one favoured, and so on. Back in those days passions ran deep. To pass the time on the train, one could do pretty much anything; every person had his or her own pastime. On the way to school some would finish homework or review their lessons. Often the kids would talk about a wide range of topics. They would pull pranks on those who slept. There were a few who had been up since five o'clock, and some even earlier, in order to catch the train. Between Coresi and Giulianesi we would challenge each other with rock, paper, scissors. Sciaretta and I often teamed up.

In Toronto, Sciaretta had become very successful. Now he owned a construction company. He came to pick me up in a really nice car. He brought me to his house – and what a house indeed – roughly fifty kilometres from Toronto, so that I could meet his wife. We had lunch

[8]The Lepini Mountains are situated south of Rome, facing the Mediterranean Sea near Anzio.

and on the way back to the hotel we stopped to admire Lake Ontario and had a nice walk. We reminisced about those years, the train, the challenges we used to have between us, our first girlfriends and the signalman's daughter. She must have been seven or eight years older than we were. She was like a princess for us. She was a rare beauty. When she boarded the train in the spring wearing her black shirt and white blouse she drove all the males nuts, regardless of their age.

We spent a day filled with memories and emotions, telling each other stories of all sorts – another day spent in Canada that I will never forget. The next day, after a few official meetings with members of the Lazio community, John Romano picked me up. John came to Canada from Minturno[9] more than forty years ago. He had worked hard and was now the owner of the biggest foundation laying and transportation company in all of Toronto. You could say that he is one of those Italians who built a major part of Toronto, one of the biggest cities in all of North America. He had all kinds of different machines and lots of trucks at his company, and he had bought quite a few acres of land in Concord, where he had a huge, classy palace, not a normal house, on Jane Street. Concord, which was amalgamated with the municipality of Vaughan, has roughly 10,000 people and is located about forty kilometres north of downtown Toronto.

John had many friends and family members back in Minturno, where he went to relax for a few weeks each summer. He had a really pleasant wife and six daughters. He reminded me of Uncle Pasquale Ciardi, who made Aunt Santina have seven or eight kids just to have a daughter and, to make sure he didn't mix them up, he started calling them Quinto (Fifth), Sesto (Sixth), Settimo (Seventh). Romano's story was similar: he had all those daughters in the hope of having at least one son. John and his wife were as hospitable and as wonderful as they were nice. They wanted to start a buffalo farm, and he knew

---

[9]Minturno is a very old and famous town 120 kilometres south of Rome.

that I could help them. John asked me for some advice and wanted to know who he should contact. I gave him the numbers of some breeders from Pontinia, a town that ha lots of buffalo farms. Who knows what he could achieve! I spent an amazing and unforgettable day with this Italian family.

VI

Friendships in Toronto

My days were busy, running here and there, and time flew by. Suddenly, I remembered that I had not called Fiorina to let her know that I had decided to spend the weekend with her and Flav.

When I got to the hotel, it was already ten o'clock and the following day it would be Friday. I was unsure about what to do. At last, I made up my mind and decided that I would visit Fiorina. All the things that I had to do I had done. As far as saying goodbye to Tony, Leonardo and Rita, I could do that in the morning. After all, they were the best friends that I had in Toronto, and Tony was also a consultant for the Lazio Region. Since I hadn't seen Elena yet, I figured I could go tomorrow for lunch. I found some courage, picked up the phone and called.

I heard Jadwiga's Polish accent. I could tell that she was happy to hear from me. She informed me that Fiorina was not home. She also told me Fiorina was worried because she hadn't heard from me at all, and that when she got home she was planning to call me. I told Jadwiga that because it was already late Fiorina could call me in the morning. Then I added that, if it is not a problem, I would enjoy spending the weekend with Fiorina. Jadwiga wished me a goodnight and told me not to worry, that she would pass the message on to Fiorina.

Imagining that tomorrow would be another busy day, I prepared my luggage and a small carry-on, putting everything that I might need for a weekend at Fiorina's cottage. I went to bed, read for a bit, but soon weariness took over. I shut the light and fell asleep right away.

Suddenly the phone rang, causing me to jump. I was awake. I turned on the light and looked at the clock. It was nine a.m. I could not believe it. I had slept for ten hours straight!

"Hello?"

"Pietro, how are you? It's Fiorina."

"Hey, Fiorì. You must be amazed that you're waking me up at this hour."

"I'm sorry, but seeing how it's nine o'clock, I was worried that you had to go out. Sorry if I didn't call you back when I got home, but it was two o'clock in the morning. I was at dinner with Flav and some friends in Hamilton. Jadwiga told me that you are coming with us to the cottage!"

"It's such a pleasure to hear from you. Yes, if it's not a problem, I'd like to spend the weekend with the two of you; however, if you're leaving today, I'm free around five."

"Don't worry, we won't be leaving before seven o'clock. So I'll send Flav to pick you up around five thirty?"

"Thanks, Fiorì, but it is better if I take a taxi. That way everyone's free and I can leave as soon as I'm ready. So, I will leave the hotel and bring my things with me? You told me that Sunday you would be able to drive me to the airport…"

"Sure, don't worry. We'll be waiting. Come as soon as you can."

"Okay! I'll see you later."

"See you later, then!"

Even if Fiorina's call had made me jump out of bed, I felt euphoric – as if I had had too many drinks. I got up, stretched and quickly showered. I shaved and got dressed quickly because it was getting late. I quickly checked to be sure I wasn't leaving anything behind, and I was off. It was already ten o'clock, so I didn't even stop to have coffee. I left the hotel, got into a taxi and asked to go to Woodbridge, to Cianfarani Travel Agency, owned by my friend Leonardo.

Leonardo hailed from Ciociaria, Lazio Region, precisely, from the city of Sora. He arrived in Toronto in 1950. He tried almost everything before he found the right path to success. He started by offering services to Ciociari and working as a notary. Up until a few years ago in Toronto you didn't need any particular qualifications to do that. He started a travel agency on College Street, which became part of Little Italy over the years. Not only has it become a meeting place for Ciociari, but also it has been representing all Laziali for a long time. Many years ago, when he came to pick me up at the Toronto Island Airport on the lakefront, the first thing he proudly showed me was his license plate: "Lazio1." In Ontario you can pay a little more to personalize your license plate. He still has it today.

As soon as the Ciociari in Woodbridge had outnumbered the population of Sora, his business grew and he moved the location of his agency. Not only did his whole family work at the travel agency, but it also provided a job for many others. Leonardo always introduced himself to everyone with a smile. Then a smirk would appear on his lips and he would squint. He seemed sly and bad, but you realized almost right away that it was just an affectionate pose and that he was just playing, a reciprocal understanding.

Leonardo was already waiting for me. He introduced me to his family and workers again and told me that Tony and Rita were waiting for us to get a coffee together. We got into the car and turned onto Pine Valley Drive and then onto Highway 7. After a couple of kilometres, we turned right and we arrived at 200 Whitmore Road, a little square with a variety of different offices, boutiques, bars and restaurants. Tony had an office there, as he was the manager of Patronato Epasa, one of the largest social services offices for Italians in Toronto.

Tony was short, a bit chubby, with intelligent-looking eyes. He was Leonardo's brother-in-law, having married one of his sisters. He went to school in Italy where he became an accountant and then came to Toronto. He worked with Leonardo for quite some time when he still had the agency on College Street, and later he opened his own agency, Patronato Epasa. At Tony's agency one found a mix of Ciociari from different little towns, but also Italians from all over Italy. The agency addressed a variety of Italian citizens' concerns and offered all kinds of assistance, including help with pension matters. It was like being in Italy.

For years Tony had been a "consultore," a quasi-permanent representative for the Lazio Region. So, along with running and managing his own business, he also saw to the interests of all the people from Lazio living in Toronto and the rest of Ontario. He always seemed busy and without a minute to spare or any free time for himself. But when it came to hanging out with his friends and having fun, he found the time. He knew everybody and was sort of Don Giovanni with the women. He was waiting for us with Rita, a young woman who was born in Canada but with Ciociari roots. Rita, a somewhat chubby brunette with charcoal black eyes that shone like stars, was cultured and *simpatica*. Even though she moved slowly, she was full of life, and when she looked at you, it was as if she could see right through you. Every time I saw her I was enchanted by her. She taught high school and did some research and wrote some good stories about Ciociari who had immigrated to Canada after the war.

When we met Tony and Rita, they greeted us joyously. We barely had a chance to finish saying hello than we were already off to get coffee together. We spent an hour discussing the different problems in the community and the measures that should be taken to strengthen the community and to make it a better place for everyone, including the children. We talked about the different projects that the Lazio Region could fulfil and so on.

Time, however, went by very quickly and although the company was amazing I really had to leave. We said our goodbyes, hoping to see each other as soon as possible. Rita insisted on driving me to Joso's, a restaurant on Davenport where Elena was waiting for me. Rita drove an SUV, which she steered smoothly around the streets of downtown Toronto like a professional driver. Calm and quick, she chattered happily about everything: school, her family, dreams and so on, including things that maybe should not have been said. But we were close friends and had known each other a long time. We had been through and done many things together. We were at Joso's in no time. We parted with a warm hug and a few tears. Who knew just when we would be able to see each other again? Inside the restaurant, I saw Giovanna, one of the pretty waitresses who knew me. She quickly went in search of Elena. It was one o'clock and all the tables were taken.

Joso's isn't just any restaurant. The menu is a mix of typical Croatian, Italian and seafood dishes. I can say that the kitchen, and I mean the cuisine, is absolutely amazing – it's finger-licking good, no doubt about it, and I beg anyone to differ – in addition to the pleasant atmosphere. I've been to many restaurants all over the world, where people go to eat, not because the cooking is good but because there is so much to enjoy or to consider, either the ambiance or the other patrons. Joso's exudes a warm, cosy feeling. They make you feel like part of the family. But the pleasantness, the art, the culture, the class and the elegance that one finds there is hard to find elsewhere. It is like one big masterpiece, from the food and the furniture to the amazing dishes that they serve – and the waitresses, each one prettier than the next. The extraordinary person behind all this Joso Spralja. A rare man, Joso is a Croatian from Zadar, a city by the sea, and is himself a man from a family of fishermen. He is a jack of all trades, and I've had the pleasure to meet his wife, a skilled chef and a woman of rare sweetness.

Joso arrived in Canada in 1961 when he was thirty-two years old. He knew how to sing, play the guitar, paint and sculpt. He even restores and preserves art pieces. To earn a living, he went around singing and performing in different bars, pubs and restaurants. One night at the beginning of 1963, while he was singing at a bar at 71 Yorkville, he met a singer who had come to Toronto in 1954 from Israel. She was eighteen years old. She had seen and lived through pretty much everything. She was born in a little town in Poland, and when she was still a child, brought to live in Palestine. She almost didn't make it out of Auschwitz, which unfortunately took the lives of thousands of her people. She knew how to dance and sing.

She and Joso got along right away. She already had many songs in mind. She taught them to Joso and from April 1963 they started performing together in different pubs, bars, hotels and theatres. They were even invited to sing on television and radio shows. They garnered applause and praise, singing and playing all over Canada and England for four years. Then their paths diverged, and each went their separate way. Malka Marom was her name, and she stills sings. She does a lot of other things too. She wrote *Sulha*, a charming novel. Joso also continued to sing and play music, paint and sculpt, but he started thinking that the time had come to do something else, and so he opened a restaurant specializing in Croatian cuisine.

It was the only Croatian restaurant in Toronto. Joso renovated a wooden building near Yorkville, one of the richest and most fashion-able neighbourhoods in downtown Toronto, and he turned the place into a living work of art. On the walls he hung different paintings and placed all kinds of amazing sculptures that he made or painted himself. He turned that old wooden house more into a museum than a restaurant. With a home-style menu, but at a very high level, especially in terms of fresh fish, calamari, shrimp and shellfish, Joso's quickly became one of the best restaurants in all of Toronto, frequented by the upper classes, and rich and famous artists.

As soon as you sit down to eat, you feel that you are eating in a museum. In some of the paintings, there is the figure of the same nude woman. Her blond hair, light-coloured eyes and full breasts are delicately painted with different backdrops, much in the way an art teacher would paint. The girl is Elena, Joso's daughter. Only later did I learn this. You can tell that Joso's paintings honour his daughter, even as they reveal a certain sensuality, fertility and joie de vivre.

In fact, Joso's kids, Leo and Elena, are artists like their father. They went to school in Toronto, began helping out in the family business from a very young age. Leo sings, plays, paints and has taken photos that are displayed in a gallery, and is like his father in many ways. Elena draws using different techniques and can create masterpieces out blown glass. Some of the objects that she created are on display in the restaurant. Elena was our waitress the first time that a friend of mine took me to Joso's. This friend had immigrated to Toronto from Pisterzo[10] when she was three years old.

From that very first visit I became fast friends with Elena. Maybe it was the amazing setting, or the friend who had brought me, or a pinch of jealousy and the fun that I was having, and so a huge affection and a sense a respect grew between us. I returned with friends and gave Elena a copy of my book on Bressani as a gift. She introduced me to her father and her mother, Angiolina. Joso gave me a catalogue which contained all sorts of different artworks that he had created.

---

[10]Pisterzo is a township 80 kilometres south of Rome.

Such a nice, special gift. Since then, every time I'm in Toronto, I never leave without going at least once to eat at Joso's restaurant.

As soon as I walked in, Elena, with her arms wide open, greeted me. She was even prettier than the first time I saw her. She had gained a few pounds, but she looked great. Her face revealed her age a bit more than it did before. She spoke in proper Italian. Elena was from the Dalmatian coast, but her family roots were Venetian and Italian, not to mention that she had also married an Italian.

"Oh, Pietro, how are you? It's been a while. It's good to see you again." She gave me a warm, friendly hug. Coming back to the restaurant and seeing her again always gave me the same feeling, like diving under blankets to warm up when you are freezing. She took me upstairs to a little square corner table reserved for me. This time I brought her a little gift, a bottle of red wine from Cori. She gave me a kiss as sweet as honey, then had to leave me with the waitress to return to her post at the entrance in order to greet the clients, to see what was happening on both floors and to surveil the service of the more important clients. Every now and then she came by to check up on me and make sure everything was alright.

All the tables were occupied, and apart from some small talk, everyone was eating in silence. It was like eating in church, or as I said before, a museum. Everywhere one looked, one saw works of art. Wherever one glanced, one found beauty and sensuality. Giovanna, the waitress seemed happy to be serving the owner's friend. She looked like a Madonna and also seemed to be part of the museum.

When I was almost finished my lunch and most of the other clients had left, Elena came to sit at my table to have a chat. We told each other what we had been doing for the past couple years, our kids, family and work. She also talked about the works of art that she had made out of glass, how she made them using her imagination, and about the artistic photos that she takes, just like her brother and father.

She seemed pleased, I could tell. Her eyes shone as she spoke. Running a restaurant does bring an owner a lot of personal satisfaction, along with a lot of money. Joso's was a high-end destination for the affluent, and it kept her, her brother and the whole family well off. On the other hand, they all worked together to keep the restaurant going.

One could see the soul of the artist in every word she said. When she talked about the glass art and the colours, her face literally glowed. It was her passion. You could say that I watched her take her first steps. I was one of the people who went to her first important art exhibition in Montreal, in 1993. That was the night she promised she would have dinner with me. It was December, just before Christmas. I had turned down many invitations from other friends who had wanted to spend the evening with me; I already had made plans, I said. Instead, I waited by myself for hours and hours in the huge hotel room at the Ritz-Carlton, but no Elena. When I went down to eat, I found a note at Reception explaining that she wouldn't be able to make it because she had left for a friend's cottage up north to spend Christmas Eve. She said that she tried to refuse the invitation but it had been impossible.

I'll never forget that time in Montreal all by myself, alone and depressed. Anyone could read the way I felt by my downcast demeanour. I left the hotel and walked for two hours in the middle of a nearly blinding snowstorm along Rue de la Montagne. I walked across Boulevard de Maisonneuve, down the famously rich and elegant Rue Saint-Catherine and up Boulevard René Lévesque. I walked the entire downtown core of Montreal. The streets were full of Christmas decorations and festive lights. All the bars, coffee shops and other gathering places were open and seemed to invite people, beckoning them to have fun. No need for signs. It was well understood that it was a holiday.

Once I calmed down, I went back to the hotel. I stopped to get a bite to eat and exchanged some small talk with some other people who were also by themselves at the hotel's café, where one can always find people who are just passing through. There were a lot of beautiful women looking for company, but it didn't even enter my mind. After a while, they each found some man and left together. When I finally went to bed, it was really late, and as soon as I lay down, I was out like a light. The whole evening had been awful.

Here I was years later, reminding Elena of that day years ago in Montreal and how she had abandoned me. She looked at me and I could see that she was sorry. She gave me a kiss. We had a quick toast and I started getting ready to leave, for it was already late. She told Giovanna to call me a taxi and I said goodbye and kissed her hand. Then, we gave each other a sweet, friendly hug after taking a picture. I hurried back to the hotel. Saying goodbye to Elena always leaves me with a bittersweet feeling that is hard to explain.

It was already four o'clock when I got up to my room. I washed up, closed my luggage and went back down to the reception desk. I paid my bill and asked if they could call me a taxi. Fiorina would be waiting for me. I didn't feel like conversing with the redhead driving the taxi, who was chattering away. It occurred to me that she might be Irish, but unfortunately my head was buzzing. I had just left Elena, and the thought of Fiorina seemed to leave me speechless, thinking of all the things she had yet to tell me.

VII

Adolescence: First Signs of War

The redhead with the pleasant face, who drove like a professional race car driver, had given up on asking me questions. Lord knows how her curiosity must have gnawed at her; however, I had too many things on my mind to pay her any attention. Instead of taking Yonge Street, she took the Gardiner Express and went up the Don Valley Expressway. Without me even realizing it, we were at John Street, near Markham, and soon after, the redhead, now silent, turned on Dean Bank Drive. With a somewhat satisfied and mischievous smile, she dropped me off at the path that led up to Fiorina's house. I hadn't even finished paying and getting my bags than I saw Flav coming towards me in a hurry. As the taxi slowly drove away, Flav took my luggage to a flaming-red Mercedes. Jadwiga came toward me, a sunny smile on her face. We greeted each other like affectionate siblings and she told me to come into the house to wait for Fiorina, who would be ready in a couple of minutes. I followed her in.

Once inside the house, Jadwiga told me that she would be coming with us. She asked me if I would like something to drink. I was thirsty so I asked for a glass of water. Meanwhile, Flav appeared and asked for some orange juice. Flav really was one big, fit man – wide shoulders, slim without a gram of fat, a square jaw and shiny black eyes, just like his short buzzed haircut. He told me that it had been a tough week, but overall it went well, and now two days of total relaxation were really needed.

Fiorina descended the staircase. Everything seemed more familiar, easily recognizable and beautiful. She wore tight-fitting jeans with an ash-grey sweater that hugged her curves. Her black hair hung loose and straight. Who would believe that she was seventy years old? She carried a jacket and a windbreaker on one arm; on the other a big gym bag, which Flav quickly took from her. Fiorina smiled as she approached me and held out her hand, which I gently kissed. But then she kissed me on the cheek. She spoke in English, asking me how I spent the past few days and how was I doing. She explained that we had to leave right away because it was a long trip and soon it would be dark.

At first I responded in English. But I have to admit that I felt a bit awkward. My head was full of words in Corese, so as we were getting into the car I said, "Fiorì, isn't it better if we speak in Corese?"

She laughed for a moment and, speaking to me in English, she told me not to worry for it was going to be a long trip. Flav and Jadwiga had finished locking up the house. Fiorina let Jadwiga sit in the front seat beside Flav, who would be driving. She let me in first and she joined me in the back seat. We were off. Flav slowed down a little to wait for the automatic gate to close behind us. Down the road I could see a few parents riding bikes with their kids and others speed walking. Flav sped up and we headed towards Yonge Street. We drove up the street and eventually we turned left to head east on

Major Mackenzie Drive. When we got to Highway 400, we turned north, right after Canada's Wonderland, the big amusement park just north of Toronto.

Flav and Jadwiga were already having an animated conversation. They were speaking too fast in English for me to understand. I was able to make out only a few words.

"Have you ever been up north? It's beautiful, peaceful and colourful, and we can relax," Fiorina said.

So I told her all about my trip to Midland the year before. It was July. It was so hot and sunny that one could have easily suffered a heatstroke. The sky really seemed to spread out before me when I had looked across Georgian Bay, standing at Sainte-Marie among the Hurons.[11] I was utterly transfixed by the beauty of the water and the landscape.

"I'm so happy that you could come. Not only are you from the town where I was born, but I must say that you've grown on me and I find you fascinating. Besides, having guests stay with us adds flavour to the fun. Every now and then Flav, Jadwiga and I reminisce about the special times we've had and remember the people that we have taken to heart."

"Fiorì, I'm sure you've realized that I enjoy spending time with you as well as being interested in your story, so much so, that I put aside spending these days with other close friends. Without any regrets – even though every time I see them I am filled with many sweet and delicate emotions, which has just happened to me with Elena, the owner of Joso's restaurant."

"You know the owner of Joso's? A few times I went to eat there with important clients of mine. Not only is the food good, but it's also got an amazing atmosphere if you want to spend an evening among

---

[11]Sainte-Marie among the Hurons was a French Jesuit settlement, the first European settlement in Ontario, from 1639 to 1649. It is now a historical site.

friends. I don't know Elena personally, but I've seen her. I know that she's the owner and that her father painted nude portraits that make that place seem like an art gallery, a restaurant of rare beauty. Even though I'm a woman, I must say that she's an amazing lady full of charms. She greets all of her clients so warmly."

"Of course, I have known her and the father and the mother for quite some time. The family is principled, rich in ideas and has a passion for art in their souls. I really enjoy going to Joso's and I've always felt at home there."

"Maybe sometime we could all go to eat there together, if you come back I hope."

"I'd love to."

The highway was packed with all kinds of cars, especially in our lane. Everyone was going north, leaving the chaos of the city behind for two or three days. Whoever was lucky enough to have a cottage up north wasn't willing to give up going there to spend a weekend. Even Fiorina, whose house was in the suburbs, surrounded by green spaces and away from the noise and traffic, always found time to get away, to head towards places of solitude, far away from the everyday life and home. Here, whoever can afford a cottage has one. It is like an obsession and kind of a ritual that starts Friday night and ends Sunday night or Monday morning, when everyone goes back to work. I reflected on this and realized that even in Italy today people are starting to do the same thing.

Then, to coax Fiorina into continuing with her story, I said, "So your childhood years before the war were worry-free, just like everybody else?"

"Up until the first bombs were dropped on Rome I didn't have any fear, anxiety, and I was pretty much worry-free. The days that I spent in Cori were the most relaxing. If it was up to me, I would have been always in the streets playing. When I was in Cori, one December morning I woke up and found blood all over my legs. I was thirteen years old. My mother hadn't said anything to me about a woman's period. The thought that something terrible was happening to me paralyzed me with fear. I called to my mother, crying and scared. My mother came to see what was going on and then smiled at me happily, and told me that it was nothing to worry about. I was growing up. With a soft voice she told me that what was happening to me was a mystery and was the vital strength of womanhood. She also said that it would continue happening to me once a month, every month for years. It was something that touched women in everything that made one a woman and influenced the different parts of a woman like her body, her mind and her soul.

"It didn't take me long to realize that something had changed in me, something that now made me a part of the grownup world. It seemed like I had become important. I even felt different. I also noticed that my breasts started to become fuller. One day, on the way home from school, a boy who was a few years older than me was walking home with me because we lived near each other. We had walked together many times before. At one point he started touching me. I didn't understand. He pulled me underneath a doorway. He kept trying to hug and kiss me. At first I was breathless, then I felt afraid. I was scared like I'd never been before. My instincts made me yell out and the guy left me alone, saying that I was just a tease. Once I got home I told my mother all about it while I took a bath. My mother stared at me and I felt her eyes penetrate me, as if they were burning right into my soul. Later she hugged me and said comforting words to me, the way mothers always do. She started telling me all about the problems that girls my age faced. She helped me understand what a woman's life was like.

"I went to a high school in Rome. I liked going to school. But unfortunately I knew that the war had arrived. For obvious reasons some girls and boys didn't attend school anymore. Everything was divided and weighed. Basic, everyday supplies were hard to come by and everyday life had become difficult. For the Christmas holidays we went to Cori. When we were there, they told us about Loviciotto. He had been drafted into the army, and then sent to the front. We got no more news about him. Loviciotto was one of the people I used to crush grapes with when we were younger and with whom I was friends.

"My father was no longer playful and the funny person that I loved. Before, when he used to come home from work, he was always happy. He would joke around with me and my mother, he'd ask me how school went, he would look over my notebooks and quiz me and would teach me many things. Now, he came home dead tired. His face was always sullen and worried. He didn't bring me the little gifts that he always used to surprise me with.

"My father was friends with a German officer, Hans, who worked at the German Embassy. He would come over often for dinner and would talk with my father and mother until it got late. He was younger than my father and he was an optimistic and cultured person. He knew more Italian history than we did. He usually had some Italian book under his arm when he arrived. He liked different writers like Leopardi, Pirandello and Dante. Before the bombs started to drop on Rome, in my house, especially when Hans was over, we would talk about art, history, theatre and literature. Sometimes Hans would show up with tickets and would take all of us to the theatre. I noticed that he would stare at my mother intensely, almost as if he wanted to devour her with his eyes.

"After the first bombing of Rome, his interest in my mother became more obvious. Not only had I noticed because I was older and because I had started to understand such things, but because the way he acted had changed. The bombs that fell on San Lorenzo had changed the way many people acted. We lived near Termini Station, in a building that was on Via dei Mille. My mother didn't even protest, almost as if those hot glances that Hans threw her sort of flattered her and she liked the attention. I understood fully many years later why we women are flattered and drawn by the attention of men. But all that attention and all those glances really bothered me, and I became cold and mean towards Hans."

Fiorina had been speaking with her head on the car seat head rest, her eyes closing and opening as if she were drifting in and out of a dream.

I took one of her hands and squeezed it. She squeezed mine back and for a while we sat in silence. Flav and Jadwiga were in the middle of a conversation. I tried to listen and make out some words, but I didn't understand much. The car sped north. At certain points, we passed colourful forests. The colours merged as the sun started to set. Soon they would totally disappear.

Fiorina resumed her story. One could see that she was in pain as she spoke, but you could also hear the liberation that she felt as she related her story. It really is true when they say that we are our past, and that no matter how hard we try, we can't remove it, just like we can't live without it. The life you lived in the past stays deep inside you and when you least expect it, it comes to the surface. I could only begin to imagine all the memories that were floating around in Fiorina's head.

"My father told my mother that at the office everything was nuts and no one knew what was going on. Moment by moment, everyone worried about what would happen. The Americans had landed in Sicily. Father hadn't heard from his brother, who had sold everything and gone to work in Canada as an engineer. From one day to the next it seemed that he had aged ten years. At home all they talked about was salt, sugar, coffee and flour, which were hard to find. My mother had started working at a notary's office. Even my days at school were no longer carefree. I felt older and no longer a child, more like a grownup, like my parents."

"Fiorì, I was much younger at the time. But as far as the sky and the earth shaking and ready to explode and the disaster that we were about to face, I sort of understood what was happening. I remember my whole family in tears at the square on the mountain side of the town, waving goodbye to my Uncle Pacifico as he disappeared into the bus that took him away to join the army. I never saw him again. No one knows if, how or where he died, somewhere in Russia."

Fiorina gave me a warm look and squeezed my hand and again a strange silence fell over us. Fiorina resumed her story.

"To think that just a few months before I was happy, I had everything at home, every day in Rome, and when I was in Cori I felt like a princess."

"What else did you like about Cori? Which memories are pleasant ones for you?"

Fiorina closed her eyes and paused before she answered. In the meantime, a lot of different memories of when I was a boy sprang to mind. I closed my eyes and all of a sudden I remembered the time I was at St. Oliva Kindergarten and I pooped in my pants. Lisetta, the janitor, came near my desk and smelled it. She pulled me out of the class and told me to go home. I have always wondered, if she shouldn't have cleaned me up. What a strange place the world was back in those days. I must have been no older than four or five at the time.

Once outside, I headed towards the bend near Uc'Arcanio, which took you to the beginning of Via dell'Impero that led to Via Regina Elena, which is now St. Nicola Street, and then to my house. But I hadn't even finished passing the kindergarten's wall, when suddenly I saw my Aunt Filomena standing in front of me. A bit embarrassed, I tried to hide behind the trees by the street. But my aunt was too smart. She saw me right away and walked up to me saying: "You did it again. Hurry up and go home to change." It must have been something that happened often if my aunt had said that to me. But I only remember that episode and that one time she saw me. It was as if I could see everything happening before my eyes.

"I liked the folklore feasts that took place in Cori," continued Fiorina, "especially the different saints' feasts. There were many. It was almost as if they had all gathered in Cori, which was full of big and small churches inside and outside the town. My mother liked going to the horse races at Colleucci[12] in honour of the feast of St. Anthony. She always tried to get seats near the finish line. All these memories of different feasts are buzzing in my head. After all, my mother used to always take me along. I loved going to the races, even if I also remember being short and it was hard for me to follow the race. Sometimes my father would sit me on his shoulders and I could see better. I remember looking at the jockeys with my mouth wide open, wondering how the jockeys seemed to be one with their horses. There was always a bunch of people, and if the horse that won was the one that my mother wanted to see win, she would glow with satisfaction."

Fiorina's face became even more radiant and beautiful as she told her story, especially when she talked about her mother, and so I let her speak without interrupting her.

"Another feast that I really liked was St. Nicola's Feast. From the town to the valley, up the mountain, one followed a big, long procession of men, women, boys and girls of all ages. To get to the little church was quite a hike, but also a delight. While walking, you would bump into a friend and others along the way. People would bring food and drinks and sit cross-legged underneath the olive trees before and after Mass. Everyone was happy and took part in the party. All the stress, hard work and even some of the sorrow would disappear. I also remember that on one side of the church there was

---

[12]Colleucci is in the valley side of town.

75

a big stand. The stand sold homemade wine and *ciambelle*, little buns with chunks of prosciutto in them. I loved the buns full of *porchetta*[13]. It was also my father's favourite. That's probably where I got the habit.

"The highlight of the feast was the *palio*. The feast organizers used to go all over town collecting money for registrations. On September 10, St. Nicola's Feast Day, they would pull out the names of the participants. On top of a pole they would place the prizes – quite a bit of good fabric for clothing, sometimes it was even enough to make wedding dresses. One year, I couldn't have been older than ten, the winner was my mother. As soon as she saw me she started laughing. You can't even imagine how beautiful my mother was. When she was happy, no other woman, no matter how beautiful, could compare to her. And my father loved her so much that he seemed even happier, almost as if he were drunk.

"There were a lot of different games. Yet everyone waited for the pot race. They tied a cord to a pole on one side of the street and then across to anther other pole on the other side. From the rope fifteen pots were hung stuffed with all kinds of different things: water, ashes, beans, salami, mice, lizards and anything. No one knew what was in them. The players wore a blindfold made of cloth over their eyes. Then they gave you a stick; sometimes the shorter players sat on someone's shoulders, some sat on donkeys, some stood on their own feet. They would bring the players near the rope where they would swing the stick, trying to hit the pot. Whatever was in the pot that broke, the player could keep. People would die of laughter when someone broke the pot full of ashes, or mice, or lizards. One time they even put a snake in one of them. You should have seen the confusion that it caused among the people, while the poor snake tried only to slip away and escape. Everyone would yell: 'Hit it, swing lower, swing

---

[13]Roast suckling pig.

higher, and smash it.' This would happen especially when the players had to swing at the pot, even though they weren't underneath it."

We had arrived in Barrie. Flav said: "We're hungry up here! What do you guys say if we stop to put something in our stomachs? It's already seven-thirty. Or we could stop at Penetanguishene. But it would be late and it will already be dark. Pietro, what do you say?"

"For me, whatever you guys decide to do."

"Then let's stop here. Jadwiga and I ate only a little bit of fruit and yogurt today. We won't stop at the gas service station restaurant; instead we'll go to the usual restaurant beside the lake."

"Whatever you say, Mom. I was also thinking about going to the same place."

Flav drove another ten kilometres and then exited the 400. We entered Barrie. We had already driven for more than a hundred kilometres. Barrie is a modern and nice city, full of restaurants, parks and different places to spend your free time. Near Barrie there are illuminated ski trails for night skiing. Skiers come from all over, not only from Ontario. The city has about a hundred and fifty thousand residents, having grown substantially in the last ten years. The majority of the people who live here are young. All kinds of people moved here from all over, thanks to the many job opportunities and, often, new professions. It seemed like a fun wonderland made for entertainment. Located on the shores of Lake Simcoe, near Kempenfelt Bay, it is in the middle of an absolutely marvellous green space. Highways 400 and 11 are the main streets that pass through Barrie, bringing people who want to enjoy themselves. Moreover, these two highways open the way to what is called amazing northern Ontario.

Flav went down to the lake and then drove up and down Lakeshore Drive. There's a beautiful lookout on the lakeshore, and lots of green spaces right down to the lake. He turned onto Dunlop

Street, then on to Bayfield Street, and then he parked beside a restaurant that served meat and fish.

The restaurant had a chic atmosphere. It was packed with tables that had been set with care. All the furniture was dark oak wood. The walls displayed a lot of nice paintings – landscapes of Lake Simcoe and various forest scenes. You could tell that Fiorina, Flav and Jadwiga were well known, because they were quickly and warmly welcomed. We sat down at a table and the owner, Tina, came over to our table. They all spoke English and from what I understood from their conversation, and the bit that Flav and Fiorina told me, Tina was from Friuli and her husband, an amazing chef, was from Sicily. It was an Italian restaurant that served dishes from all over Italy. Jadwiga and Fiorina ordered a steak, Flav an omelette, and I ordered some fresh salmon. To drink, besides water and coca-cola for Jadwiga and surprisingly for Flav, we ordered a bottle of red wine from Ontario.

Jadwiga wanted me to tell her about the days I had spent in Poland with my Polish friends. She was all ears when I talked about Krakow, Wadowice and Zakopane. Storytelling happens naturally when people get together around a table, over a meal, and it's always nice to retell some stories. They stir up pleasant emotions, good for both body and soul. Even Flav and Fiorina were paying attention and seemed amused, as they listened to what Jadwiga and I were saying. Fiorina and I finished the entire bottle of wine. We ended dinner with a chocolate dessert. Tina filled some shot glasses with liqueur for us and set them on fire. The flames shot up and then slowly grew smaller and fainter. It was a real showstopper!

When we left the restaurant, Tina and her husband came out to say goodbye to Fiorina and Flav. I watched them exchange goodbyes like old friends who saw each other every day. It was getting late. We all got back into the car. Flav headed back towards the lake, where the water was still and mirror-like. You could see a full moon and a crystal clear sky. Everything seemed beautiful to me. My eyes were feeling heavy and started to close. Flav passed through Barrie and turned back onto the 400. After roughly thirty kilometres he took the 93. The food, the wine and the fatigue kicked in and I fell asleep. I slept quite a while and when I woke up I noticed that we were driving alongside a body of water, another lake or a bay. One could see lights on the other side.

"Sorry Fiorì, I fell asleep. Just like a newborn that dozes off. Where are we exactly?"

"Oh, don't worry. The wine we drank made me sleepy as well. We're driving along Penetang Bay. We passed close to Midland and were driving by the site of one of oldest European settlements in North America."

"I know this. We are in the land where the Huron lived for many years. I know Father Bressani's story. A few years back I wrote a book on him, *The First Italian in Canada,* and I brought several copies to Quebec and Ontario with me. I even left a copy at Sainte-Marie among the Hurons Library in Huron. Who knows if it is still around?"

"Unfortunately, I don't know Bressani's story, although I have heard of him. There's a high school in Woodbridge, Ontario, named after him."

"Hopefully, I can arrange to send you a copy of the book. In Toronto many families from the Lazio region have a copy. But in 1992 when I came to launch my book on Bressani, I didn't know that there was a certain Fiorina born in Cori. To think that Father Bressani was one of the first Jesuits to make it all the way over here, and who wrote one of the most important documents bringing to the light one of the first and most important Christian missions. He was born in Rome, at Trastevere and taught in Sezze, a town near Cori, and probably to get to Sezze he passed by Cori."

"It's unbelievable, I feel emotional just thinking about it. You have to get me a copy of this book. I have goose bumps."

"Of course, it is an interesting story that moves you emotionally too."

"As you can see, we are leaving the bay behind, which is part of Lake Huron. We passed Champlain Road and now we're driving on Military Road. We're not far now. After a few kilometres we'll be driving along the shore of Lake Farlain, and it will bring us right to my cottage."

"This really is an amazing place. I also know where we are. We are heading towards the Penetanguishene Peninsula, where the lakes were formed by glaciers. The biggest of these is Lake Farlain. It's about 35 kilometres long and six or seven kilometres wide on the southern side of the park. It is so beautiful that there are no words to describe it. I'm talking about Awenda Provincial Park."

"Here we are! We're already on the east side of the Farlain lakeshore. How far are we, Flav?" Fiorina asked her son in English.

"About two kilometres."

The car turned left. It stopped in front of a wooden gate that was painted white. Flav stepped out and opened the gate. Jadwiga got out as well. Flav jumped back in and headed towards a gravel road. Then Flav stopped again and waited for Jadwiga, who was closing the gate. We continued on the road. After two or three hundred metres we arrived at a cottage. Flav drove around it. He stopped in front of an automatic garage door.

We all got out of the car. Someone turned on the light. The garage was pretty big, able to fit two large cars comfortably. There were some pieces of furniture full of bags and containers. Hanging on the walls were skis and other winter things. On the other side there was a beautiful wooden staircase, probably leading to the upper floors – a way in from the garage directly into the house.

Flav unloaded our luggage and said to his mother: "Go upstairs. I'll deal with rest of the stuff."

But Jadwiga and I took our own luggage and we followed Fiorina, who had already climbed the stairs and was opening the door to the house. We entered a room, a sort of living room/dining room. Even with the drapes drawn, you could tell that one of the walls was one huge window. In the middle of another wall there was a fireplace. There were rectangular and round tables, a television, and the kitchen was partially visible from the doorway. A bit off to the right of the entrance there was another beautiful wooden staircase leading no doubt to the bedrooms upstairs. This was more mansion than cottage!

Fiorina, Flav and Jad, which is how they usually addressed her, started a fire. It was late, but if someone wanted to relax and have a chat, they would be warm. Flav surely had already turned on the gas heating system, which really is necessary for the cold nights. In all our conversations with Jadwiga, Fiorina, Flav and I spoke English. When I didn't know a word, Fiorina helped me out. Once in a while, when they came to mind, I said a few words in Polish, which made Jad laugh happily.

"Pietro, come upstairs with me so I can show you the room that you'll be sleeping in, and the other rooms too."

Jadwiga put her bag down on an armchair and moved towards the fireplace. I followed Fiorina. The stairs brought us to a hallway that was a few metres wide with a number of doors. On both sides there were windows with white embroidered cotton curtains. Fiorina opened the first door in the hallway and told me that this was the room where I'd be staying. The room contained two beds. Then she showed me the bathroom that was directly across from my room. She instructed me to leave my bags and things so that she could show me the rest of the floor.

She opened the second door and let me in. It was a huge room with a queen-sized bed. This was her bedroom. It seemed fancy and luxurious. She also showed me her ensuite bathroom, which was also quite big. Moving away from her room, she opened another door directly across the hall, which was as big as the room that was for me and which also contained two beds. This was Jadwiga's room. The tour continued with yet another bedroom, as big as Fiorina's, but this one containing three beds. And there was another upstairs bathroom too.

The house was absolutely marvellous. Full of furniture and bigger than most houses that people live in every day. I thanked Fiorina, who led me back downstairs again.

Jadwiga had a nice fire going. Fiorina told me to sit down and relax in one of the armchairs near the fire. She took the chair opposite me. In front of the fireplace there was a three-seat sofa. In the meantime, Flav returned from the garage with his luggage and his mother's as well. He took them both upstairs right away. Even Jadwiga went upstairs with her bags. After a few moments they both returned.

"Well, Mom, shall we drink something before going to bed? You know, to welcome our guest. What would you like to drink? Pietro, do you prefer something strong or something light, some juice or something else?"

"To tell you the truth, I'd really like a cup of tea if it's possible."

Even Fiorina and Jadwiga decided to have some tea and Jad set off to boil the water. Flav went over to the liquor cabinet and took out a bottle of bourbon and a glass. He put down the bottle and headed for the kitchen, returning with the glass half full of ice. Flav turned on the television, which was a bit removed from the fireplace. He surfed the channels and finally stopped on one showing a movie.

Jad brought me and Fiorina our tea, and then went to sit next to Flav on the sofa. Fiorina sipped her tea. Her face was relaxed and beautiful. We looked at each other in silence, almost as if we were trying to read each other's thoughts.

To break a bit of the awkward silence that had fallen between us, I piped up: "Fiorì, this really is a beautiful house."

"We've had it now for about fifteen years. I really like coming here. There's a lot of peace and quiet, relaxation, not to mention that I sleep. I sleep like a baby when I'm here. I love going on boat rides on the lake, bicycle rides and walks in Awenda Park. It's only a couple of kilometres from where we are. Every now and then I like going for an excursion on Georgian Bay. I come here often, even during the winter. I also enjoy doing cross country skiing through all the trees."

"I have broken your silence."

"No, come off of it! If I hadn't taken a liking to you or if I considered you a bother or if I didn't like talking to you, I certainly wouldn't have invited you. Instead, I'm glad you came. It's almost like a light inside my soul went on, when without realizing it you got me talking, bringing me back to my past. It's kind of like cleaning all the skeletons out of my closet that have haunted my dreams for so long. It feels like I've been living in Canada forever."

"Speaking of which, we were talking about the feast of St. Nicola. Why don't you tell me about some other feasts?"

VIII

Fiorina Tells Her Story

"I already told you about the different feasts they had in Cori to honour the saints, and I really liked them. They made me feel like a cartoon character brought to life. My mother turned into a kid again among all those people, walking from stand to stand or stopping to watch people playing games. She always came back with some sweets or other things that she would buy at the stands. I followed her because I was just like her. As far as buying things, I still have that habit today. Whenever I went to some big store or to some feast, at some point I always found a souvenir of some sort in my hand; I'm like a magnet and objects are metal.

"I also liked the feast of St. Rocco. I probably enjoyed it because of the ring race that always kicked off the celebration. I was hypnotized as I watched the jockeys astride their horses, dagger in hand, galloping fast as they passed underneath the poles that held the rings. These rings were no more than three centimetres in diameter. You would feel a hot rush of exhilaration and the mad roar of the fans course through your body when a jockey triumphantly raised his dagger in the air having successfully captured one of the rings.

They used to say that only on the day of St. Rocco would the women of the valley side of town, Cori Valley, flaunt themselves in order to find a husband. Even the boys that lived on the mountain side, Cori Mount, would come down to the valley that day. Every now and then, there were arguments and fists would fly, often turning into real fights.

The Accrocca family would come over to my parents' house in Rome. They were all really nice. Livio worked for the railway; his wife must have been a seamstress because she used to alter my mother's clothes. They had two sons. I remember the older brother well, Elio. He was a university student. He was nice, very pleasant – and he was a poet. Sometimes he would recite one or two poems, and my mother seemed to hang on every word that came out of his mouth. It was Elio who talked about the girls flirting on the day of St. Rocco and about the fights that involved the boys from both sides of the town."

Fiorina told her story and I listened as if I were under a spell. I could have never imagined that she knew Elio Filippo Accrocca, the famous poet from Cori, known in all of Italy and throughout Europe. But Fiorina had no way of knowing this since she had left Italy half a century ago. I felt very emotional.

"Fiorina, what you are telling is absolutely incredible. I'm starting to think that between you and me there's some kind of strange string that brought us together. Elio – Elio Filippo Accrocca – was a great friend of mine. I said was, because he's with God now. He died on March 11, 1996. He was a major poet who was in the spotlight, famous not only in Cori and Rome, but also known in countries all over Europe. To me, he was like a big brother. He was the one who gave me the push that I needed to publish my first book, a collection of poems, *Amori di carta e inchiostro*[14]. It was Elio who wrote the preface

---

[14]English title: *Loves Made of Ink and Paper*

and who introduced and praised my book. I often wonder if it was earned or not."

Fiorina stared in disbelief, her smile was radiant. "Well, then you have to let me have a copy of this other book as well. You'll end up adding to my book collection. As far as Elio goes, I remember him as if he were a dream. He was a very affectionate, pleasant and playful person. When he got his degree, they invited us to their house to celebrate. I will never forget that day, especially the huge bowl of homemade fettuccine with the tasty tomato sauce made from leftover chicken meat, and the atmosphere of celebration that was in the air. One of the few happy days spent in Rome after the war. That Sunday at his house, of all the poems that he had written, he read one that spoke of the Madonna of the Rosary. It was a feast that was held in the town. My mother loved it. The poem was about girls who show off their curves. I also remember that during the feast you could smell the crushed grapes and roasted chestnuts."

"I know that poem."

Affiorano le case sui vigneti
Oltre il confine della valle, gonfie
Nel ventre di lucertole in calura.

È l'ora in cui le rondini in amore
Boccheggiano dai nidi e le ragazze
Scoprono i fianchi come le puledre
Che corrono alla festa del Rosario.

Al mio paese aspettano settembre
Le donne che lasciammo di sedici anni
(adesso ne hanno venti sui seni colorati come olive).
Aspettano settembre per potare i petali ricolmi.

Houses appear before the vineyards
Beyond the edge of the valley, filled
with lizards in heat.

It is a time when swallows in love
Frolic in their nests and the young girls
Uncover their hips like fillies
Running in the feast of the Holy Rosary.

In my town they wait for September
The young ladies that we left when they were sixteen
(now are twenty with breasts the colour of olives)
They wait for September to prune the petals in full bloom.

"It is part of the collection of poems that Elio wrote, in the first book that he published. The introduction was written by Giuseppe Ungaretti who, in addition to being Elio's professor, was also one of the most important Italian poets of the century. The title of the book by Accrocca is *Portonaccio*. It is a small book of poems that is famous and important in Italian literature. It also talked about the war, the bombs that fell on Rome, about St. Lorenzo, Cori, and first loves."

"It's beautiful. That is the one, the poem that you just recited just now, was the one that my mother liked. I'd really like to have a copy of this book."

"I hate to say it, but it's practically impossible. It's half a century old, and you can't find it anywhere; however, the same poems were republished in other books years later. If I come back, I'll bring you some of these books or I'll send them to you."

"That's not a bad idea, that way I could read them sooner. Another feast that I liked was the thistle feast."

"I'm not familiar with that one, although I'm from Cori too."

"They used to celebrate it on the same day as St. Michael's Day. I liked it because for two to three days my father was always in Cori. Along with St. Michael, they celebrated the so-called Snail Soup Day. My father loved eating the soup that they made with the little white snails that lived on the thistles. He would eat tons of those snails. They would cook some just for me, because my grandparents and my parents would put all kinds of hot pepper in the sauce. Now I love hot pepper and spicy food, but when I was younger, I just couldn't handle it."

In the meantime, Jad brought us another cup of tea. The movie had ended. Jad and Flav said goodnight and headed upstairs to crash on their beds.

"We'll also be coming upstairs to sleep soon. As soon as we finish drinking our tea and wait for the fire to burn out. Goodnight, my dears."

"Goodnight!"

"Even at the Feast of the Rosary there was a horse race from the Madonnina up to the Croce[15], and if my mother could, she never missed it. I remember that even the feast of St. Francesco was really nice. I liked listening to the priest. The entire large square in front of the church would be full of people who came from all over. There were so many people they spilled all over Via Nuova[16]. Then the priest would start to speak. I didn't understand much of what was said, but that sea of words, of threats, of persuasion, of sins and stories about the saints enchanted me. Everybody was silent. Everybody listened. What an amazing silence; eyes that stared straight ahead and all ears listening to what the priest had to say. After the priest had finished his sermon, the people seemed a bit different, like when you have just finished eating and you feel full and satisfied.

---

[15]Madonnina and Croce are two landmarks in Cori Valley.
[16]Via Nuova is a large road, built in 1910, that crosses the town.

"During the feast of St. Francesco there were always amazing concerts. The orchestra played classical music. My grandfather, who was a huge opera fan, never missed it. He always used to bring me with him. I liked the music, but when the concerts were long I would fall asleep sitting on his shoulders. I used to dream that I was in paradise, and I really was."

Once Fiorina had started speaking, it seemed that she would never stop. But I liked it. In my mind I relived all the saints' feasts that I had gone to when I was a kid. Every now and then I added a few words myself, but it was nice to drift back to the past listening to the river of words that came from Fiorina.

"During the summer a nice feast was St. Oliva. Maybe that feast and the feast of the Madonna of the Soccorso were the only ones where the people from the valley and those from the mount came together – all Coresi. It was also the feast with a few organized games like the horse ring race. But I must say that the other two games left me speechless. The feast took place in the middle of August. There were all kinds of watermelons, big and small. Those who sold them would place the watermelons out in the middle of the street. Then the fun began. Someone would run and grab the watermelon and then they had to sit on it to break it. Normally, the boys from Cori were the ones who did it. All the people would watch and laugh.

"Then there was another game, the race to the top, the so-called Climber of the Pole, the greasy pole. In the little town square, in front of the church of St. Oliva, they would plant a wooden pole that was fifteen metres high. Then they made the pole slippery by covering it with grease. At the top of the pole they planted a wheel. They tied different kinds of gifts to the wheel. Gifts like prosciutto, sausages, packs of pasta, clothes, ashes and charcoal. Whoever managed to climb to the top of the pole grabbed one or more gifts and pulled them down the pole. The crowd roared with laughter when some poor climber would grab the bag full of ashes. It wasn't easy trying to climb up the pole. Some climbed up the pole and at some point, due to the grease and fatigue, would slip back down. Some of the younger climbers tried to cheat by pulling out little sacks of dirt from their pockets, which they would smear on the pole in an attempt to get the grease off the pole. After a while, they were able to clean it off a bit and finally climb up.

"Everyone had fun. When I relived these memories in my mind, I realize now that those were games that belonged to other times, to another world, a life that was full of misery and struggle."

"You are right. Often we don't realize that we have fun at other people's expense. Up until now you've never talked to me about the feast of St. Maria of the Soccorso."

"I already told you that it was one of the only feasts where all the people from Cori were united: the people from the Valley and people from the Mount altogether. Everyone followed the procession. It went from St. Maria of the Valley, the most important church in Cori Valley, all the way to the Sanctuary. Rain or shine, it didn't matter. My grandmother and my mother always went to the procession.

"Up until I was five or six years old, I followed the procession and walked with them. Afterwards, when I was older, they let me walk with the other girls. I enjoyed it. My parents were Catholic and every Sunday we went to church. They had me go to catechism class. I knew all the prayers by heart. That's why I could daydream while I was in the procession, distracted by people in the street or at their windows. I still managed to say the various prayers though. I followed the procession from beginning to end, from the valley to the Soccorso, reciting the different prayers with the rest of the girls. My grandfather and my father would wait for us at the town square in Cori Mount.

"It was quite tiring to walk for a couple of hours from the valley up to where the Madonna was. Not only did I like watching the people who were out in the street, but I also liked to see all the windows that were decorated, often with velvet and tons of flowers. But what left me breathless were the different designs of flowers that lined the street where the procession passed. The day before the feast, boys and girls would go out in the fields and pick all kinds of flowers of varying colours. After, some talented person would place the flowers on the ground to form an image. Sometimes it was the figure of the Madonna, or the saints, or Jesus Christ, or some other figure. Sometimes, instead of a figure, the flowers were scattered like carpets. They were really beautiful. Who knows if in Cori you can still find all this? I myself have seen how much the world has changed over here."

"The feast and the procession of the Soccorso are still the most important of the town, but ever since I was a boy many things have changed."

"The thing that I remember most was the people who walked through the whole procession barefoot. Not to mention that everyone would be wearing their best clothes for the occasion. But as you walked down the street you would see a lot of misery. Especially from the town square in Cori Mount up to the Sanctuary, you would see a lot of unfortunate people, some with no arms, some with no legs, blind people, and so on, all begging for a bit of spare change."

"Some things today aren't the same as before, but there are still plenty of things that one can see that makes your heart cry."

"The world is really a strange place. All that misery and all the thoughts and good intentions that came to mind during the procession seemed to disappear in front of a big plate of homemade fettuccine. On that day they tried to make sure that even the poorer households were able to put some fettuccine on the table." Fiorina paused. "Maybe we should go rest up? It's past one a.m. Tomorrow we'll be up all day."

"You're right. It's time to go to sleep. Even if I never want to stop listening to you speak."

We got up and went upstairs. In front of the door to my room, Fiorina kissed me goodnight and bade me sweet dreams.

IX

Bombs Rain Down on Rome: The Drama Begins

I was dead tired, but inside, my soul was calm. Talking to Fiorina and listening to her tell her story really did do me good. When I was with her, certain images of Cori, even if I had removed them from memory a few years ago, came back to mind. It felt like they had always kept me company – everywhere, far away from Cori and even in Italy.

The room that Fiorina had selected for me was beautiful. Beside the bed and the wooden closet there was a sofa, an armchair, a table with a chair, a bookshelf full of books, and against the wall at the foot of the bed there was a television. I could not wait to lie down. After using the bathroom and doing what I needed to do before bed, I undressed quickly and slipped under the covers. I was curious to see what books the bookshelf contained, but I felt exhausted. As soon as the lights were off, all sorts of thoughts started dancing in my head – about Fiorina from Cori, who had been living for the past half century in Canada, about this strange friendship and attraction that had started to grow between us, and about Flav, too, and the peace and calm that Jadwiga inspired and the special friendship they both shared. Then my fatigue kicked in and soon I fell asleep.

Often after a few hours of sleep it happens that I suddenly wake up and it takes me a while to get back to sleep. Then I'll start to toss and turn under the covers. And so at some point, I began to hear sounds coming from Fiorina's room. I sat up, listening intently. The strange sounds seemed to be moans, and the image of Fiorina and Jadwiga with their arms around each other's waist while they walked back into the house flashed before my eyes. Men are curious creatures too. I got up and did something I was really not supposed to do – I leaned close to the wall, straining to hear through the wood. I understood almost right away that what I was hearing were moans of pleasure, continuously and repeatedly. I remained frozen, but the creaking noises that the bed was making were familiar. It was the noise that a bed makes when a man and a woman are making love.

The first thought that came to mind was that Jadwiga had gone into Fiorina's room, and from what I heard it didn't seem plausible. I didn't understand. Someone was making love in the next room. The moans of pleasure were unmistakably female and it couldn't have been that Flav had gone into Fiorina's room. After all, it was her son! Or maybe someone else had arrived in the middle of the night? However, I was pretty sure that they would have told me if that had been the case. Maybe everything was just a dream. Was it possible that Flav and Jad had moved into Fiorina's room and Fiorina went to sleep in another room? Why would they need to do that? What if both of them had gone into Fiorina's room?

I felt weird. Not only because of what I was hearing, but because of what I was doing. It's true that it's hard to control yourself when you're curious; but it was shameful to be spying the way that I was, and I shouldn't have been snooping into other people's affairs.

However, my curiosity kept me glued to the wall, even as my guilty conscience chided me to move away from it. The silence that followed helped me out of my dilemma. I jumped back into bed and, after tossing and turning for a while, my mind full of thoughts, I fell asleep again.

The morning after, when I opened my eyes, I noticed right away that it must be late. From the window, even though the shutters were closed, I could see the sunlight filter through. I looked at the clock. It was already nine thirty. I sprang out of bed. I walked over to the window and opened the shutters. It was a beautiful sunny day. From the window I could see the lake. A few hundred metres separated the house from the lakeshore. Out on the lake sailboats were visible. Surrounding the green fields were huge maple and oak trees.

I went to wash up and shave. My mind drifted back to what I had heard the night before. Once dressed, I headed downstairs. Not a soul around. Maybe they're sleeping in, I thought. Or maybe they've already gone out? From the huge window I caught a glimpse of a pleasant woodland scene, the rear of the house and a deck in the direction of the lake. I felt as if I were in some sort of paradise.

Since I didn't see anyone and I didn't know what else to do, I decided to go outside. The air was cool, cool and delightful enough to revive the dead. The view was absolutely amazing. Not only the lake with the sailboats dotting it, but all around me, the trees full of warm fall colours, everything was so beautiful. Some of the trees must have been thirty metres high. There were birch trees, ash trees, red and white oaks, lots of different evergreens and maple trees, including the kind that makes sweet maple syrup. For centuries maple syrup was honey and sugar for those who lived here before the arrival of the Europeans. It is the leaf from the maple tree that is on the Canadian flag. The leaves on the trees were already turning red and yellow, even though fall had just begun. This spectacular scene took my breath away.

I was heading towards the lake when all of a sudden, in the middle of the trees, Fiorina appeared to be walking quickly. She was wearing a snow-white sweat suit. On her head she wore a white baseball cap. She saw me and waved. I walked towards her. She walked towards me too, a happy, peaceful look on her face. She seemed more beautiful than ever. Calm and relaxed. She opened her arms and hugged me tight.

"Good morning. How are you, did you sleep well? After I wake up in the morning here, I like to jog in the woods."

I figured that I must have dreamed everything last night. Yet, I found it hard to believe that Jad and Flav went into her room and she went to sleep somewhere else. However, apart from some minor problems, I really had slept well.

"Yes, really well. It was a long, deep sleep. As soon as I woke up I noticed it was late. I didn't hear or see anyone in the house, and so I decided to come outside."

"Jad and Flav went for an excursion to Georgian Bay and then to buy some groceries. They'll be back around one o'clock. Come, let's go inside, I'm sure you'd like a warm cup of coffee and milk and maybe a piece of cake. If you feel like going this evening to see the sunset at Georgian Bay I'd be happy to take you there."

"Thank you, you are always kind and generous and if it doesn't bother you, I must say that this morning you seem even more beautiful than ever."

"You are really nice and no, it's not a bother. Actually, I like it when someone compliments me, thanks. Let's go," she said, her eyes smiling as we headed back to the house.

All of this seemed so natural to me, as if I had always lived here and had been Fiorina's friend forever. She warmed up some milk and what seemed to be a litre of coffee. Then she put out jam, apples, butter, cookies, some sweet bread and different fruit juices. I filled a glass with orange juice. I drank a cup of milk and coffee with a bit of bread and butter. Fiorina drank only a glass of orange juice.

"Well, Fiorì, I guess we can say that you had a happy childhood. At least until the war came."

"You are right, especially when I was in Cori. My grandmother and grandfather used to spoil me from morning 'til night, and they always let me do what I wanted to do. Near my grandmother's house lived a family of farmers with many children. The youngest one was a girl my age. Her name was Mimma. I wonder if she's still alive. We were always together when they didn't take her to the fields. She didn't go to school. She finished Grade Five and then she stopped. Ever since she was a just girl she did all the housework, while her parents and her older brothers and sisters went to work in the vineyard or in the olive grove, or somewhere else. The family had a pig that they grew and fed.

"During acorn season, while I was at my grandmother's house in Cori, Mimma came one day to tell me that they were all going to the woods to pick acorns and did I want to go along. The acorns were used to fatten up the pig and to make the meat tasty. I told my grandmother that I wanted to go along. They didn't want me to go for a number reasons: I would have to wake up in the middle of the night, it was cold, I wasn't used to it and it was really tiring. Nonetheless, I kept begging and pleading until they decided to let me go.

"We woke up and left before you could see the first light of dawn. I was so happy I could barely stand the excitement. My grandmother prepared my lunch bag and inside it she put an omelette sandwich and a bottle of water. It was such hard work and so tiring that I was dead tired. It's true, I wasn't used to it! For Mimma, it must have been a regular day, just like any other. But I had never felt so tired in my whole life. I understood what hard work meant, even if Mimma's family tried to coddle me. They told me to sit down and rest, and protect myself from the cold. On the way back, they sat me on the donkey so that I could rest a bit. I liked that. But I also wasn't used to riding on an animal. When we got to my house and I got off, I couldn't move. I had bow legs and my back was stiff. After leaning on my grandmother for a bit I started to take my first steps."

While I slowly sipped my cup of coffee, I took in Fiorina's words as well as her eyes. My cup of coffee seemed never-ending, as Canadians drink coffee by the litre, just as Italians drink wine. Fiorina's words could be read in her eyes as they flowed out of her soul. While Fiorina told the story of how she had spent a day picking acorns with Mimma's family, the days after the war came back to mind, when I used to go with my father, mother, sister and brothers to pick acorns and chestnuts for Ruzzica[17], our pig. He got his name when he was a just piglet. He had been playing with me and my brothers and had literally rolled down the stairs. I told Fiorina and we both had a good laugh.

"When I was in Rome and I ran into my girlfriends, I had fun telling them about the days that I spent in Cori. They were all ears, as if they were listening to a fairytale. One thing's for sure, those days of fairytales ended too soon. In Rome, in my high school, between students and professors all we could talk about was the war. Now and then someone disappeared and no one knew what had happened to them. They had overthrown Mussolini. I didn't even recognize my father. One day he told us that he had to go to Milan on some mission. My mother didn't want him to go; even Hans who worked at the German Embassy and who knew more than we did told him that it wasn't a good idea. However, my father left anyways saying that it was useful for his career and maybe away from Rome he would have

---

[17]Ruzzica in Corese slang means little wooden wheel.

a better understanding of what was happening. Besides, he said, he would be gone only ten days.

"I had already turned fourteen and so I was old enough to understand. But all the things that were happening were confusing. We didn't have problems as far as money was concerned. The notary that my mother worked for paid well, as far as I could tell. One morning, while I was at the oratory with my friends, we heard airplanes flying low, followed by loud noises that I had never heard before, the sounds of bombs exploding. Everyone went running home. It was August 13, 1943. I will never – and I say never – forget it.

"As I neared my house, I saw Hans get into his car and drive off. It was a strange sight to see him there during the morning hours. My mind confused, my heart beating a million beats a minute, I ran up the stairs to my house. My mother opened the door. Looking at her face and her appearance, I thought she might have been high or drunk. Her eyes were strange, her hair was a mess, and she was wearing her nightgown. It wasn't like her to show herself in that way. Especially at that time of the day and with visitors. I became even more confused when she threw her arms around me and hugged me tightly to her chest. She started saying, 'My poor girl, were you scared? I heard the explosions from the bombs they dropped. What bad, awful times we are living, and your father insisted on leaving. Lord only knows where he is. Mother Mary, please let him come home.'

"I could tell that she was agitated. My heart kept beating even faster. She felt it and hugged me even tighter. I reacted by saying, 'But what happened to you? Your hair's a mess, you are wearing your robe. You know that daddy knows what he has to do. Do you have to go to the notary's office or not?'

Normally, she would go right after lunch. She closed the front door and then went to the kitchen to drink a glass of water. She sat down. I was all sweaty and dirty, so I took off my dirty clothes and started washing my clothes and myself. She looked at me with such sad eyes. I told her that I had seen Hans leave the building in a big hurry. She looked at me even more upset. She sat down next to me and hugged me, almost crying. She told me that we wouldn't be seeing Hans anymore because he was leaving that night. He had been called back to Germany.

"Finally, it's about time!" I exclaimed. "As far as I'm concerned, he wasn't at all pleasant."

Even my mother said, 'Finally, it's about time' with a strange look on her face and her eyes lowered. Then, all of a sudden, she started to cry.

"Ma, ma, why are you crying? What happened?"

"My daughter, my ..."

Fiorina's eyes were glassy. She came closer to me and then she squeezed my hand. The moment had arrived. She was about to tell me the part of her life in Italy that had been hell for her.

"Pietro, you have no idea about what is coming out of my soul! It has been buried and hidden inside for so many years! Every now and then in the past I had nightmares or some flashes in my mind...but I can feel that telling my story helps me feel better... even if it brings back a pain that I thought I had gotten rid of forever."

"Fiorina, you're giving me a gift, the gift of a great friendship."

She squeezed my hand even tighter.

"My mother squeezed me to her chest and then she let me go. She looked at me with an expression that I had never seen. 'Fiorì, you're old enough and you need to know that Hans came to say goodbye. He told me that I was the best out of all the people that he had met in Rome. He said that he liked me, that for some time now he had realized that he had fallen in love with me, and that he couldn't leave without making love to me, and that I needed to give him this gift. You probably noticed all the compliments that he showered on me, even when your father was around, and that they didn't bother me at all. Unfortunately, we women are like that. Sometimes we're strange. But I had only ever been with your father, and I had loved only one man, your father. I told him that he had been a good friend of the family, that it had been a pleasure getting to know him and to have him over as a guest. It had been nice walking around Rome sometimes without your father, but what he wanted to do just couldn't be done. I had a husband and a daughter. Then he started coming closer, touching me and caressing me. The more I kept telling him to stop, to go away, wishing him luck in Germany, the more he insisted. Then he changed and became angry. He started to threaten me, he started hugging me tighter. I tried to push him away, to move away. I almost started to scream. Then he pulled out a gun and pointed it to my head. He said that if I wouldn't make love with him, he would have to kill me and then he would have to kill himself. You have no idea how fast my heart was beating, and my blood seemed to boil.'

"I looked at my mother as if I didn't know her. Tears were welling up in my eyes. I've already told you that it had been a couple of years since I had my first menstrual cycle and my mother had slowly explained how women are made. She helped me understand the functions of the different body parts and she had already taken me for my first visits to the midwife. Mentally, I was older than my actual age. I guess you could say that I was already a little lady. But I didn't have a boyfriend yet, and up until then there had been a few innocent caresses with the boy that I had told you about, the one who had pulled me under the doorway and tried to touch me. I was a little bit behind some of the girls who went to school with me. I remember hearing them talk about things that they did with the older boys – things that sometimes left me confused or that I didn't quite understand. Instead, what my mother was trying to tell me transported me to another world.

"My mother told me that Hans forced her into having sex with him. She felt desperate because of it. Then she told me that at least it had happened on a day when she couldn't become pregnant. She told me that she felt tortured and couldn't give herself any peace. She felt even more desperate because at some point there was no need for the gun because she let herself go. She couldn't believe it, she continued making love to Hans as if it were natural. She no longer thought about her husband or her daughter. She didn't think about anything. Then Hans left. Only the shame remained, and it started to gnaw away at her. Right after all this, I arrived…

"An immense silence fell upon us. My head was spinning. It was full of a thousand different thoughts. I kept looking and watching my mother, who fixed herself up a little. She had also calmed down. She prepared lunch. We ate. I thought about my father and wished that he was at home with us.

"She got ready to go to work at the notary's office and before she left she said, 'Fiorina, don't tell your father what happened. He would die. Hans left and certainly we won't be seeing him again. It is better that only you and I know, and that you also will have to bear a bit of the cross. For that, I am really sorry. Try to relax, be calm and study.' My mother left and I remained alone. I mean really alone. Who could think of studying?"

Down Fiorina's face a few tears rolled, but a few smiles appeared. She let me hold her hand tight. I felt upset. I didn't know what to say or what to do. Fortunately, Fiorina was an extraordinarily strong person. She got up and pulled me into the kitchen, telling me that it was time to start preparing something for lunch.

"War can destroy everything and everyone. When it happens, no one has respect for anyone, or for laws or rules. Life is already full of traps. But with a war in progress, you don't understand anything, and everything becomes uglier, without any order whatsoever. My dear Pietro, I never could have thought a few months earlier to see not even a fraction of everything that followed. No more than a month before, I had witnessed the fall of Mussolini, who seemed omnipotent, a saint and a benefactor. Oh, all the misery that one could see in Cori or in Rome! The people who thought that things could have been done differently, and my grandfather, who couldn't stand by or stay quiet when he saw people who were treated badly. My father, a few years before the war, had said to all of us that Il Duce could straighten the legs on dogs and that in Italy there was respect and order, and whoever wanted to work always found something to do. It was only later that we found out that none of this was true, that order and respect were only for the lords, the rich, the sirs. Those who were in power could do whatever they wanted. All the poor people had to live with the unliveable. After, we started to understand that whoever tried to rebel in any way ended up badly and that the Aryan race, which they taught us about at school, was crap.

"The fall of Mussolini took place in the middle of the summer. I was in Cori. My grandmother had brought me to the Sanctuary of the Madonna of the Soccorso. It must have been the day after the fall of the Fascist regime. While we were coming back from the mountain where the sanctuary was, we ran into people who were coming and going in and out of a building, hauling things past the gate of an olive grove belonging to the Celani family, where there was a summer camp. The people had carried away everything that there was. Anyone could understand that something big was happening. My grandmother had a worried expression on her face and had started to walk quickly. At the square of Cori Mount there were groups of people talking. From one of the bar cafés, some people came out with a poster of Mussolini. They placed it against a wall near the gate to the building they called the Cazzetta and everyone went and spat and swore at the poster. Right in front of the gate there was an elm tree that was as tall as a building. Underneath the shade of the elm tree there were many people. There were no police officers anywhere. There was great chaos.

"My mother was waiting for us at my grandparents' house. She told us that while she was waiting for us to come back, her worries were eating away at her. She told my grandparents that we had to leave right away and go back to Rome where my father was. That's exactly what we did. Even in Rome we found everything upside down. Every day things got worse, starting from that horrible day with Hans and my mother and the bombs that fell on Rome."

Fiorina seemed to come back to the present. She worked in the kitchen preparing the food and setting the table, while she continued telling her story calmly. From the big window the sunlight and even a bit of warmth filtered through. The weather seemed to get better as the hours passed. I felt at home, and I had become part of Fiorina's world.

Another hour went by before we heard the sound of Flav's car. It was one o'clock. Jad and Flav came back, all happy and festive. They greeted me and Fiorina warmly. They had bought a fresh salmon, which must have weighed five or six kilos, and they put it in the fridge, saying that we would barbecue it on Sunday. Seeing Jad and Flav that happy, everything that I had heard the night before came back to mind. Who knows if they were the ones I had heard making love? But how could that be? In Fiorina's room! I started to wonder if I had really dreamed everything.

Fiorina had already finished getting lunch ready. We all sat down at the table together and Flav and Jad told us all about their excursion. They said that it was an absolutely marvellous day, and the colourful autumn foliage had been a sweet sight for the eyes. They had stopped to drink a juice in a bar-restaurant in Penetanguishene. There was a flyer full of specialties and all sorts of different wines that made your mouth water just reading it. Jad seemed particularly young and full of energy. She kept herself busy bringing dishes and clearing the table while we ate. Fiorina remained seated. A few times even Flav got up. It was easy to understand that Jad felt like part of the family and was treated as such.

As soon as we had finished eating, the three of them got up and started cleaning off the table. I also wanted to give a hand, but they sent me to sit on an armchair. Then Jad prepared a coffee. Not a little cup of coffee for espresso, but a mug full of coffee for each of us. Fiorina told Flav and Jadwiga that she wanted to take me to see the sunset on Georgian Bay and asked if we all wanted to go to dinner at the bar-restaurant that they had gone to earlier that day. We would have to leave right away, however. Everyone went to their own room to wash up and get ready, and in roughly forty minutes we were leaving.

X

Christmas 1943 and Images of Cori

I was the first one to go downstairs. I stepped out into the early autumn air. How sweet! From Fiorina's house you could see the blue mirror-like lake surface shine. I could also see a few sailboats scattered on the lake, which was surrounded by the colourful woods. This place was really amazing, calm, silent and made for relaxing. Jadwiga and Flav came down next. They were so cute. To me they seemed like a couple. Lastly, Fiorina. Wow. Before she was dressed all in white and now she was dressed all in black, both pants and jacket. Around her neck she had tied a red silk scarf. The more I looked at her the more she seemed to be made to be admired: a sort of sensual magnet, a prima donna.

We all got into the Mercedes, Jad and Flav in the front like before and Fiorina and I in the back. Fiorina took my hand and squeezed it. She looked at me with a warm, affectionate expression, almost gratitude. I felt myself starting to be uncomfortable. I don't know if it was due to shame or a sensual pleasure, or something else. The car followed the lake until we arrived on the opposite side facing Fiorina's cottage. Then the car turned right on Awenda Park Road.

Jad and Flav spoke quickly in English, as though they were the only ones in the car. They spoke so fast that I wasn't able to understand a single word. I squeezed Fiorina's hand and said: "Fiorì, do you feel up to continuing with your story?"

Fiorina looked at me with a sweet expression.

"You really want to know the whole story? Well, I've already started, might as well finish. A few days after the bombs were dropped and everything else that had happened between my mother and Hans, my father came back from Milan. He walked in after dark. My mother threw her arms around his neck and it seemed like she didn't want to let him go ever again.

"My heart was pounding and beating fast. A tear slid down my face. It was a tear of fear, as well as a happiness that I can't explain. My father had come back home: handsome, strong and protective. He held me up to his head and, looking intensely at me, spoke my name twice: 'Fiorina, Fiorina.' I threw my arms around his neck and I started laughing and crying at the same time. My mother looked at me with a happy yet worried expression. My father told me not to worry. He said that he knew about the bombs, and that the important thing was that we were altogether.

"That night being together was fabulous. It was a sensation that I had never felt before. I spent the whole night watching my father and my mother, and I kept thinking about what had happened between my mother and Hans. It was as if a nail had been driven into my head, reminding me that my mother had made love to Hans – not only because she had been threatened, but because at some point she had actually enjoyed it and she hadn't thought about anything else, not about me or my father."

Flav slowed the car. We took a pleasant drive. The park was very beautiful. The Canadian forests are breathtaking in the fall, full of colour, and every tree – maple, birch and oak – a different colour. Every now and then in between the trees you could catch a fleeting glimpse of some animal or bird.

After a few moments of silence, and with all the thoughts that were floating around in my head, I turned to Fiorina and said: "Those days must have been horrible for you."

"They were ugly, sad days, I must admit. I watched my father and mother and kept thinking that I would have liked to talk about it with my mother in order to understand how and why the world was made the way it was. Sometimes it felt like I had something stuck in my throat, but I pretended that it was nothing. Not even when I was alone with my mother did I ever ask or talk about that day.

"The days slipped away, one after another. Whatever happened that day, ate away and consumed me quietly on the inside, not to mention all the other things I had to think about. Everyday life in Rome became harder. Both my father and mother worked. I went around to the different shops and tried to buy and gather everything that was needed. I always attended the oratory and I kept going to school, even though those carefree days that I had spent there just a few months earlier were gone. They no longer existed. I had fewer and fewer classmates, and they had all kinds of problems.

"During the month of September Rome was in chaos. The king abdicated and deserted his country. The Germans were in complete control. All over Rome people were talking about the battles that were raging at Porta San Paolo. There was a sinister sense of fear that went around the streets. My father's face became more worried and darker every day. My mother relied on her strong character. It was almost as if that day with Hans never happened. She still sang and hummed as she cleaned and did her various chores and the housework. She was good at lighting up my father's face, and a few nights I even heard them making love.

"We stayed in Rome until Christmas Eve, when all three of us left for Cori. We spent the holidays at my grandparents' house and we managed to get some peace and quiet. I still remember well that we spent the whole night playing tombola and the goose game. Even Mimma came with her family. Unfortunately, our conversations were rife with worries. Cori was also controlled by the Germans. You could see them everywhere. They had taken over houses and buildings, either limiting or restricting the owners and some they had even thrown off their own property.

"Before midnight, around eleven o'clock, we all went to see the birth of the baby Jesus at the Church of the Madonna del Soccorso – me, my mother, father, grandparents, Mimma and her family. A few days earlier it had snowed. You could see the white snow still on the ground in the garden; however; that night the sky was calm, clear, no clouds and full of stars. There was an icy wind blowing, and it felt like it was slashing your ears. Nonetheless, the church was full of people. It wasn't like the year before. The people's prayers seemed real and came right from their souls. We all took communion. The emotion in the church was so thick that you could cut it with a knife. On the way back down to the town it seemed that we were walking in a procession, although in the other direction.

"All people could talk about was the war – all those who had gone to fight as soldiers and those who had been called now to fight, all the suffering of the families, the families that cried for their loved ones who had been victims of war, and about the food card that was needed to buy food. Every now and then you could hear chants against Mussolini. The sad truth is that those were my last carefree days in Cori and in Italy. Mimma and I were no longer young girls, but we weren't women either. Even if it was freezing cold outside, the

110

last days of December were spent mostly playing in the streets or at home. We played as much as we could without thinking too much about the fact that the sky was about to fall on our heads."

Even if Fiorina was telling me about the worst times of her life, she appeared calm. Maybe the fact that she was telling her story did her soul good and brought peace to her heart, something that all the money in the world, a big house and all her friendships couldn't provide her. Here in Canada she obviously had a lot of good friends.

Jad and Flav were talking; I don't think they understood what we were saying. We travelled on about twenty kilometres when Flav brought the car to a stop in a parking lot where several other cars were parked and where a few single-storey cottages stood.

We all got out. There was an entrance to a campsite and other services, offices and a notice board containing information about the park. Fiorina linked her arm under mine. We all headed towards a dirt path, Jad and Flav ahead of us. A couple of times Fiorina asked Flav the name of some bush or some tree that she wanted me to know. Walking in the middle of all those trees, away from streets and cars, underneath the swoops and glides of the birds and next to Fiorina made it an even more pleasurable place than it already was on its own. We walked along quite slowly. While we walked Fiorina continued telling me her story.

"I remember that those days flashed by. In the morning I would go to my grandfather's shop. He would sing opera to me while he hammered away. He really did like music. I would sit on a stool as if I were a doll and listen as if hypnotized. I also liked listening to him talk to the clients when they came to place their orders – wooden tubs to make wine, wooden barrels, kegs, butts – or to bring some item to be repaired. Though the war wasn't that far away, and despite all the Germans in the streets, the town seemed peaceful. Everyone kept doing exactly what they had always done every day. They got the provisions they needed for their households and did what was necessary for their vineyards, olive groves and shops.

"My grandfather said that it was a good season for olives. A lot of the olive trees were laden with olives. During the day the carriers would pass by, their sacks full of olives. Sometimes they rode donkeys, mules or horses, taking kilos of olives to the oil mill. Those were days of hard work for everybody. At dusk, all the workers would return home together. The women would put the woven baskets under their arms and the men their olive harvesting tools. They were so tired they could barely stand up. Yet a lot of young people would go around town singing. I was especially impressed to see young girls my age work so hard. I also knew for a fact that there were some eleven-year-old girls who worked full days. Those weren't easy times. From morning till night, when the people headed home from work, the streets were packed. On the little street on the way to the Madonnina, there were so many people that there wasn't enough room to walk. The streets of Cori filled with people until evening. Then everybody would go home and have warm soup before going to bed, because the next morning everyone had to wake up early for another day of hard work.

"The work was tiring and difficult. The people left so early in the morning that it was still dark outside and they would come home when the sun had already set. To earn some bread to eat there wasn't a time limit. One day after lunch my grandfather took me with him to the oil mill of Loici Scolaro, which was on Via Ninfina. He was taking olives to be crushed, the olives that he and my grandmother had gathered at an olive grove of about sixty trees that was called the Vattiodro and located a kilometre or so from the Fontana Mannarina[18].

"The oil mill was crowded. Everyone was wearing worn-out clothing that was covered in dirt and grease. The oil mill employees had greasy faces. There, in the middle of all this dirt, I must have

[18]Fontana Mannarina is located in the countryside around Cori Valley; it has a spring and fountain.

seemed like a little princess from some other world. Outside it was very cold, but inside the mill it was hot enough to make you sweat, thanks to the big fire. Every now and then they would throw another piece of olive wood on the embers. My grandfather had brought along a loaf of bread. He asked me to toast some bruschetta[19]. Before pouring fresh olive oil on the bread, I rubbed some garlic on it. That distinct odour of garlic and oil and the taste of the bruschetta made at the oil mill are gone forever, although on certain hot days it almost seems like I can smell the fragrance under my nose."

I stopped under a tall maple tree. I looked at Fiorina. Now she was a beautiful Canadian woman; yet, hearing the things she said made her seem more Corese than I was. She wasn't the only one who would never smell those aromas again. There are still a lot of oil mills in Cori today, but they are not like the ones from the past.

"Listening to you is like reliving the days when I was a boy. Right after the war my father brought me to the oil mill under the Cazzetta building at the town square in Cori Mount. I liked the warmth, eating the bruschetta at the oil mill, the fire, the aroma of freshly crushed olives, watching the crushed olives, which they would place in the containers and stack so that they could be crushed. They would throw hot water on the paste and then tighten the press, and slowly the oil came out."

I told Fiorina that I felt like I had always known her.

"How is it possible that the oil mills aren't the same and they no longer let you toast your bruschetta?"

"Yes, Fiorì, even that has changed. The bruschetta today is toasted at home or you can order it in a restaurant; however, they use gas to heat the grill and they no longer are toasted on the olive wood embers. They still are tasty, but the flavours that one could only find at the oil mill are gone and only the memories remain."

---

[19]Bruschetta is a large slice of toasted bread flavoured with garlic and oil, and often with fresh tomatoes.

Flav and Jadwiga were a few hundred metres ahead. Fiorina and I started walking again. The forest is always beautiful. Every now and then there were stretches of swamp – wetlands. Different areas where there was water and the trees were of a different kind and fewer in number.

"The last time that I went to an oil mill was during one of the holidays. A cold and beautiful day, but inside it was heavenly, warm due to the fire burning and all the people that were there. At some point my mother, my grandmother and my father arrived and even they asked for a bruschetta. My grandfather wasn't near the embers toasting bread. He said that it had been a really good year for the olives and that he had a lot more olive oil than he needed for us at home, so he sold some to the owner of the mill. Our oil was brought to the house and stored in the cellar. It was December 30. I remember it well because the day after was New Year's Eve.

"The morning of New Year's Eve I was with my grandmother in the kitchen. My mother and father went to visit some friends and buy some things that were needed for that evening. I enjoyed being in the kitchen with my grandmother. That night my grandparents' friends and Mimma and her family were coming over. We prepared a lot of food. We made different dough mixes for deep frying; then we filled two big serving bowls of fried broccoli, fried codfish, fried potatoes, and fried pumpkin. My grandmother took the big wooden board that we used to roll out the dough and placed it on the table. We started mixing flour and eggs to make some *tagliolini* – little square pasta pieces for the chicken soup to be ready to serve if someone preferred them instead of the *stracciatella*[20] soup, which was served before the homemade fettuccine that my grandmother had made the day before. She had made four sheets of *sfoglia* – puff pastry. These flaky pastry sheets were each a metre and a half long, which she laid

---

[20]*Stracciatella* is a soup with eggs cooked and beaten into little bits in the chicken broth.

out on her bed to dry. After they had dried, they were rolled up and my mother cut them into little slices. The fettuccine that were still rolled up were placed to dry on two wooden rectangular bowls. As soon as the sfoglia dried off a bit, my grandmother taught me how to cut them really thin to make them into tagliolini.

"At lunchtime my grandfather came back from his shop and my mother and father came home as well, and we were all together. When they saw me all covered in white flour, my father started laughing and my mother said that she raised a little baker. My grandfather, as always when he was happy, started singing one of the many operas that he knew. We had a light lunch because everything else had been prepared for dinner, including a kid that weighed seven or eight kilos. It had already been cut into pieces and seasoned so that it could be cooked after lunch."

As Fiorina spoke, my mother appeared before my eyes, when she was in the kitchen, preparing something to eat for the whole family for some feast, the kneading trough full of bread loaves on top, at the bottom, where the wicker doors were, fried food: broccoli, pumpkin, dried salted codfish, artichokes and fried potatoes. I tell Fiorina this as she puts her arm under mine and we stroll among the trees behind Jadwiga and Flav.

Without realizing, we must have walked a kilometre or two, because Fiorina turned to me and said, "I hope you aren't already tired, because we're almost at a beautiful spot where, at this time of year, and especially when I have a guest that I like, I love to walk to. We're almost there. In the meantime, we can continue the story about my *other* life."

"To be near you and to listen to you tell your story, I could walk indefinitely. Can't you tell by the way I'm listening?"

"That night my grandmother's house filled with people. There were at least thirty people. We were all tightly squeezed in around a table laden with all kinds of different foods. Mimma and I were the happiest of everyone there. My grandmother, with my mother's help as well as mine, my father's and grandfather's, had managed to prepare everything. Everyone brought a gift. A bottle of some type of wine to taste, cooked figs, dried apples in slices, long slices of crunchy cookies made from honey chestnuts and almonds, ring-shaped cakes and an assortment of sweets, and sponge cake. Someone also brought a bunch of grapes, still attached to the stem. They had preserved them for months in the cellar. They were a bit soft but were really sweet. My grandmother was overwhelmed. 'You didn't have to bring all this stuff!' she exclaimed.

"But there were a lot of us and we all had a good appetite. From the stracciatella soup to the sausages, I had never seen so much food disappear in one night. The sweet dessert pizza with ricotta and ground coffee, which was served at the end, made me lick my lips. The price of coffee had gone up and it had become very expensive and hard to find. All the coffee Mimma's mom had managed to find, she had used to make the sweet pizza, which was consumed in a flash. Afterwards, they made coffee from toasted barley or chicory grass roots, like they did every day in the poorer households. Who knew how long they would have to make coffee that way? It was an amazing New Year's Eve feast. Even if every now and then they talked about the war, the bombs that were dropped on Rome, and despite the things that could still happen to us, being together in my grandmother's house made us feel calm and safe.

"Once we had finished eating and cleared off the table, and after the dishes had been washed, my grandmother pulled out the *tombola* and we started to play. There was plenty of wine for the adults and enough sweets for everyone. The happiest moment came after three or four games of tombola when Mimma won. She started singing and she threw her arms around my neck. We went to bed at three in the morning, even though once in a while the light would go out and we had to light candles and a few oil lamps.

"The next day was a feast day and no one had to go to work. We had fun and it felt good being together. Mimma and I probably had a little more fun than the others. We had never stayed up that late before. When I did go to bed, I barely managed to change my clothes before literally falling asleep like a sack. My grandmother woke me up the next morning around eleven o'clock to go to Mass. My mother and father had gone to the Madonna because on the way back they wanted to stop by the Tratticci's house, the shepherd, to say hello and to wish them a happy new year. His farm was located at the last curve before you reached the sanctuary. My grandmother brought me to Santa Maria Church in Cori Valley. The church was so packed and there were so many people that you couldn't even move. In front of the church young boys had formed circles, but there were even older men who were playing. They were betting on the dice game. The winner was the one who threw both dice that had a higher number, therefore the higher sum. They played the card game *sette e mezzo* and the tower coin game.

"I liked watching them play the tower coin game. All the players placed the metal coins that they had on the table. Then they formed a circle to count out and see who would be the first one to throw the round stone at the tower of coins. The player who had to throw the round stone would patiently stack the coins on top of each other, making sure that they had the same side up. Once he had taken aim and thrown the stone at the coin tower, the player could take all the coins that had landed with the reverse side up. If no coin fell on the reverse side, it was the next player's turn. The circles where the men played *marone*, or tower coin game, were many, and you could find them in other places, not only at the open space near Santa Maria Church. That's why all the coins that you saw in Cori were scratched up or bent or both. Only men played these games, like the dice game and the coin tower game. The women were only allowed to watch, which was unfortunate for me because I really would have liked to play the coin tower game."

I couldn't believe what Fiorina was saying. She seemed to be enjoying herself while she told me all about New Year's Day 1944, talking about folklore games brought up the fact that the women weren't allowed to do what the men did – even things that the women would have liked to do.

At some point it seemed that we'd been walking in that forest forever and while we walked all of a sudden, out of nowhere, what we had been talking about became real. What Fiorina was telling me had really happened, and some things that she said I felt as if they had happened to me too, only at some different place, with different people, and Fiorina and I weren't that distant or different from each other.

XI

Georgian Bay, the Allied Landing at Anzio and Nettuno – Bombs on Cori

A few frogs began to croak in a nearby swamp, as if a concert were about to commence. A little while later, almost as if someone ordered them to stop, the frogs fell silent, and a few metres ahead I could hear Jad and Flav's voices. Even further away, I could hear the voices of the other hikers. Fiorina smiled at me and started speaking again.

"After New Year's Day, we stayed another two days in Cori. Then we left for Rome because my mother and father had to go back to work. And besides, I too had to study and do some homework. So for Epiphany I was already in Rome. It was my last *Befana*. I was old enough to know that the gifts that the children found near the fireplace in the morning hadn't gotten there on a flying broom, but were placed there by parents. I went to sleep right away after saying goodnight with a mischievous smile on my lips.

The next morning I got up right away. My mother and father were still sleeping. On the table in the living room my eyes fell on a package that had been wrapped with coloured paper. It contained an outfit, a pair of shoes, a scarf and lingerie. Everything was brand new. The lingerie was exactly what young women were wearing then, and it was the same one that I had asked my mother to buy me a few months ago. As happy as a kid on Easter morning. I ran to their bedroom. They were already awake. And I must say that it rained hugs and kisses for everyone that morning.

"The next day school started. I was happy. But my Latin professor, who was also the youngest of the professors, the one that my girlfriends and I had a crush on, didn't show up. The rumours were that he was Jewish. He had managed to hide it from everyone until a few weeks prior to his disappearance. Then, one of his friends had betrayed him, and now no one knew if the fascists had caught him and handed him over to the Nazis to be shipped off to the concentration camps, just as they had done with all the people from the ghetto. Some said that he had managed to get away and was hiding somewhere.

"It was only years later that I learned the truth about those camps, that they had coldly exterminated large numbers of people. To be more precise, they were left in chambers to suffocate until they were dead and then their bodies were burned. Jadwiga has told me unbelievable stories about Auschwitz, Poland, in Oswiecym, near her town. A few of our classmates were also missing, maybe because they were still on vacation, or for some other awful reason. Who knows? When I left for school, I was happy. But I went home with my heart in my throat and my head felt heavy as if I were hung over.

"Even at home things weren't easy. Rome was full of Germans. They were the ones in charge, in command. From my father's reasonings I understood that those who were against the Germans and fascists became more dangerous. If the latter caught someone who opposed them, they would make them wish they'd never tried. You could say they were lucky if they didn't end up in the cemetery. My father had never gone against the government, but he agreed with my grandfather; he didn't like things that were unfair. When he started seeing people around him disappearing for no good reason and the bombs falling on Rome, not to mention everything that they were doing to the Jews, he started asking questions. Now he had new beliefs. He recalled how they had started hunting Jews and throwing them out of schools and offices. He said that watching everything that had happened and not doing anything about it was cowardly. Everyone had been blind. My father seemed to be another person. It also seemed that he had aged ten years in a few days.

My father lamented the misery people had to endure just to survive day after day, while only few were able to live a rich life. All this was right there, before everyone's eyes, but no one did anything about it. In addition, now that the Germans were in charge, bombs began to fall from the sky and people didn't know what to do. Sometimes at home I would hear someone grumble that the worst thing was that we didn't know what bad things were still in store for us. There was often a depressing atmosphere at home."

I hugged Fiorina tightly. I myself felt that I was reliving everything that I had seen and heard as a child, almost as if I were dreaming. My mother and father's hard work. And even my brothers' hard work. I said all this to Fiorina. And she looked at me with sad eyes. In the meantime, we had reached a clearing. Flav and Jadwiga, a few hundred metres ahead of us, turned and motioned to us to hurry up.

Fiorina hooked her arm back under mine. She squeezed it a bit and then continued.

"And yet, everything that happened at school and at home, the hard times, the anxiety and uncertainty were nothing compared to what was about to hit us. On January 13 there was another bombing. As soon as my fear passed, I ran straight home. I found my mother already there. We hugged each other without saying a word. When my father got home, he told us to go to Cori because we were safer there. It was now clear that they would continue bombing Rome and we could die. Cori was a little town. They wouldn't bother touching it. He said that he was going to stay in Rome so he wouldn't lose his job; it was what he had to do. For the first time, we were in tears when we said goodbye to my father before going to Cori.

We got to Cori in the middle of January. The train station was full of German soldiers. It was after lunchtime. In the town the streets were full of strangers, people from somewhere else. Girls my age I didn't know went home holding baskets under their arms. There were a lot of mules, donkeys, a few horses and a few wagons, all full of sacks that contained olives or big containers full of olive oil. The aroma that I smelled was really different from the odour that I smelled in the streets of Rome. There was the stench of animal manure, but there was also the ubiquitous aroma of crushed olives, from the oil mills, from the containers and also the smell of fresh olive oil that people were taking home to conserve.

"My grandparents, as always, were happy to see us arrive, even if this time it wasn't a vacation. Everyday life had become difficult for everyone everywhere. My grandfather said that a lot of clients owed him money. Too many families cried because their children were fighting in the war far away, while some families were already in mourning for the loss of their children. We were worried for my father, who had remained by himself in Rome. At home people talked about the families that had left for Rome when they had the chance because they thought that they would be safer there, since Cori was full of Germans and no one knew what could happen. No one knew what to do anymore. Whatever you did, you were wrong. It was all pointless. My mother was also worried about me because I couldn't go to school."

The trees had thinned out considerably. Jad and Flav had stopped walking and we had almost caught up to them. Behind them there was a strangely tinted light. It was brighter than the light we had seen walking through the forest; yet it was a bit weak because the sun had started to set and was quite low. We arrived on top of a cliff, which seemed to be a balcony overlooking Georgian Bay. Georgian Bay is the most eastern extension of Lake Huron. The sight before our eyes was absolutely breathtaking and unbelievable. The sunlight hit the water at an angle and the lake had assumed different colours. First, a dark white colour appeared on the lake surface under the cliff, which turned to blue, then greenish-purple and pink towards the horizon. The sky was mottled with a scattering of clouds, which were yellow-ish-reddish-purple, depending on the angle of the sun's rays. It filled one's eyes and one's soul.

All four of us were standing at the edge of the cliff, about forty metres high. A path led to a staircase of a hundred and fifty-five steps, which allowed people to descend to the pebbled beach below. But it was too late to climb down that staircase. The trees – oaks and maples – although less dense there, came right up to the edge of the cliff. Underneath the rocky cliff, on certain spots along the beach, a few birch, cedar and fir trees could be seen. Thousands of different birds that I had never seen before sang and cheeped all around.

"Fiorì, first of all let me thank you for bringing me all the way here. Everything is absolutely beautiful. There's so much to take in. I don't know where to look."

"Yes, it really is beautiful. Sometimes we come here even during the winter. The colours are different then, but the long walk is encouraging and the panorama is always magnificent and enjoyable. Watch and see how the colour of the water changes as the sun gets lower and lower."

We stood silently, all four of us, watching the sky and the lake mutate slowly. When I asked the name of the island that one could see far off, Jadwiga recounted the story.

The island came into being thanks to Kitchekewana, an ancient god that the Hurons believed in. According to the tale told over the years, Kitchekewana was a giant god who lived and defended the whole island and all the people who lived around Georgian Bay. He was as tall as a building and wore a hat that was made out of thousands of bird feathers and his outfit was made of hundreds of furs. The necklace that he wore around his neck was made out of logs. One day, according to the legend, the other Huron gods realized that he was always angry. They thought that if he had a girlfriend he might mellow. And so they started going from village to village, visiting all the different tribes to try and find the prettiest and liveliest young girl. In truth, Kitchekewana was in love with Wanikita, who apparently was of unearthly beauty. He tried to declare his love for her, he tried wooing her, and he wanted her to be his; but she had fallen head over heels in love with the most handsome warrior from her tribe and she didn't want anything to do with Kitchekewana. When Wanikita said no again, Kitchekewana went crazy. One day, he was so distraught that he dug his fingers into the dirt and grabbed everything that he could grab and threw it into the lake. That's how Georgian Bay got the thirty thousand islands, which makes it such a rare and beautiful bay. The five holes that his fingers had dug became five little bays within the greater Georgian Bay: Midland, Penetang, where we had been, Hog, Sturgeon, and Matchedash.

We all stood and listened, spellbound, as if every word Jad uttered was true. As she told us the story, her face was so beautiful that she herself could have been Wanikita. The sun set lower and lower by the minute. We clapped our hands for Jad and, like a tour guide, she continued: the island's name is Giant's Tomb Island, and it is the place where the giant Kitchekewana is buried, or at least that's what people have believed for centuries. And there's more. They also say that the spirit of the god continues to inhabit the whole area, and it is thanks to him that the colours of the trees, the water and the sky are so beautiful and fascinating. Jad added that sometimes the blowing of the wind sounds like an angry voice that yells, and the song of the birds seems like the cry of a sad lover who finds no peace.

And then she burst out laughing.

Tightly squeezed together, we all enjoyed the marvellous sunset. The water seemed even ruddier, thanks to the pink and purple clouds and sky. Everything was red one minute, then it faded to grey.

I saw Flav put his arm around Jad's waist. My mind became confused again. I didn't know what to think. Obviously, there was a bond between them. Exactly what, I didn't know. Fiorina put her arm back under mine and said it was time to go back to the car before it got dark. We walked back at a much faster pace. A lot of birds still sang and a few frogs croaked as well. Flav and Jad led the way and we followed in silence. By the time we reached the car it was dark. All around us there was a great stillness. Then we were off again. Flav and Jad never tired of chatting. But Fiorina and I remained silent, reflecting.

Fiorina turned to me and said, "When you return to Cori, you will have many things to remember…"

I was sure that I would not easily forget the emotions I felt, everything that I had seen in Toronto, and all that Fiorina had been telling me. They would stay with me for the rest of my life.

"You left off talking about the bombing of Rome, and about all the fear and confusion," I said.

"My mother and I believed that if we left Rome and went back to the town that things would be calmer and safer. But life had become difficult even there. Whoever had home-grown or homemade things still managed to have something to eat; but everyone felt the weight of having to ration food items, from flour to salt. The only good thing was that I could meet up with Mimma often, even if she worked inside or outside the house from morning 'til night. Who knows what happened to her? What a hard worker she was! The more time went by, the closer the war got to the small town of Cori.

"My grandfather kept saying that no one understood anything anymore. A few stray Italian soldiers had come back to Cori and the homeland. The king had left Rome. Mussolini had created a new government and continued his part in the war with the Germans somewhere in Northern Italy. The German soldiers who were in Cori acted as if they were on vacation. Often you could hear airplanes flying by. Some people said that the Germans and the fascists had lost the war. However, it was just as easy to believe the rumours circulating that the Germans were about to get some secret weapon that would allow them to win the war, which would also explain their nonchalant behaviour.

"There was so much misery around. Bread, rice, sugar – everything was rationed. If you wanted to buy a piece of meat at the butcher shop you needed to have a pass, a stamped coupon, and you had to wait in line. I used to keep my grandmother company while she waited in line. The streets of Cori weren't the calm paradise that had kept me safe and sheltered from the miseries that happened elsewhere. People no longer gathered wool and copper for the soldiers, after all, the poor only had their eyes left to cry with. The real problems began on January 22. There were continuous explosions coming from the direction of the sea, and it was obvious that it wasn't the sound of thunder. One night, at 3:00 a.m., my grandmother and mother got up to look out the window to see what was going on. Even I was awake.

"My mother said that maybe it would be better if we all went to Rome where my father was, but my grandparents said that no one should go anywhere until we knew what was going on. They told me to go back to bed. My mother lay down beside me to help calm me. The morning after, everyone was talking about the bombing and the explosions the night before. Some said that the Americans had just landed on the shores of Anzio, and that they would arrive in Cori, and in no time they would reach Rome. You could also tell that the Germans around Cori were no longer on vacation. It was a constant coming and going of men and machines and cannons never seen before. Everyone was afraid and worried, but also resigned. We began to convince ourselves that the German soldiers would have to leave Cori. Instead, the days passed and it was clear that the war was so close that it was in our homes. Cisterna and the coast along the sea had been hit by cannon fire. With all the fear and confusion no one imagined that the bombs and the cannon balls would reach Cori, even though we knew that they had bombed Sermoneta close to Cori on the 19th. That morning around nine thirty a.m. we heard the planes fly overhead. They bombed Velletri.

It was really cold in Cori. You could hear the explosions of the cannons and every day the air forces flew by. We were right in the middle of the war. We heard that the bombing on Velletri had claimed roughly a thousand lives. On Sunday morning my grandparents and my mother took me to Mass at San Francesco Church. There were a lot of people from Cori Valley and Cori Mount. On the way there and back we talked to many people. Even Mimma had come with us. We weren't worry-free like we had been a few weeks before. A whole week of fear had caused us to grow up a lot faster. We listened carefully to what the grownups said. The concern was so thick we could have sliced it with a knife. The cannons didn't stop, but it seemed that the bombs and the cannon balls wouldn't reach Cori. Everyone went to work as they had always done, picking olives or doing other back-breaking tasks. Shoe shops, furniture shops, the saddler and the carpenter – everywhere people went to work as usual, but they were on high alert."

While Fiorina talked, I took her hand and squeezed it. All the images of those days came back to mind. I had gone back to when I was a boy. It was impossible to forget those days if you had lived them, especially when someone talked about them the way Fiorina did. As I listened to her, my heart raced.

All this time Flav was talking calmly to Jad, who was even calmer. We were driving by the park on Kettles Beach Road and were about to turn on Champlain Road. It seemed like we were always driving in the middle of the forest. Every now and then you could catch a glimpse of a nice home, its windows brightly lit. On the left-hand side there were pathways here and there that broke off from the main road. At some point, we followed a large curve to the right and the pathways then broke off in that direction. Flav turned on Beach Road, which skirts the lake for a distance. While the houses were beautiful, the real beauty was in the plants and trees in the forest, now in shadows. Even though it was dark, the passing headlights would momentarily illuminate the autumn foliage. Now it was night time, and listening to Fiorina seemed even more intriguing.

"Those last days of January flew by, between cannons and the noise of airplanes that passed over our heads morning to night. It was cold. We would spend most of the day in the kitchen by the chimney where the fire was always on. My mother allowed me to study. I was always reading or doing homework. My mother told me that I had to prepare so that one day I could be independent, and studying would allow me to do it.

"On Saturday my father was coming to Cori. That way, once we were all together we could decide if it was better if we all went back to Rome in view of what was happening in Anzio and Velletri, which weren't far from Cori. Maybe I could continue going to school and also finish the year. On Saturday night we went to wait for my father where the buses arrive. We were happy, after all it had been a long week without seeing each other. It felt more like years. When I saw him get off the bus my heart was racing. I ran towards him and hugged him tightly. I was so happy that I almost started crying.

"That night there was a festive spirit in my grandparents' house, despite the heavy discussions and the worry. My father told us that living in Rome with the Germans and the fascists, not to mention the old and new resistance fighters, had become really dangerous. A lot of simple things were no longer available. Long line-ups at all the shops. Everyone was waiting for the arrival of the Allies. The news that they had arrived on the coast of Nettuno reached Rome in a flash and from there spread everywhere like the wind. The people thought the Allies would conquer Rome in a few days. But my father said that a week after they had arrived there was still only disappointment and fear. All that was certain was that their front was stopped at Cisterna and Aprilia. The Germans there acted like they were the owners of the land. They had become worse than ever and were very sure of themselves. It was a good idea to wait a few days before returning to Rome. On Sunday morning my grandparents went to city hall, where someone was distributing flour. My mother, father and I went to Mass at San Francesco Church. We took our time, slowly and calmly wending our way back home along the Via Nuova. We had almost reached the Lanara[21] when all hell broke loose on Cori. We

---

[21]Lanara is a landmark along Via Nuova.

heard the airplanes arrive. They seemed like they were flying on our heads. And then everything seemed upside down. I could hear the bombs exploding close by, a lot closer than when I had heard them in Rome. I squeezed my mother tightly.

We moved away from the road and stood underneath an olive tree. All the noise from the planes and the bombs induced fear. The whole world seemed to tremble and shake. We watched as a bomb fell on the little yellow house belonging to the Giupponi family on Via Nuova. Thick black smoke rose up over Cori. Once everything calmed down, and the sky seemed free of planes, we hurried home as fast as we could. As we passed the Giupponi's house we saw the door still burning. Our hearts were literally in our throats when we got home. Everyone we ran into was in a great hurry. I also heard people saying that we had to leave the town because they'd be back to bomb it again. At home my grandparents were wild-eyed with worry. They hugged us for so long that it seemed like they didn't want to let go. No one knew what to do. We found out almost right away that at San Pietro Church there had been a disaster. The bombs had hit it right on and there were several casualties. It was clear that we had to leave the town. We couldn't wait any longer."

XII

Evacuees on the Mountain Somewhere Between Cori and Rome

While Fiorina talked, Flav continued chatting with Jadwiga as he drove. That first bombing came back to mind. I used to live on Via Regina Elena, which is now Via San Nicola. I was with my little sister playing in little square by our kitchen window when I heard the bombers fly overhead. I saw the bombs explode in front of Giupponi's house. The little yellow house on Via Nuova was set on fire by an incendiary bomb. To one side of the little square, underneath an olive tree in front of our kitchen, my older brothers and my father had made a bed out of hay. Up until this day I don't know how I managed to do it, I was so scared. But with a quick jump, I grabbed my sister and we hid both under the bed of hay. We clung to each other underneath that hay bed, until our mother came and pulled us out crying, 'my poor children!'

I told all this to Fiorina, who squeezed my hand as if she wanted me to know that even though we didn't know each other back then we had both seen and lived through the same things. We could really understand one another.

Fiorina continued.

"To leave and go back to Rome wasn't simple, nor was it safe to stay in our house in town. My grandparents wanted to go to their cottage near their vineyard at Fontana Mannarina, near the olive grove called Vattiodro. Mimma came by to tell me that she and her family were leaving town. Like the rest of the people moving away, they were going into the woods to build some kind of hut or cabin for shelter. People thought that it was too dangerous to go towards the train station where they had their olive groves. It was almost as if we all had to go off to war. My grandfather talked to some people he knew who owned a few mules, so that they could help him bring some of the materials that were needed to build a shelter. My father went along to give them a hand. Everyone hoped that the Americans would advance in a few days.

"Within two or three days the majority of the people had left the town. Almost all of them went up into the mountains. There were rumours that the heads of the town council had gone to Rome. No one knew who was in charge. Goodhearted volunteers tried to help out. They dug and pulled the dead out of the rubble of San Pietro Church and the houses that had crumbled. They brought the bodies to the cemetery and helped the injured. Some were lucky enough to find transportation to take the seriously injured to Rome.

"Everyone helped one another. Thousands of people were scattered in the woods. The bombs and cannon balls continued to hit the town. Unfortunately, there wasn't any good news anywhere. It wasn't easy to find food. Whoever had cows or other animals killed them for meat. The people traded amongst one another. There were also people who did what was known as "black market." This meant that they went down the mountain and back into town to find necessities. Some went all the way to the townships of Norma or even to Carpineto and Montellanico. Misery and hunger were widespread and felt by everyone."

Flav's car had left Beach Road and turned onto Andrew Lane. We were really close to Penetanguishene. Fiorina calmly continued talking about those last few days of January 1944. Back in those days I was just a kid, but I had seen and heard a lot. Listening to Fiorina, I could feel the sound of the bombs shaking my soul. I saw myself walking after Giggetto, my father's mule loaded with all sorts of stuff. Together with my mother, my grandparents and my brothers, we walked down Via delle Fontanelle, now Via Leopardi, with the flow of people all heading for the mountains.

I remember the faces of men and women, young and old, and everyone carrying something. Their eyes were wide open and they wore strange expressions on their faces. There were some who struggled to carry the injured. I recall seeing a woman covered in blood, sitting on a chair that two men had brought. I was full of fear and questions. She was like a Christ figure who had come down from the cross. Whoever thinks about starting a war should die before they are even born. Fiorina noticed that my head was spinning with so many thoughts. She let a bit of silence fall between us before she started speaking again.

"My grandfather, with the help of my father and others, built a hut near the Pezze[22] where many were gathered."

"Fiorì, this is absolutely unbelievable. I was one of the evacuees at the Pezze, on the land of my uncle Pippo, my aunt Vincenza and her sister Giustina, my grandmother! The land wasn't really theirs.

---

[22]Pezze is located in the Lepini Mountains, outside Cori.

They rented a plot of Giupponi's land to let cows and pigs graze. They even had a cabin and a hen house."

"Is it possible? Maybe we ran into each other in the middle of all that chaos! It must be a sign of destiny that we really had to meet. Only you understand me and with you I can remember those days of fear and misery. A few days later, my mother and father started looking for a vehicle with which we could get back to Rome. They thought that it was better if they went back to work and that we would all be better off in a big city. We couldn't take the train there. They found a truck that someone lent them and it was going to take us to Rome. We exchanged goodbyes with my grandparents who looked worried.

"Back in Rome life was not easy, nor was it calm, even when looking for food. I went back to school. My parents did everything so that I wouldn't miss many classes. We spent the whole month of February in Rome. We didn't know what was happening in Cori while we were gone. We knew only that the Allies and the Germans were between Cisterna and Campo Leone. Fighting alongside the Germans were Italian soldiers who had remained faithful to Mussolini. The number of people who died and the number of injured were very high.

"Saying that school continued is just a way of saying it wasn't the same anymore. Rome had been bombed another six or seven times. No one had any way of knowing where and when they would drop another bomb. If we heard the warning siren or planes, we would run and take cover. We would find each other huddled together tight with people we knew or didn't know and it didn't matter.

"At the notary's office where my mother worked, work was drying up. But the more free time my mother had, the more she thought about her parents who had left their house and were living somewhere in the woods. At the beginning of March we decided to travel back. Cori was reduced to a mountain of rubble and debris. The bombs had brought down and ruined almost all the churches. San Pietro, Santa

Maria in Cori Mount and Santa Caterina were gone. Many of the homes had been totally destroyed. It was like hell on earth, literally. The majority of the people were completely desperate; however, my grandparents were happy to see us in the woods of the Pezze. I was older now and I would often go with them from the mountain to the town to look for flour, water, beans and fava beans. One time I even went with them all the way to Norma to get a bit of corn flour. The planes continued to fly overhead. We saw the planes in a nosedive on top of Cisterna, over Littoria[23] and over Cori. The cannons never ceased. The Germans, who had given things to the people, like leftover food, now began behaving like animals."

Flav's Mercedes ran up kilometre after kilometre. After we had passed Andrew Street, Champlain Road and Robert Street, we were at Main Street in Penetanguishene. We drove almost all the way down the street. Then Flav parked near a restaurant. As soon as we walked in I understood that Fiorina, Flav and Jadwiga were regular customers there from the way the staff welcomed them like family.

I was confused, I felt dumbstruck and my soul was torn. Fiorina's story and all the memories of what I witnessed and felt on my skin made me feel like everything inside me was turned upside down. A little peace and relaxation was exactly what I needed now. The restaurant was warm and elegant. Almost all the tables were occupied. It was like being in church. Everyone spoke in a whisper. Being the last to arrive, we caused some havoc. We hadn't even sat down than the owner came right out to our table. He was the son of Polish immigrants and he showered Jadwiga with attention. He spoke to her in Polish. Jad told him that I was from Italy and that I also spoke some Polish. I must admit that he treated us like royalty. He brought us a bottle of Chianti, explaining that the wine was a gift for Jad and

---

[23]Littoria today is Latina.

the Italian guest. Oleg was his name, and he was very attentive the rest of the evening.

We all ordered fish, a mixed platter of freshwater fish from the lake – oven-baked and roasted carp, trout and pike. At least, that's what I understood. It was a real specialty. Oleg insisted that to complete our meal we try the dessert, a Polish cake that was his mother's specialty. Although she was in her seventies, she still worked in the kitchen from time to time.

When we were finished, he came to say a warm and affectionate goodbye to all of us. When we walked out of the restaurant it was already ten-thirty. Fiorina said that it would only take us half hour to return home. On the way we talked about the many beauties of the park, of the colours of the lake while the sun set and about dinner. Back at the house Jad and Flav rekindled the fire. Jad filled the electric kettle with water and we all had a nice warm mug of tea. Just like the first night, Fiorina and I sat in front of the fireplace, Jad and Flav went and sat in front of the television.

"Jad and Flav seem to share a special bond," I remarked to Fiorina.

"They're great friends. Flav took to Jad right away as soon as she came to work in my house. During the feast days they spent a lot of time together. Especially since Flav's wife went to live in Montreal, where their daughter is studying medicine."

"Oh! Flav's married?"

"Yup, it's been twenty-five years now. The woman he's married to is French Canadian. Even if in the last few years they've been living separate lives, they still keep in touch."

"How is that?"

"It's a complicated story. I don't know if it's right that I tell you. But if we have time and most importantly, if I feel strong enough, I'll tell you."

Fiorina's face seemed to darken, but only for a moment, because it lit up right away as if by telling me her story a heavy weight was lifted from her shoulders.

"The last days of the war you were in Cori?"

"My grandfather had made a really nice wooden cabin, and there were also four beds made of hay. He had made them into bunk beds, one on top of the other, two on one side of the room and two on the other. We slept comfortably and had plenty of space for all five of us. In the middle of the room there was a fire that we kept going day and night. Sometimes the humidity and cold seeped into your bones. That, however, wasn't the worst part. What was worse was the sound of the planes flying, the bombs exploding, the cannons firing, and not knowing what to do. Food was scarce and there were many sick and injured people due to the attacks on the Germans. My mother wanted to bring my grandparents to Rome, but they refused to move. They said that if they had to die, they would rather die in Cori.

"One day there was a little celebration under a chestnut tree, a baby had been born. The mother, who was an evacuee from Cisterna, decided to call her Libera, which means freedom. Who knows what happened to her? Every day that passed, things seemed to get even harder. Time went by and the food supply dwindled. I forced myself to eat the bitter leaves of brambles and clematis. Some of the more courageous people went all the way to Rome to try and bring back food and whatever medicine they could find. Instead of city hall for a bit of flour and pasta, now they distributed it on Via delle Fontanelle.

"Every now and then a German ambulance took some of the seriously injured to the hospitals in Rome. Some people had managed to find an old radio. They were able to listen to foreign radio stations and spread the word that the Nazis and the fascists had lost the war and it was just a matter of days before they would surrender. Meanwhile, Cori was full of soldiers and army trucks. Across the entire region right down to the shore all you could hear were the explosions and the cannons that continued firing. Not a day went by without hearing planes flying overhead or without hearing explosions, near or far.

"My father returned to his job in Rome, and to check on the house and see if it was better for all of us to go there. My mother tried to convince my grandparents to go to Rome. A few days after my father left, in the middle of the woods of Cori, the apocalypse seemed to have arrived. All of a sudden we heard the planes. They were really close. It seemed like they were right over our heads, that's how close they were. The explosions of the bombs followed. Everything shook. We were in hell. It was April 12. Entire families were killed. There were many injured, both old and young. The living buried the dead as best as they could. A few of the seriously injured people were taken to Rome. Exactly how they managed to bring them there, I don't know.

"My grandparents were almost convinced that we should all leave for Rome, but we had no idea how we could get there. On the other hand, few people managed to leave Cori. After a few days, my father came back. In Rome there had been another bombing near our house. The desperation gnawed away at us and the fear of what tomorrow could bring ate away at our soul. The days went by. The German soldiers were in control of Cori, but you could tell they were panicking and scared. All the arrogance and calm they had displayed earlier were gone.

"In the middle of April, my father went to Rome again to get a better understanding of what they said on the radio, if it was true or not. Rome was an open city and they couldn't continue the war inside Rome even with all the bombs they had dropped. My mother and I remained in Cori and we went to the Fontana Mannarina where my grandparents had their vineyards to try and find something to eat. I had learned to balance and carry weight on my head like all the women in Cori. Sometimes I risked going around with other girls and boys. In Cori you had to walk over, in the middle, or alongside all the ruins. The bigger and stronger men were captured by the Germans so that they could work for them, looking after the animals, like the sheep and pigs they had managed to round up and which were slaughtered later on.

"The fear of the bombs and what the Germans could do, or what could happen if the Allied Forces broke the German lines at Cisterna, were all things that kept us awake night and day. The days seemed to overlap without us even noticing. My father came back from Rome at the end of April. He stayed a few days in the town and then left for Rome again. It was considered a free city. They said that they wouldn't have fought, but no one knew what the Germans would do before they retreated. At least that's what people thought. One would see Allied planes in the skies overhead. It was better to wait a little longer before returning to Rome.

"On the day of the feast of the Madonna del Soccorso a lot of people went to pray to the Sanctuary, but the bombings continued just the same. It seemed like there was nothing that tied the earth to the sky, if there ever had been something."

It was late. Flav and Jad turned the TV off and said goodnight. They were going to sleep. Fiorina and I stayed up a little while longer and then we also went to sleep. In front of the door to my room Fiorina gave me a goodnight kiss and wished me sweet dreams.

I was dead tired, but my mind was full of thoughts that kept sleep at bay. I was also listening carefully, recalling what I had heard the night before. Curiosity isn't only for women. Then fatigue took over and I fell asleep. During the night I woke up more than once and every time I didn't hear anything strange. I thought that maybe I had dreamed everything from the night before. But how could it be? What about Flav and Jad, who seemed to be made for one another?

Had they really gone to sleep alone? Why was Flav's wife living in Montreal? Then my eyelids became heavy and slowly closed. The next morning the sunlight woke me up. The shutters on my window had not been closed. It was nine o'clock. I jumped out of bed as if I were a giant spring and hurried off to the bathroom to wash up and shave.

XIII

May 1944, the Allied Landing, Rape, the Midwife

Before going downstairs all cleaned up and rested, I looked out the window and saw Flav and Jad, both of them wearing tracksuits, fixing a big grill under a maple tree. Once downstairs, I saw Fiorina, also wearing a tracksuit, running around in the kitchen. She came towards me with a brilliant smile on her lips.

"Well, hello! I hope you slept well. Do you have any preferences for breakfast? We've already had breakfast and we all went for a jog in the woods. Flav and Jad are outside preparing the barbecue, and then they're going for a drive. They're going to Midland. Do you want to go with them?"

"Good morning, Fiorina. You really do have a beautiful smile."

"If you say it again I just might believe you."

"Fiorì, not only do you have a beautiful face, but you are very beautiful."

She came close and gave me a kiss.

"You do know how old I am, right? I'm in my seventies! Well then, what do you want to do? Do you want to go with Flav and Jad?"

"I wouldn't change you for a woman in her thirties!"

Fiorina had a hearty laugh.

"Right now, all I need is a bit of creamy coffee so that I can warm my stomach up. I would like to go and see Midland again; however, I prefer staying with you because I can't wait to hear the rest of your story."

"Whatever you prefer, I'm happy with that. It's a nice day and we can go for a walk along the lakeshore."

Jad and Flav came back inside and they joyfully greeted us. Jad said good morning to me in Polish and asked if I wanted to go with them to Midland. I told her that while I certainly would like to go, with the little time that I had left in Canada, I wanted to spend it talking to Fiorina.

Flav, in a playful way, said they were a little jealous, but it was understandable. They went upstairs to change. Fifteen minutes later they came back downstairs, said their goodbyes and left. Fiorina finished cleaning up the kitchen. Then she went to freshen up, saying that in about ten minutes we could go walking; the salmon was prepped to be grilled on the barbecue.

The day was awesome. The sun shone brightly, the sky was clear, not a cloud in sight, the temperature just right, and the splendid autumn colours filled one's eyes. Out on the lake sailboats were criss-crossing the water in all directions. Fiorina came out wearing a white sweat suit and a little red hat. She linked her arm under mine.

"Let's go."

We walked silently for a while, then Fiorina picked up where we left off the night before.

"There were days just like this one that May many years ago. Full of sun, warmth, even if we were in the middle of a war. But the world would soon be turned upside down, which would then bring me all the way here. The Germans got worse day by day. One could see it in the way they rounded up the animals, by the way they tried to capture men (who kept trying to hide) to serve them, and by the way they always gave less and less food, even to the people who worked for them. You heard different stories going around that they had started their retreat from Cassino. People said that the city and its sanctuary had been totally destroyed by bombs, and that it was just a matter of time before they retreated from Cisterna and Campoleone as well.

"Mid-month my father had come to take us back to Rome. But with all the bombing and cannon fire, the mopping up operations and the fighting, the trip was a big risk. We couldn't do anything, because right as we were deciding if we should leave or not, all hell broke loose. I think it must have been May 23. We saw the planes coming from over the mountain and head towards Cisterna. The landscape around it was full of smoke. All you could hear were explosions and flying cannonballs. A few days later we could hear exchanges of gunfire close by. The Americans had arrived.

"Word spread throughout Cori that the Germans were gone. People started climbing back down the mountain. It was like a river of people, climbing down the mountain, just like a procession. They went back to their houses, but many of those houses had been reduced to rubble. People found shelter wherever they could – in cellars or with other families. The church of Santa Oliva had been spared by some miracle. Basically, wherever there was shelter to be found people took refuge in it. Everyone helped clean the streets and clear the ruins. They helped rebuild the houses that had been destroyed.

"Even my grandparents' house was partially in ruins. So we thought it was better if we stayed in the hut where my grandparents had the vineyard near Fontana Mannarina. Hopefully, we would leave for Rome in a few days. This time it seemed that the Germans had left for good. In Cori and in the surrounding area you could see the poor Germans who had died, their bodies abandoned, and army tanks and trucks that had burned and were smouldering, with dead soldiers hanging from the doors. It was a real hell.

"The Americans were in and around Cori for a few days, leaving behind all kinds of food wherever they were camped for people to fight over – chocolate bars, canned meat, beans, carrots and corn."

At this point Fiorina stopped her story. We were near the lake. It was marvellous. But Fiorina's face seemed to be made of marble. She was right in front of me. All of a sudden she threw her arms around me and hugged me tightly, almost suffocating me. She was breathing heavily and near tears. Then she took a big, long breath, as if she were sucking in the air all around her. She regained her composure and then started again.

"My grandparents, with the help of my father, were fixing the house and often my mother and I would also go and help. Americans, British and Canadian soldiers passed by. The war was over. The planes flew overhead. You could still hear cannons firing near Velletri, but where we were the hell on earth seemed to be over. One morning my mother and I were all alone in the little hut. My mother had finished picking and cleaning some spinach-like greens and at a certain point she turned to me and said that we didn't even have a drop of oil. She told me to go to my grandparents to pick up a bottle. It must have been around ten o'clock. It would take me a good half an hour to go and another half an hour to come back, but I could make it in time for lunch.

"I started to head towards Cori. It was a hot and sunny day. I walked quickly. Right at Fontana Mannarina, not even a kilometre from the hut, there was a parked truck with four or five soldiers. They weren't Germans, so I picked up the pace and calmly continued on. I was happy. My father had said that as soon as my grandparents could go back to live in their house we would leave for Rome and maybe I could go back to school right away. I liked going to school.

"As soon as I was closer, one of the soldiers who was holding a machine gun in his hands started yelling at me. I felt my heart freeze over. Faster than the wind, they came towards me. They grabbed me and took me over to a grassy area near the road. One of them started touching me all over. They touched my breasts and even in between my legs. I started yelling and I tried to run. But one of them grabbed my waist. Another one arrived and helped him. They threw me on the ground while the others laughed. One of them forced himself on top of me and pulled out a knife. He pressed it against my throat and I turned to stone, like a statue. I didn't understand. Another two arrived. They held me down. They took my shirt off. They ripped my underwear, the knife always pressed against my neck. I cried.

"Then I understood what was happening. They were raping me. Two of them held my legs apart and they took turns. They were almost all dark skinned. I don't know how much time went by. I felt as if I were dead. When they left, I was still shaking and afraid. I was full of blood, semen and fear. Another two trucks drove by, but I still couldn't move. I crumpled against the fountain wall and stayed hidden. I felt like I had literally been cut open. Slowly, I started to recover. I didn't even pick up the chocolate bars or the canned meat that they had left behind.

"I got up, and instead of going towards Cori, I turned around and went back to the hut. First I walked slowly and scared. Then I sped up and started to run. My mother was outside getting some water from the well. When she saw me, all dirty and with my clothes torn she came towards me yelling. I burst into tears. I couldn't stop myself once I started. I didn't have to tell my mother what had happened. She understood right away. She also started crying. She screamed and cursed the whole world. Then she gave me something to drink and washed me. She never stopped stroking me. She kept saying, 'My poor little girl, what did they do to you, daughter of mine?' I kept crying, 'Mommy, my mommy, my sweet dear mommy.'

"Later on, around two o'clock, after lunch my grandparents and father arrived. They found us in bed hugging each other. As soon as they knew what had happened, my grandfather cursed everyone from the evil Mussolini to the King – he even cursed the sky. The yell that my father let out was really scary. I had never heard him swear, but that day he used all the swear words. Then he crossed his hands behind his head. He sat down and started crying like a baby."

Fiorina had stopped talking. She held on so tightly to my arm with unbelievable strength. She stared at me, looking at me straight in the eyes. It was almost as if she were out of breath, as if she had worked very hard and now she was dead tired. I felt as if my soul was in pieces. Fiorina's words had made my heart shrink so small that it was smaller than the tiniest bug. I no longer felt like I was in a beautiful place. It felt like the sun no longer shone and that around us everything was dark. Then, I felt like throwing my arms around Fiorina's neck so that I could squeeze her tightly against me. I wanted to take away the enormous pain that I had seen in her eyes.

We started walking again in silence. Words weren't needed. Fiorina was a strong woman. She started again and I understood that she wanted to empty everything that was in her soul. She let the skeletons out of the closet, and all the years of pain and suffering. The time had finally arrived to bring everything out in the open. She never thought it possible that she would meet someone who would listen and understand.

"I never told my son everything, what I just finished telling you. Even when he started asking questions, like who was his father and where he was. I just told him a few things to satisfy his curiosity. He understood, but he never knew the whole story, the whole truth.

"That day the war had torn my flesh and planted itself in my soul. After all the crying, screaming, swearing, the day ended with a painful black cloud over our heads as soon as my grandmother said, 'Let's hope that she's not pregnant.' We didn't even think about the bombs, or cannonballs, or the difficulties that the war had brought upon on all of us. It felt as if the sky had suddenly fallen on our heads. I didn't really understand what my grandmother's words meant, but they kept reverberating in my heart. I didn't know what other pain and suffering awaited, but I started to understand that even the ugliest and dirtiest part of life had to be faced without letting the pain and anger win.

"My father said that we had to go to the police and tell them what happened. My mother agreed, but my grandparents started talking about the shame, and that we should wait and see if I were pregnant to talk to a midwife who could get me out of this mess. After a few days of crying and headaches, we started doing the everyday things that we had always done. News reached Cori that Rome had been liberated. No more cannons. Even the planes stopped flying overhead. Yet the noise remained in our heads. We started getting ready to go back to Rome. We said goodbye to my grandparents with tears in our eyes. We exchanged goodbyes with Mimma and her family who had helped fix my grandparents' house. No one had said anything about what had happened to me. Mimma and I hugged each other tightly like we had never done before. We would never see each other again.

"All over Rome there were piles of ruins. Close to our house, which fortunately hadn't been damaged at all, there were more ruins. My father went back to work at the department right away; however, you could read all the worry on his face. After another fifteen days, my mother went back to work for the notary. Meanwhile, she had asked around here and there to see if there was a good midwife that could examine me.

My father and mother babied and coddled me even more than when I was a young child. I felt strange in a way like I had never felt before. People celebrated all over Rome, but I didn't have peace in my heart. The city was still full of soldiers and I was scared of them. The Germans were gone and the war was far away. There was a lot of misery and you could see it practically everywhere. Slowly, everything started to move again and I continued with my schooling. They let us write the exams in the school gymnasium. I wrote my exams with a lot of difficulty, but with the help of my mother and father near me and with God's help as well. The following year I would go to high school. My mother, and my father too, never got tired of telling me that I needed to study just like I needed my daily bread. How I would be able to go to high school I didn't exactly know yet. Quite a few of my classmates were missing and no one had any information regarding their whereabouts. War is like a bear that is thirsty for blood and people.

"One day my mother told me that she had found a good midwife; but we no longer needed to know what had happened inside me. Days passed and I still didn't have my period. I was pregnant. We waited a few more days, but nothing. My mother cried. My father was desperate. I realized right away that I was the calmest. One Saturday morning we went to see the midwife. It was a bad day. It rained, actually it was pouring. The midwife lived near Piazza Bologna. I thought that I would find an old lady. Instead, she couldn't

148

have been more than thirty. She greeted us kindly. She was always smiling. Before she examined me, we had a long talk. I had to tell her what they had done to me. Even she shed tears. She took to me right away and was very understanding. It was almost as if she had put herself in my shoes. Then she examined me. Despite the war, she had everything she needed to find out if I really was pregnant, or if maybe my menstrual cycle was late due to the trauma I'd suffered. There were no doubts anymore.

"Then she started talking about what she would do so that I could have an abortion. When she explained what she had to do to me, I started shaking. My face must have been the picture of fear because she started caressing me and consoling me with kind words, just like my mother. She told me to stay calm, to sleep on it, to think about it for a few days, then come back to see her. On the way back home I didn't say a word. At home we found my father. We all hugged each other and we stayed that way for about a half an hour. Only a few years later I learned that it hadn't happened to me alone. A lot of women, old and young, especially in Ciociaria, in Sezze, in Norma, and other towns south of Terracina, had endured the same hell as me. Rumours circulated that they had even raped men. I later learned that they were Goumiers, Moroccan auxiliary units conscripted by the French army from their African colonies. Whoever wants to start a war should be killed before they're even born."

XIV

The Bitter Year of 1945

"The days passed. My parents tried to be positive. They said that the only solution was to have an abortion. But I was so scared that I couldn't even sleep at night. We went back to the midwife a week later. We talked for quite some time. She too tried to encourage me. She told me that I wasn't the first and that I wouldn't be the last. We only had to decide when. The whole month of June went by and I was almost convinced. But day by day I felt a strange transformation inside of me. I was no longer scared and I felt a strange calm that gave me a sense of peace in my heart. There was some fear and a strange feeling of euphoria that, even today, I can't explain how it led me to decide not to have an abortion.

"My mother and father had taken all of my pain to heart. They were more scared and embarrassed than I was. Every now and then I heard them talking, whispering, worried and crying. As soon as they saw me convinced, they got over their fears, their desperation and the shame. They found courage and started to behave once again as mother and father. The midwife met with me every week. She understood what was going on in my heart and she was close to me. I guess you could say that we became friends. She kept me company up until the last day of my pregnancy with words of understanding, sweet words of comfort and encouragement.

"That Christmas we didn't return to Cori. My grandparents came to Rome instead. They stayed even for New Year and the Epiphany. They told me that Mimma and two of her older brothers had left to seek fortune in Australia. I was seven months pregnant. I felt like I was another person. I was calm and my parents had made sense of what had happened. I stopped going to school, but I continued studying. My parents sacrificed a lot. Yet they were both convinced that I had to keep studying. At home, with the help of my mother and father, and all of their coddling, I studied more than when I went to school. The war wasn't over and life was still hard for everyone. The midwife came to visit me at home. She assisted me and she didn't even want to be paid.

"The end of February 1945 arrived. Almost nine months had gone by. The midwife came and slept at my house every night. She didn't want to leave me alone. Flav was born at night, almost without any pain. I was a single mother, no husband, but I didn't think about it. I dedicated myself to that small child with all my heart and soul, gaining enough courage to move mountains if needed. My father wrote about everything that had happened in a letter to his brother who was working as an engineer in Canada. He had left before I was born and he hadn't returned. He had been married but had lost his wife a few years earlier. He had a big house in Canada and there were a lot of jobs. He said he would be happy if I moved there. He wrote that everything would be easier where nobody knew me and everyone minded their own business. However, I preferred to die rather than leave my mother and father. In the fall I enrolled again in school.

"My mother reached an agreement with the notary so that she worked only after lunch. We all watched over the young child, who grew bigger everyday. He was just like other kids his age, even if his skin was a bit darker. My grandmother came to Rome frequently. She taught me a lot of things, and one of these was speaking Corese even better than my mother. School went well. The year 1946 was a good, peaceful year, but in the spring of 1947 a new hell started for me. My grandfather had a heart attack and within a few days he died. My mother went to stay for a while in Cori. I didn't go to school. My father also went to Cori for the funeral. I thought of my grandfather happily hammering away on the butts, singing opera. Even now I can still see his happy face, as I used to sit hypnotized on a stool in his shop, listening to him sing and watching him work.

"After the death of her husband, my grandmother almost lost her mind. She sold the shop, the olive grove at Vattiodro and the vineyard at Fontana Mannarina, and she came to stay with us in Rome. The only thing that she didn't sell was the house. She was always saying that when it was her turn to go, she wanted to die in her house, where her husband had died, where my mother was born and where I was born. For almost a year my grandmother was also a nanny to me. She was happy to watch Flav and coddle him the whole day long. After all, he was named after her, even though everyone in town called her *Fravia*. My mother and father continued to work, and I managed to pass my second year of high school.

"Towards the end of June my grandmother started feeling ill, and she was also homesick. She wanted to go back to Cori. My mother and father went with her. It seemed as though being at home made her feel better. They asked Mimma's mother and father, who were also her neighbours, to take care of her, and they told them what had happened to me. Mimma's parents said that Mimma and her brothers were doing well in Australia. They were worried that in the end even the other brothers would move there and that they would end up alone. Life really does reserve all kinds of pain and suffering for us! It seems as if we never stop suffering.

"The month of July was very difficult. They fired Togliatti, the leader of the Italian Communist Party, and the atmosphere was ugly. Cori was in turmoil. Many people were arrested and thrown in jail because they had participated in roadblocks. Everyone was scared that there would be some kind of attack on the government. My mother spent the whole month of August in Cori. Every now and then my father would visit her on Sunday. All of a sudden at the beginning of September my grandmother fell seriously ill. Three or four days later she died.

"I didn't go to my grandmother's funeral. Flav wasn't even three years old. My mother came back completely desperate. She couldn't find peace. She went back to work for the notary. In spite of all the events, she remained as beautiful as ever – after all she was my mother! Something about her, however, had changed. She seemed always tired and worn out, even when she didn't go to work. My father was worried. I began to worry about him as well. The only comfort and joy was Flav, who started talking and running all over the house.

"I enrolled in the third year of high school, but my mind was somewhere else. I often thought about everything that had happened to me, about my grandparents and everything they had taught me, including a taste of what paradise could be, about Flav, who had been conceived by violence in the middle of the war, and about my mother and father. I could not concentrate on studying. It had been my mother who made me understand that knowledge could help me in life. While she was in Cori, my mother didn't want to sell my grandparents' house. She had a special bond with the town and it was like her family. Her roots were there. All of my grandmother's savings, which had grown when she sold the shop, the olive grove and the vineyard, were placed in an account that my mother had opened at the post office under my name. It wasn't much even back then. It amounted to a million five hundred thousand liras. Obviously, I wasn't rich. But I was a girl with a baby, and those savings could be useful.

"In the house, Flav was like a gazelle in constant movement. His grandparents did nothing but worry about him. On the other hand, Flav filled our days and brought light to our lives. When he turned three, we had a birthday party for him. Even the midwife came with her husband who was an elementary school teacher. She had a baby that was one year old. She was the only true friend that I had in Rome, and she came often to visit us. She also encouraged me to study. Every time she left our house, she would leave me with a feeling of hope. My uncle wrote from Canada. He wanted to know how we were doing and he wanted us to know that he was there waiting for us whenever we wanted to go there. Then suddenly it was Christmas. We spent it in Rome; however, on the Epiphany my mother started to feel sick."

Fiorina stopped her story. Even if what she was remembering and what she was telling me was painful, she had spoken calmly. But as she spoke about her mother, her throat tightened and she almost started crying. We were standing underneath a tall maple tree with a big, leafy crest and leaves that were almost red. It was really beautiful. A lot of birds were singing and flitting from one branch to another. As soon as I got over the rush of emotions I was picking up from Fiorina, I realized that I had never asked her about her grandparents on her father's side and so I asked. Fiorina took a deep breath.

"My grandparents on my father side, well, I never knew them. They died in quick succession when I was only two or three years old and I don't remember them. This is another reason why I learned to speak Corese, because I had a special bond with my grandparents from Cori. As far as my grandparents on my father's side were concerned, all I knew about them was what my father told me. I knew that both of them were from Pinerolo originally, and that our house in Rome had been purchased with the money that his parents had left him. My father had also talked about some other distant relatives that I never met. I guess you can say that I've always been tied to Rome, but most of all to Cori, especially emotionally. Afterwards, even Cori became a faraway shadow, like a dream that could be sweet or at times a nightmare. When I heard you on the radio, and that you came from Cori, a part of my life returned and now, as I slowly tell my story, a lot of memories are resurfacing."

The day seemed to become even hotter. The lake was a strange blue colour. You could see red and green waves shine, reflecting the many trees surrounding it. Fiorina smiled sweetly when I told her that for a few years I had lived in Pinerolo. It really must have been written in the stars that we had to meet. Fiorina sat on the grass. I sat down next to her. The birds continued their serenade. If this wasn't heaven, it was pretty close. It didn't last long, as Fiorina continued telling her story.

"My mother one day started feeling tired. She had no strength to do anything. My father took her to the doctor. When he came back home his face was as black as coal. They checked her in at San Giovanni Hospital. They didn't know what she had. The notary and the midwife came to visit her. Then they said they had to operate. It was Christmas Eve. They removed one of her breasts. They gave us a bit of hope. I went to school every day. My mother never got tired of telling me to study. It wasn't easy. Flav ran all over the house. He kept his grandmother company. Now I was the one who did all the housework and late at night I studied. I became so stubborn that I would remain glued to my books. Every now and then my father would come and comfort me and tell me to get some sleep. It was the middle of March when my mother became very ill. We took her back to the hospital. They operated on her again. My poor mother, you couldn't even recognize her. We brought her back home.

"I was always by my mother's side. Her pain must have been agonizing, but despite her state she rarely complained. She talked about my father, about Flav, and how we had stayed near her and that I didn't have to give up studying. Flav started to fuss because I was at my mother's side more than with him. Some days the midwife would come and take him to her house or for a walk with her son. I would go one day to school and then I would miss the next three. That way I might be able to write my exams. My professors knew and understood what was going on and tried to help me as best as they could.

"My heart shrank and became so small that it seemed to be as tiny as a pinhead. Sometimes my father and I would hug each other silently. There wasn't any need to exchange words. Somehow, I don't know how, I managed to write my exams and get my high school diploma. We had a party. My mother's face shone with happiness. With the last bit of strength that she had, my mother came to sit with us at the table. Even the midwife, her husband and her son, who played with Flav, had come. After a few days my mother started having difficulty breathing and in the middle of the month of July she left us. Right up until the end she gave me strength, and she left me with a smile on her face.

"I still have it imprinted on my mind. I will always have it with me. My father was even more devastated than me. In just one day he seemed to have aged a hundred years. My mother knew that she was about to die and so she told us that she wanted to be buried in Cori. She wanted to be buried in the bare ground. We brought her back to Cori. My father chose to have a solemn funeral at the church of San Francesco. The church was completely full, not an empty seat.

"I felt as if I were walking on pins and needles. I stayed glued tight to my father's side. I left Flav with the midwife. Near us sat a

157

few of my grandparents' relatives and Mimma's mother and father. Even their other sons had left to go to Australia. I couldn't take my eyes off my mother's casket.

"My father asked them to play Verdi's *Requiem*. You couldn't hear a fly when the first notes announced the *Dies Irae*. The voices from the chorus entered my body like a sword. It seemed like Judgment Day, especially when they played the fanfare, *Tuba mirum*. I felt fear and anger, which shook me inwardly. It called to me when the *Rex tremendae* played and the soloists invoked God. I wanted to yell: "What have we done to you that you make us suffer so much, what has my mother done?" That scary scream remained in silence at the bottom of my soul. My silent face turned into a fountain.

"It's difficult to understand which sins we have to ask forgiveness for while they sang *Recordare*. The tenor singing *Ingemisco* said that even he was a sinner. At that moment, my soul was being destroyed by anger. For the last four years all I felt inside and outside of me was a lot of pain and suffering. The days were a sort of a penance, and despite all this I had the love of a boy that came from a violent act. My tears stopped flowing with the *Lacrymosa*, which brought a sense of peace and calm and which helped dispel my anger. It was as if I were in that coffin, hugging my mother, begging her to return to us. I hugged my father tight. I never forgot those moments.

"Just as she had asked, she was laid to rest in the ground. The trip back from Cori to Rome was full of mixed emotions: painful because she had left us and joyful because of the wonderful memories. My mother had been my father's whole world from the first day that he saw her. Now we were all alone. It was a real blessing that we had Flav.

"My father didn't go out anymore, not even to the office. He stayed in the house. Flav kept him company, and he even managed to make my father laugh. The notary that my mother worked for was close to us and he told me that if I needed help he would be happy if

I went to work for him. My father preferred that I enrol in university. Flav was small. There were also a lot of things to do in the house. Often the midwife would come and pick up Flav and he was happy to go with her. My father's brother kept writing and telling us that we should go live with him. He had a big house. It had enough room for all of us. He also said that he would come to Rome in the spring to try and convince us personally. My father kept insisting that I had to go to university. So I enrolled in a liberal arts program.

"The university was close to our house; however, in order to attend classes I had to first find a solution for Flav. Near our house there was a lady who looked after a young child to earn extra money. For a small amount she accepted Flav too. It wasn't easy. Flav didn't want to go to her house and he often cried. Then he started to get used to it and I was able to attend some of the classes. I still remember a few classes on Ungaretti, which I enjoyed very much. There were many students attending at the time."

As soon as I heard Ungaretti's name my jaw dropped. Giuseppe Ungaretti was Elio Filippo Accrocca's university professor and thesis supervisor, as I had already told Fiorina. Accrocca was a famous Corese poet. He was Elio's teacher and friend. The first book that Accrocca published was *Portonaccio,* and it had been published with a preface by Ungaretti. I mentioned this to Fiorina again, and she stared at me, equally stunned. She squeezed my hand and for a while we sat in silence, admiring our surroundings.

XV

September 1950, Fiorina Alone, Good-Bye Cori

Certainly the place that surrounded us was ideal and made one feel good. The lake, the trees, the birds, and the soft colours of autumn entered your soul, putting out the fire of anger and pain. For years this place had been a refuge for Fiorina. She looked at me with sad yet calm eyes and then she started again.

"The year that my mother left us was coming to an end. Christmas was upon us. The notary came to visit us and once again he offered me a job in his office. My father and I decided that after the Epiphany I would try working after lunch while Flav stayed with his grandfather. Cencia, the midwife, and her family also came by to visit. We all had lunch together on Saint Stephen's Day, better known as Boxing Day in Canada. The night of New Year's Eve it was only us three at home. My father seemed to have found a sense of calm. He played with Flav and made him laugh. No one, however, knew exactly what he was feeling inside. That New Year's Eve before going to bed he hugged me tight to his chest and said goodnight with a lump in his throat. It was his first New Year's without my mother.

"A few days later he left for Cori by himself. He said, 'I'm going to visit your mom,' almost as if he were going to see her in the flesh. He came back a few days later. He was happy that he had run into and spent some time with his old friends, the friends who had brought him to Cori for the first time. They had all eaten together at their house. They had also given him a container full of fresh extra-virgin olive oil and a basket full of smoked olives.

"I started working at the notary's office. I liked my job; however, studying in university was difficult. This was something that both my father and I didn't like. I didn't know what to do. The more time passed, the more I felt attached to my job. Flav would start going to kinder-garten in a few months. That way, I would have the whole morning free to study and I probably would be able to manage the two things better. We had already taught him to read and write. I had courage to spare. After everything I had been through, nothing scared me. But it wasn't over and fate intervened once again. Right after Easter, my father had a stroke, leaving him partially paralyzed. He couldn't talk and he couldn't feel his left leg.

"At first I was desperate. Then I summoned my courage, even though I couldn't understand what the Eternal Father had against me. My neighbour watched over Flav for practically the whole day. Cencia came as soon as she could.

"I wrote to my uncle in Canada. At the end of May he arrived in Rome. I had never seen him. He and my father were like two drops of water. You could tell they were brothers. My father seemed to be doing a bit better. They would spend the whole day together. They never got tired of talking and telling each other stories. My father was letting himself be convinced that we should all move to Canada. My uncle said that before he went back to Canada he wanted to visit Torino and Pinerolo; however, the next day my father felt ill again.

"He hugged my uncle. He couldn't talk. He made us understand that he wanted to try and write. His writing was almost illegible. We understood him when he knelt in front of my uncle and prayed him to watch over the two kids. He was obviously referring to me and Flav. Flav couldn't understand why his grandmother was no longer in the bed and he didn't want to leave his grandfather's side while he was there. He called for him even more than he had his grandmother. After eleven days of agonizing pain the Eternal Father took my father.

"I didn't feel anything. I felt insignificant, like a little piece of straw that the wind tossed here and there. I tried not to cry for Flav's sake, and only for him I tried to be strong.

"On Saint Peter's day, my uncle and I went to Cori to lay my father beside my mother. Flav stayed with Cencia. It was a hot, dry, sunny day. We had a second Mass for my father at the little chapel in the cemetery. We had already had the funeral Mass in Rome. At least half of the people who worked with him in the department were present; but in Cori there were few people at the Mass in the cemetery: his old hunting friends, some distant relatives and some acquaintances, and Mimma's mother. They hugged me one by one with tears in their eyes. We left right away for Rome. We didn't even go to see my grandparents' house. I was alone with Flav and this uncle, who would be leaving to go back to Canada in a few days.

"Until my uncle stayed with us in Rome, I thought I could manage. I could perhaps continue to work at the notary's office as soon as Flav could be enrolled in school, but I would have to quit university. First without my grandparents, and now without my mother and father, the world for me had suddenly become tasteless and colourless. Flav was getting bigger and even his world had been turned upside down. I talked to him as if he were an adult. He would sit and look at me with awe. Just like me, he also felt the sudden loss of so much love and care. He no longer went calmly and carefree to Cencia's house or our neighbour's house. He always wanted to stay with me.

"My uncle insisted that it was better for Flav if we were to move to his house, in Canada, where Flav could start going to school. In the meantime, he and the notary took care of all the paperwork regarding my father's death and put together what little I had inherited, whatever my mother and father were able to leave me. I really didn't know what to do. I was scared and worried to go so far away from the only place I had ever known, with a young child, where I didn't know anyone but my uncle and only a few words of English. My uncle left for Canada. He hugged me tight and looked at me without crying, even though his eyes were full of tears. He told me that he'd be waiting for us. After all, he was also living all alone."

Fiorina remained silent for a moment. Then she got up and went towards the lake, which was calm, colourful and full of boats. The birds were singing and she turned around and called me. I got up and followed her. She smiled.

"I wonder if it's possible that life is like this for everyone. You have to believe me when I tell you that I've lived through really scary times. I've often asked myself exactly what sins I had committed that had placed me in this situation. The Catholic Church had proclaimed 1950 a Holy Year. On the occasional Sunday, I took Flav to Saint Peter's Square. You could meet people who came literally from all over the world. After the war, Rome was rebuilding in many different ways.

"I liked working for the notary. My uncle wrote me a letter every week. I talked about moving to Canada with Cencia and the notary. They both cared about me. They suggested that I stay, since soon Flav would be starting school. Things would become a little easier, but I also realized that some things would become harder for me. Thus, on a nice sunny day in August, while I was doing some housework by myself, and Flav had gone out with Cencia, I started convincing myself that it was a good idea if I went to live with my uncle. The notary was disappointed when I finally told him that I was leaving. Yet again, he demonstrated that he was a real gentleman. He helped me put together all the paperwork that was needed. I left him the power of attorney to sell the house in Cori and the house in Rome.

"One Saturday in September, before I left, I went to Cori one last time. I left Flav with Cencia and I took a train early in the morning: a diesel-powered railcar. There were few people on it. During the entire trip I kept my eyes closed and I thought about everything that had happened to me in the previous five years. Once I arrived in the train station in Cori I took the bus. I got off at the Croce and went straight to the cemetery. It was a beautiful sunny day. The sky above Cori looked like a baby blue blanket. A light breeze blew. It caressed my face, almost as if it wanted to play the part of my dear ones who were gone. I got to the cemetery without rushing, but before I entered I walked to Giupponi's olive grove and picked a handful of daisies. That way, I wouldn't have to show myself in front of my grandparents and my parents empty-handed.

"First I went to visit my grandparents. I sat close to them. I could see my grandmother in the kitchen, placing an apron on me while I helped mix eggs and flour to make homemade pasta. I pictured my grandfather at his shop as he hammered away on the butt circles, singing 'La donna è mobile.' They had really cared for me. On top of their graves, I used the daisies I had picked to spell Forever in my Heart. I said farewell to them with a tear in my eye.

"Then I went over to sit near my mother and father. They had asked to be buried in the ground. They lay there, one beside the other. Just like they had been when they were alive, united and together. Just like when they got married. They had cared for one another like two raindrops. Every time my father told me the story about the first day he saw my mother, when he went to Cori to go hunting, his eyes shone so much that they looked like two stars. His face turned on like a light bulb, and it became brighter as he talked. He had been so handsome!

"When my mother passed away, my father started literally fading away. No matter how much he loved me and as attached as he was to Flav, after my mother's death, life had simply lost its attraction, and his will to live was gone forever. I sat down in between my mother and father. All the while, Verdi's bittersweet *Requiem* kept playing over and over again in my head. In my mind, I saw the suffering faces of my father's hunting friends and the pain reflected in their eyes as my father was buried next to my mother.

"I pinned some daisies on the two crosses. I gathered a few handfuls of dirt and I placed them in my pocket. I gently passed my hands over those two mounds of dirt, caressing my mother and father who now lay below the surface and were resting in peace. I left a few tears behind, then I calmly walked away. There were no people among the graves, and as I passed I only encountered lizards crawling and birds flying. It was almost noon.

"As I left the cemetery I looked towards the seashore. The sky was so clear that you could see all the way to the shoreline of Nettuno. The water shone as it reflected the sunlight. In between Cori and the sea you could see a line of smoke left behind by the train as it travelled towards Terracina, cutting the surrounding landscape in two. I couldn't help but think that the whole scene was like my life, cut in two – all that had happened to me in the past and the new life that I was hurtling toward. I could hear the *cuff, cuff* of the train and a few birds here and there singing and chirping – sparrows, red robins, cardinals, titmice and redstarts. Other than that, an amazing silence. In a flash I passed Villa Cavatera, San Francesco and the Piazza della Croce, after which I found myself in front of my grandparents' door, as if in a dream.

"I opened the door, walked in and turned on the lights. I walked over to the windows and threw them wide open. I took a look around the room and suddenly it started to spin. I felt weak, as if I were about to faint. I lay down on the bed and without realizing it, I fell asleep. I was awakened by someone knocking on the door. A few hours must have gone by. To me, however, it seemed like I had slept for centuries. I felt peaceful and rested. Someone was still knocking at the door. I got up and opened the door. It was Mimma's mother.

"My child," she said. I saw the shutters and windows open, and I imagined that it was you. You never know, so I came to check. I'm so happy to see you. How are you, daughter of mine?"

"She threw her arms around my neck and held me tight against her chest as if I really was her daughter. Then she asked me if I was planning on leaving right away or if I would be staying a day or two. I had already decided that I was going to sleep at my grandparents' house for the last time. After all, it was also my mother's house and now mine. All my loved ones were dead.

"I had left Flav at Cencia's house just for the night. She had been a real friend to me since that first time I had gone to her house with my mother when I was pregnant. Mimma's mother invited me to have dinner at her house without thinking twice. When I accepted, the wrinkles on her face from years of hard work, suffering and passing time softened."

Fiorina stopped talking. She lifted her face up to the sky with her eyes closed. She took a deep breath and, gathering her strength, she opened her mouth, slowly letting out her breath with all the pain had she carried with her until now. Then she gazed at the calm blue lake. She was part of the beauty and the surrounding landscape.

I held my breath because I was afraid that all of this might disappear with all the emotions running wild in my heart. One could see that inside Fiorina's soul she was reminiscing about those last hours that she had spent in Cori half a century ago. I placed my arm under hers so that we could start walking again. She looked at me and smiled. A very sweet smile that seemed to contain all the flowered meadows of the world. I became immersed in it because in that smile I could imagine all the love that a person possessed. After a few minutes, Fiorina continued with her story.

"I told Mimma's mother that I would go for a walk in town and that I would be back for dinner. She told me that she was alone. Her husband had died, and only her oldest son still lived in Cori. All her other sons and daughters had moved to Australia. Costina, for that was her name, left content. Back inside the house I closed the windows, freshened up and went out.

"There weren't many people in the streets after the lunch hour. Here and there I would pass a group of women near some entranceway or at the foot of some steps leading down to the street. They chatted away amongst themselves. Some balanced trays on their lap as they were shelling broad beans or chickpeas, or sorting and cleaning wild chicory and other vegetables. At the top of some of the steps there were women with spools to spin wool. They all said hello as I passed.

"Humanity and its warmth! Here, people without even realizing, were attached to one another. The days flowed one after another automatically, like the beads of a rosary being recited. It had been my mother's and grandparents' world. I guess you can say that it had been my own to a degree as well. I was about to leave that world forever. I wanted to take in everything that I could before leaving for good. The women said hello politely and I did the same with a smile on my lips and an ache in my heart, certain that I would not see them again.

"I walked down Sipportiche[24]. I went by the Piazza Ninfina; there was a line-up in front of the fountain. The people all held jugs of some kind that they filled with water. Almost all of them were women, young

---

[24]A medieval arcaded street in Cori Valley.

and old. They looked at me curiously because they were all wearing work clothes, since it was a work day, and I wasn't. There were a few mules and donkeys outside the ironsmith. Maybe they were there to get their shoes fixed or maybe to medicate some wounds that the saddle had caused. The ironsmith knew me because he made the iron rings that my grandfather put on his wooden butts. As soon as he looked up from the piece of steel that he was hammering, he recognized me and said hello. He wanted to know how I was doing, how life was for me in Rome, after all the things that had happened to me. I remembered my grandfather like it was yesterday. Tears came to my eyes. Then I graciously said goodbye, without letting him know that it was the last time that we would see each other.

"I walked along Via Ninfina. After a bit, I turned on Via delle Rimesse, where you could find cellars, which were often barns, and where everyone was working and cleaning to fix the big butts that were needed for the grape harvest. I ended up near the agency where once tobacco had been processed and stored. I walked by Piazza Romana and then slowly down Santa Maria in Cori Valley. I stopped in front of the church. I closed my eyes and in a flash I saw myself as a young child. It seemed so real. I was between my mother and father. It was the feast of the Madonna. The procession was just about to start. All the people, young and old, started to form a line and walking slowly. A lot of people held lighted candles in their hands. Some women and even a few men walked barefoot."

Tightly squeezed to Fiorina, I gazed at her face. Her eyes were closed. A tear fell from her eye and ran down her nose. But Fiorina's face was serene, relaxed, beautiful. The lake was calm. Not even the leaves on the branches of the trees moved. A few birds could be heard singing here and there. I felt my heart racing with emotion.

Fiorina opened her eyes. A few tears continued to fall down her cheeks and nose. She smiled and then she started telling her story again.

"I felt the tears run down my face until they reached my mouth. I opened my eyes again. Someone went in and out of the church. Underneath a platform a few boys played marone, the coin tower game. I didn't have a lot of time; I wanted to walk through the town of Cori one last time. I walked down the stairs that brought you to the Mattei town square and down Cacania. On the way back up I paused because of the spectacular view, but every now and then you would see houses that had been levelled by bombs despite the fact that the war had been over for some time. Accompanying me on the hill that day were some farmers with their mules and donkeys in tow. The farmers' faces were roughened by the sun and fatigue. In one of the squares there were groups of women, some with baskets full of chicory or beans to clean, some knitting, just chatting or rocking a baby. They said hello to be polite, but clearly they were surprised to see someone walk by all dressed up on a work day at that hour.

"Meanwhile, I felt as if my heart was no bigger than a kernel of grain and I couldn't help but wonder what would become of me and my son a month from now in a world that was completely different. Deep in thought, I suddenly found myself on Via Nuova and immediately on the Ponte dei Feri[25]. The sun was splendid after lunch. Far away I could see the shoreline. I turned on the path beside Arturo Piccioni's shop and I walked up to Saint Oliva Church. At the small square boys and girls were playing. The church door was open. There were five or six people inside. I looked up at all those beautiful paintings on the ceiling, and for a while I stopped to ponder the one depicting the escape to Egypt.

"I felt like I was the Madonna on that small donkey with her child on her lap wrapped in a cloth that seemed to want to walk on its own,

---

[25]Ponte dei Feri is a landmark bridge built out of cement and steel along Via Nuova.

while the hands seemed to hold him without touching him. The baby's face didn't look like a child's, but a man's. They seemed to be running away from a land of tears. It looked like the baby boy understood that they would be better off where they were going instead of where they were now. The Madonna's eyes were slightly closed. Her lips betrayed the hint of a smile. Her head was tilted towards her son, worried about what tomorrow could bring, just as I was worried.

"Behind the donkey carrying the Madonna was Saint Joseph. He was old. His beard was white. In his right hand he held a stick, which he was leaning on, while in his left hand he held a basket containing food. Saint Joseph looked at the people who were walking in front of him. But he seemed distant. It looked like he wanted mother and son to stop and stay where they were. The church of Saint Oliva was the one that my mother liked. She always brought me to see it when I was a child. Standing in front of that painting I suddenly realized that I had crossed Cori just to secure the memory of seeing it with my mother.

"After Saint Oliva, I went towards Cori Mount. At the turn of the bend of Uc'Arcanio I took Via Impero. I climbed all the steps without even realizing it. Before I got to Via Saint Nicola I stopped to watch a group of girls playing hopscotch in front of the houses that were under the garden of the town square. Before the war, those little houses weren't there. They had probably been built as shelters for families that had lost their houses. A young boy about the same age as my son kicked a cloth ball. Some older boys were close by, tossing balls or spinning tops.

Once I got to the main square in Cori Mount, I started off towards Laco[26] and the Soccorso, when I heard someone call me. It was the woman from the shepherd's hut, where my mother used to bring me for a taste of ricotta cheese. She had a basin full of wet clothes that

---

[26]Laco is a landmark in Cori where before and for some years after the war there was a little lake. Later it was filled with the debris of bombed-out houses.

she had washed at the Fosse[27] under the Cazzetta building, beside the garden gates. After we had exchanged hellos, she remembered my grandparents, my mother and father. She told me that she had also ended up alone when she was a child. She told me that my parents were good people and that she had known only misery and hard work and pain. She asked me what I was doing in Rome by myself. I hesitated but couldn't resist, and so I told her that I was about to move to Canada where my uncle lived. I still hadn't said a word to anyone in Cori. It was getting late. I said goodbye. I had to give up going all the way to the Soccorso, even if I wanted to say a prayer there for all the dear ones that I had in the cemetery.

"I walked at a faster pace so that I could go and see Saint Peter Square and the Tempio d'Ercole. I walked passed the Telemaco tavern in Cori Mount. Outside, there were about thirty men sitting around a few tables drinking wine. A few of them were playing cards. They looked at me curiously. A few boys in front of Paracatorio's cafe started saying things about me. They felt like joking and playing around, but inside of me my soul was all tangled up and confused. But how could they have known?"

Fiorina leaned on my arm and looked at me with eyes that shone. Whether they shone due to the painful memories or out of the gratitude she felt because I was listening to her, I could not know.

A great silence fell between us. At the same time, however, it was almost as if a river of words tied us together. A light, brisk wind had lifted and caressed the water of the lake causing it to sparkle and glint as if lit by fireflies. In the middle of the lake two boats seemed to chase each other very slowly. A variety of birds seemed to sing a lullaby that only they knew. It would have been a real paradise if it weren't for that river of words so full of tears.

---

[27]Fosse was a popular name for the public wash-house.

XVI

Last Supper in Cori

While we walked on, we had wandered further away from the cottage. Once we had reached a distance of a few kilometres, we turned around and started to head back as Fiorina continued telling her story.

"I remember the shops and boutiques as if it were a dream. Meddio's food store, the barber, Attilio the saddler, Giovannotto the blacksmith, Sdannillao the butcher, the Coronati's shop with Luigino, called 'the Little Hunchback,' who was a friend of my father's and who just like my father liked hunting and doing crossword puzzles. I wanted to go in and say hello, but I didn't have the heart. I reached Monte Pio[28]. Some women and a few boys were in line with their jugs to get water from the fountain. Those who had already filled their jugs had placed them on their heads and were chatting with friends as they walked away.

"The coopers were outside the shop hammering away at their new butts. Lord only knows how many times I had seen my

---

[28]Monte Pio is a famous fountain monument and a landmark in Cori Mount.

grandfather do the same thing. It was almost harvest time. You could still see hay, but also the damage left from the war. The town was still full of piles of ruins. The part of town closest to the sea was gone. Even the convent and numerous houses were gone. As for Saint Peter's Church, only the bell tower and the nearby Temple of Ercole dating from the first century BC were still there, thanks to some miracle. Saint Peter's Square had become larger. It was full of kids playing.

"I looked out below. It was beautiful – on one side the purplish colours of Monte Arrestino and on the other those of the Faiola. The sun was still high enough that it lit all the roofs of the houses in the valley. Here and there the holes created by bombs could be seen, as well as houses that had yet to be repaired. Poor people, they had been through a lot and only the Lord knows how many of them, like me, had received wounds that were deep enough to cut into their souls.

"While walking and thinking, my throat became dry and I wanted to take a drink from the Saint Anna Fountain. Instead, seeing that it was late, I turned onto Via Piranesi and took a shortcut so that I would reach Via delle Pietre. In the cellars, on the steps and in between the houses there were people working. A group of women and kids stood along the lane of Via De Rossi-Via Cavour. The older ones wore blouses, underskirts and aprons. Almost all of them were knitting. There were at least fifteen people. They almost seemed like a big family. You could see donkeys and mules climbing up, followed by men and women. You could read the fatigue on their faces, but there was also a sense of peace, satisfaction and resignation. These same feelings had made me decide to leave and end up who knows where.

"I hurried along. A few saddlers and some carpenters were still closing up their shops. I walked down the Stretta Stracci, the staircase that cut the curve of Via Nuova, the small alley of Straccia, then Via Puzzo. I cut across Via Laurienti, walked down the path of Vento and across Via Colonne, and went to the small San Salvatore Square so that I could look out at Pozzo Dorico. I didn't go inside the church because I was dead tired. As quick as a rabbit I hurried towards my grandparents' house. Once there, I washed up and lay down for a bit on the bed. Around seven o'clock I knocked on Costina's door.

"'How are you, daughter of mine? You're beautiful! Come, let's go in. I'm sure that Peppe and his wife will be here soon. She's a good woman. Let's sit down at the table while we wait. My dear daughter, Peppe's the only son who's still here out of the whole bunch. Even Mimma, who is the youngest, is living with her older brothers in Australia. One by one all the others left, as well. Her brothers are all construction workers and she works as a waitress in a restaurant. They wrote and said that all was well and that she's happy. Every time she writes she sends what money she can. Children. Oh, my children! I know now that I will not see them ever again!'"

"Costina broke out in tears but regained her posture almost right away. She told me that she didn't want her eldest to see her like this. She said that she was happy reading the things that her sons and daughter wrote. They were all doing well. They worked a lot and they weren't lacking for anything. Costina's house was big, especially now that she was by herself. The kitchen was long with a big table in the middle that could seat at least ten people. Even the fireplace was big, with a fire burning away in it. Costina was finishing cooking chicken soup with tagliolini. Basically, Costina had prepared a feast.

"She told me that Cesira, Peppe's wife had been widowed when her first husband, who was in the army, died in Russia during the war. She married Peppe only a few months ago. He was older than her by a year. They got by with what they had, which wasn't much, a little vineyard that Cesira had and a few things that Peppe's brothers had left him. Cesira's late husband had left her pregnant and now her daughter was six years old.

"Cesira and Peppe didn't bring her with them to the dinner because she was with her grandparents on her dad's side. Cesira was happy because her daughter really loved Peppe and the family was growing together nicely. The only thing that worried them and caused them pain was that all their brothers and sisters were so far away, and that they didn't know if they would ever see them again.

"I felt like I was part of the family and so it was easy for me to tell them what had happened to me and that I had decided to move to Canada. They stared at me with their mouths and eyes wide open and without saying a word.

"Then Costina blurted out, 'My poor daughter, my poor child… what kind of world is this? I raised my kids and then I had to watch them leave one by one. I only have my dear Peppe and this saint of a woman Cesira, and that young dear child who never saw or knew her real father all because of Musolinaccio's cursed war[29].'

"Costina's words choked me up, thinking about that poor child, my son, and how he had come into this world. Costina had prepared a feast, but at times it felt like a funeral wake. And yet it was an evening that I'd never be able to forget. It was almost like a going-away party for me, as I was about to leave the town of my parents, where I had spent years of carefree days as well as days of real pain and suffering, which are hard to explain."

I tightly squeezed Fiorina's arm, in silence. I heard her relate details and emotions that were so real that I felt like I was Fiorina. Believe me, I had heard many stories, stories of immigrants and other sad stories. As a boy I had seen friends with whom I had played who had left for faraway places. I myself had been far away from my family for at least ten years because I was working in Northern Italy, spending the best years of my youth with people and a way of life that was completely different from the things that I had known my

[29]Musolinaccio is a pejorative word for Benito Mussolini, the Italian dictator.

first twenty years. But Fiorina's pain and suffering were greater than mine. Now Fiorina had transmitted hers to me. I felt as if they were mine. But I couldn't find the words to tell Fiorina. After another a few steps without saying a word, Fiorina started again.

"It was Peppe who wrote and read the letters for Costina. He read the latest letter that Mimma had sent from Australia. It made us laugh when she described the different things that had happened to her with regard to English, and it made us cry as she wrote about her mother and Cori. She was doing well, but you could tell that she was homesick for her mother and Cori. It ate away at her, even if she had all her brothers there with her. She couldn't help but think about her mother and father as soon as she had a bit of free time, about the hard work and sacrifices and everything they had been through.

"Silently I thought to myself what kind of homesickness I would feel for Cori and Rome, seeing as I no longer had any close relatives or anyone for that matter. Soon it was time for bed. The next morning I had to wake up at five to get ready to leave. I told Costina that I would leave the house keys by the door and if she could give them to the notary when he came. I wanted him to sell it for me. I also asked if she could close it up as best as she could, even if she had to nail wooden boards to the windows. We hugged each other, our eyes filled with tears. Then Costina threw her arms around me and held me tightly to her chest as if it were her daughter who was moving far away.

"Back at home I threw myself on my bed and managed to fall asleep despite all the thoughts floating around and the fact that my heart was beating like a train. I woke up the next morning before the alarm clock even rang. I opened the window. A brisk wind blew and it brought a breath of fresh air. It seemed almost like it wanted to caress me. From the street you could hear the hooves of the mules and donkeys as they went by. The people had already left town on their way to work in the vineyards and olive groves.

177

"I got ready in a flash, I closed up and locked up the house as best I could. I took my bag, which contained the few things that I wanted to bring with me. It also contained the two handfuls of dirt that I had taken from the cemetery. I closed my eyes and, as a tear slid down my face, in a second I saw the twenty years of my life flash before me and the world that I was about to leave behind. What would happen to me and my poor innocent child?

"I walked out of the house and I remained dumbstruck. On the steps I found Costina waiting. 'Oh my child! Last night I didn't manage to sleep at all, and so I got up to say goodbye. Here's a bag with some things. There's a container of olive oil, a loaf of bread, cooked figs and a bag of dried apples. I thought they could be useful. Go on ahead. I'll bring it for you to the bus stop.'

"I never, ever forgot that moment, and when I stop to think about it, in my mind I see that Costina has my mother's face."

At that precise moment Jadwiga came running downhill towards us. Lunch was ready. Fiorina started walking back at a faster pace. I watched Fiorina walking away. With that red baseball cap and her ponytail sticking out, her shoulders, her long toned legs, and that tight white sweat suit, she looked no older than forty.

She turned around and shot me a devastating smile. "Hurry! Barbecued fish is best when it's hot."

Retelling her story had caused her to shed a few tears. Yet you could tell that it also made her feel good. To tell your own story is to relive it many times over.

XVII

Fiorina Moves to Canada

Following closely on Jad's heels, we soon found ourselves underneath the maple tree, where Flav was getting ready to take the fish off the grill because it was already cooked. The aroma drove one mad. The fish was enormous and it was served with tasty potatoes that had been cooked in foil. Jad and Flav had already set the table. We sat down and ate like pigs.

Of course, you couldn't forget the wine. But all that eating and drinking made me feel a little drowsy. Fiorina noticed this and insisted that I take a nap. The other three were wide- awake and would clear up and prepare for our departure. At first I said no, but I could not keep my eyes open, and so gave in. I went in to rest. I think the intense emotions I had felt that morning contributed to my state. As soon as I put my head on the pillow, I was asleep, much like a sack of potatoes dropped to the floor.

As soon as I woke up, I sat bolt upright. Forty minutes had passed. It was so quiet that you could hear a fly buzz. I didn't know what to do and so I packed my luggage and headed downstairs. There was no one around. I walked outside and I saw all three of them sitting on the ground under a tree. Nothing could tear these three apart, I thought to myself at the time. As soon as they saw me coming, they got up and greeted me warmly, asking me if I had rested well. They invited me to have a coffee with them. Everything was ready for my ride to the airport.

As always, Jad and Flav walked in front of us, Fiorina and I followed. She took my hand. We sat down on the couch together while Jad and Flav went into the kitchen to make coffee. Fiorina and I started chatting. We told each other how happy we were that we had met, and that we had managed to see into each other's souls as if we had known each other our whole lives. What a shame that the time had flown by and it was almost time for me to leave for Italy. Jad and Flav returned with what seemed like a gallon of coffee in four full mugs. After, they all went to their rooms to change. Fiorina was the first one down the stairs. She came towards me wearing brown pants and a jacket with a white blouse underneath. A red ribbon held back her dark hair. I thought that she looked like a fairy all dressed up.

"Would you rather sit down and relax or do you prefer to go for a short walk near the woods?"

"Yes, let's go for a walk. But if you don't mind, I'd like you to continue telling your story."

She looked at me with eyes that shone mischievously and con-spiratorially, as if she had been waiting for me to say just that.

"All right. I'll continue telling my story as long as you promise to come back and visit me when you come back to Canada."

"That's an offer I can't refuse!"

We walked outside as if we were glued to one another's side, just like a real couple.

"Now, where did I leave off…? Oh, right! As I hugged Costina tightly before getting on the bus, I felt as if my heart had been suddenly thrown away. It was a Sunday. On the bus there were only a couple of people, the driver and a delivery boy. I sat down and closed my eyes and in that precise moment I realized that it was for real, that I was about to leave that world behind forever. I started thinking about Flav, a young child without a father, whom I was about to take far away from his home and everything he knew. I didn't even know where we were going or how I was going to manage to travel with him and carry several pieces of luggage. I started to wonder how I would meet my uncle and what it would be like living with him, what kind of job I would find, how Flav could go to school where they spoke a different language.

"The trip to Rome took no time it seemed. The train was almost empty. As soon as I arrived, I went straight to Cencia's house to pick up Flav. I hugged him so tightly that I started to hurt him and he cried out. As I looked at Cencia, my eyes filled up with tears. She told me that Flav had behaved well and had fun playing with her son. They had both spent the whole afternoon after lunch running around Villa Borghese Park. Cencia kept trying to convince me to stay. I cared for her, and she would remain in my soul thanks to all the love and true friendship that she had shown me. However, my mind was made up. I still had a strange feeling that I couldn't explain. A voice inside of me was saying that I was doing the right thing: it was time for me to leave the last twenty years behind me, move on and stop dwelling on the past.

"What you need to know is that I got where I am today after many years living here, and that there is a sea of difference between space and the passing of time. Both of them hold one's life together and the experiences that we live. You can't say no to the day that you come into the world; however, you can say no to the place where you were born, and go live somewhere else. This was something that I understood right away, and so nothing and no one could change my mind. I wasn't leaving because I had bought the travel tickets and all my papers were in hand, but because it was better, after everything I had lived through, that I move on. I needed to move on and leave everything behind, even if I had people who cared for me in Italy.

"In all these years I have never felt homesickness, resentment or jealousy. I felt it in my soul during difficult times. But ever since I met you, I have been able to comb out the knots inside of me. You got me to tell my story. I realized that, even if I wasn't homesick, the truth is that if you leave the place where you were born and grew up, it's something that you take with you wherever you go. It is always part of your destiny and it makes you who you are. A part of me can't believe that after half a century we are here talking in dialect and using words that my mother and grandparents used, the Corese dialect, words that I had used when I was a girl."

While Fiorina spoke, a light wind came from the lake and mingled with the songs of the birds who were keeping us company. Inside my soul there was great confusion, and emotions and impulses of all kinds jostled as I relived Fiorina's story. A lot of bittersweet impulses. I had heard many tragic stories in my lifetime, stories from people all over the world, but Fiorina's story was unique, and I was caught up in it, like a fly in a web. I squeezed her arm in an attempt to convey my feelings to her. She acknowledged this and smiled, then continued talking.

"The paperwork was done. This was my way of escaping a life that had become a river of tears. As soon as the notary understood that I really had decided to leave, he helped me as if I were his own daughter. After all those years, he had remained close to my mother. He prepared everything. He had me get a passport at police headquarters. He went to the Canadian consulate for a visa. He also helped me withdraw my savings. Those savings represented the hard work of a lifetime, my grandparents' and parents' lives to be exact. A small amount of the money he changed into dollars. The rest of the money he transferred to my uncle's bank account in Toronto. This was why I had left him the documents of both houses, and I insisted that he sell the house in Cori and the one in Rome. The notary, however, wanted me to keep the one in Rome at least, in case I was not happy in Canada and might want to return to Italy. He assured me that he would continue trying to sell the houses and that he would send me the money as soon as he sold them. That saintly man kept his promise and eventually sent me the money, even if I almost totally forgot about it.

"Tuesday arrived in a flash. It was the 12th of September. We woke up early. The notary came to pick us up with his car. Cencia was with us because she had decided to come with us and the notary to the Naples port. I had spent the night somewhere in between being awake and asleep. Even now that we were about to leave, I felt as if I were hanging between night and day. I woke Flav and washed and dressed him. He was calm – almost as if he wanted to make everything easier. I had told him a fairytale, that we were going far away, where our uncle lived, a place full of nice things. I locked up the house and gave the keys to the notary. I placed my hand along the doorway as if I were saying goodbye to someone who was dead, and I felt myself shake all over. A life had come to an end. Actually, all the many lives I had lived. Even if you couldn't see or understand what I felt inside, Cencia and the notary must have felt it as well.

"We got to the train station, and quickly got on the train to Naples. The sky was cloudy, an ash-grey colour. Even the sky looked wrung out. It was daytime already. Looking towards Cisterna and the mountains, I could see the houses of Cori, which at first seemed to come towards me and then disappeared in the distance. A cocktail of emotions swirled through my mind. A few tears fell from my eyes. I couldn't stop them. It was a good thing that Flav was sitting near the other window with Cencia. The notary squeezed my hand, as if he wanted to protect and encourage me.

"There are no words that can animate a moment in time in one's life. My mother and I had worked and known the notary for so long that, as time had passed, our relationship with him became more familial. I knew that he wasn't married and that he never treated my mother like just another employee, but rather with a lot of affection. My mother had told me that many times. Now that we were so close, I thought to myself that maybe there was more to it than that, at least on his part.

"Once we reached the station in Naples, the notary got us a taxi that took us to the port. We had to embark the steamship Vulcania. It was scheduled to leave at 2:30 p.m. It was so big that I can't find the words to describe it. There was so much confusion. It seemed like complete chaos to me. The place was teeming with people, not only the departing loved ones that were about to embark with every conceivable type of luggage in tow, but all the fathers, mothers, sisters, brothers and friends who had come to say goodbye. There were no calm or happy faces. One could easily understand that they were leaving to seek fortune elsewhere and they probably wouldn't be coming back. Everyone knew that they were leaving a life of hard work and misery, but no one knew what they would end up finding, or where they were heading. The worst part is that they were leaving behind pieces of their heart and parts of their soul, which would be forever attached to the towns and the people that remained behind. That's how it was for me. It was clear that they were leaving places they knew well and that they were experiencing mixed emotions. All those tears, sobbing, crying and desperate yelling that came from both those who were leaving and those who were staying pierced your heart.

"But the time had come. Before getting on the boat, Cencia and the notary gave me a parting gift: we all went to eat in a traditional restaurant near the port. It was nice to spend some more time altogether, but we consumed sadness and melancholy with every forkful of pasta. Then, finally came time to say goodbye. This time Cencia and the notary shed more tears than I did. Inside, however, a tempest of emotions raged, emotions that I could not explain.

"Cencia hugged Flav tightly to her chest as if he were her son. Tears streamed down our faces. In my heart I knew that a whole new world awaited me; yet a part of me told me that we would never see each other again. I see them still, their arms raised, waving us goodbye as the ship left the port. That is the last image I have of them. I squeezed Flav tight as I watched Naples become smaller and smaller. Everyone on the boat had wet eyes, each one with their own personal sorrow. I had never felt so alone as I did in that moment. But that wasn't exactly true, because with me there was a young child who still had to grow up. I came to the realization that we would both have to grow together.

"We went straight to our cabin, and I quickly understood that I wasn't the only one facing difficulty and uncertainty. There were two other women there, or perhaps I should say two girls, because the truth was that they couldn't have been much older than me. Cettruda from Carpineto, who was six months pregnant, was on her way to Ottawa to meet her husband. Carmina was from Pisterzo. She had married a man by proxy through the consulate, who had left a year or two earlier and was waiting for her in Montreal. I barely remember what they looked like. There was so much misery that they would have even gone to hell and back. They had left their fathers, mothers and younger brothers and sisters.

"My heart aches just thinking about them. They hadn't thought twice about leaving. Carmina hoped to find an honest man waiting for her and a job, so that some of the money they earned could be sent to their dear ones at home, just as other immigrants had done before them. Yet, their anxiety ran deep. Even the girl from Carpineto had left her parents and a younger sister behind. Now, however, she thought about the child growing inside her.

"As for me, I didn't have any family to leave behind. However, I was leaving Cori, Roma, Costina, the notary, Cencia, and all the places that I knew and where I had spent the first twenty years of my life. Not knowing what would happen to me and Flav in this strange new world was crushing me, just as an olive press might. Luckily, Flav was calm and worry-free, snuggled up beside me. By the expression on his face, I could tell that he was confused. But he looked curiously around him because everything was new, and that kept him occupied.

"When it was our turn, we went to eat, and afterward we returned to our bunks to sleep, each to their own thoughts. Flav didn't want to sleep in his bunk and so he came and slept with me in mine. Two days out, we stopped in Palermo to let other passengers on. I learned this going from one bridge to another, meeting different men and women during lunch and dinner. The trip was turning into a vacation. Along with their luggage, everyone had brought worries, tears and sadness. There was plenty of food, and you didn't have to work to get it. Many people with me weren't used to having all that free time and all that food. Little groups of people from the same towns gathered together. People played the accordion, or the guitar or the harmonica. Some sang. They would meet up on the ship's deck to play and sing, trying to pass the time in a cheerful way. It was only years later that I came to understand that, despite their sadness and tears, those days spent on the ship were probably the best days for many people for years to come.

"The ship also stopped in Lisbon. Some people stepped off the ship to take a look around. Flav seemed glued to me, quiet and calm, but I didn't feel like getting off. It was just the two of us in the cabin, because Cettruda and Carmina had left the ship for a while that day.

As soon as we set sail from Lisbon, we hit bad weather, the biggest storm that I had ever seen. The rain was so heavy it seemed as if someone was literally throwing buckets of water over the decks. Quite a few of the passengers got seasick and never left their cabins. They didn't even leave for meals. Cettruda got sick. Her face was waxen. She even refused water. Gradually, she started to feel better. We were lucky enough, Flav and I, that neither of us felt sick.

"The trip lasted thirteen days. We got off at Halifax, at Pier 21, on September 25. It was a beautiful day; however, all around us there was much confusion. I understood that it wasn't going to be easy. Some personnel spoke Italian. Slowly, they started organizing everything. They split us up into groups. It was hard for us to communicate even amongst ourselves, seeing as how many people spoke only dialect. We were also tired, worried and confused. Many people did not know what to do or how to meet up with the people who were waiting for them. The others, who didn't have anyone waiting for them, were frantic to find out how to get to where they needed to go. They were showing customs personnel pieces of paper with addresses written on them. We were all displaced people.

"After a few hours they slowly managed to sort through the paperwork and told us that we could legally enter the country. They started accompanying one group after another to the trains. Finally our moment arrived, mine and Flav's. I was about to say goodbye to Cettruda and Carmina when we realized that we were on the same train car. It took two days to get to Montreal by the train. We said goodbye to Cettruda and Carmina. Carmina had arrived at her destination and found her new husband right away. Who knows what has happened to them. My first impression of him was that he seemed like a good person with a certain charm. By contrast, I recall Cetrudda as if in a vision, a dream. I remember that her eyes were full of tears as she walked towards the train bound for Ottawa.

"Flav and I boarded our train for Toronto. We spent the night on the train. Flav was tired and a bit grumpy, and everything seemed to bother him. Finally, he fell asleep. I managed to fall asleep soon after. The train sped along under a clear night sky. I remember that I could see the full moon. Every now and then I'd open my eyes and the moonlight kept me company. Thank God, we arrived in Toronto at Union Station."

Fiorina stopped. She looked at the lake's calm surface, the water reflecting different shades of green rather than blue. It was as if she was hoping to see everything that she had told me about in the colours of the lake. From the few graceful and slow sailboats that sailed across the lake, one realized that the lake was not only populated with trees and birds but with people as well.

It was almost time for me to leave and I was worried that I wouldn't be able to hear the end of Fiorina's story. Her story had seeped into my soul – that elegant woman who had maintained her beauty after all those years. It was clear that she had lived through difficult times as well as fortunate ones. Or perhaps she had been able to triumph over the evil that she found on her path.

Sadly, though, I had to leave. An overwhelming sense of sadness fell upon me. I thought to myself that what I had seen and heard had made me richer as a person. I was coming back to this part of the world a few months later, to Quebec, and I would do everything in my power to spend a few days with Fiorina, in the hope that she would be neither tired of nor bothered by telling me the rest of her story.

Silently, Fiorina glanced at her watch. She linked her arm under mine, let out a long breath and said: "We've got to be going."

I couldn't help but reply: "Was your uncle waiting at the station? What happened next?"

"As soon as the train stopped I felt a tight pain in my chest, from dejection or happiness I was not sure. We had arrived in our new world, after days and days of travelling. I had wondered (and worried) if my uncle would be there waiting for us, and what would I do if he wasn't? I did have his address, however, and I calmed myself down by thinking about the money in my pocket. Actually, it was in a little pouch that hung around my neck. I felt lucky because I had seen so many problems and so much misery on the journey. Many people had no money at all. Others felt rich enough that as soon as we disembarked in Halifax they went around giving anyone who had helped them with their first needs ten dollars each.

XVIII

At the Royal York Hotel
and Her Uncle

Fiorina stopped and bent down to pick a maple leaf. It was barely yellow but had fallen from a tree that was as tall as a building. She handed it to me with a look in her eyes difficult to fathom, as if she wanted to laugh and cry. "Bring it with you back home, that way you won't forget me."

Fiorina remained still, in silence, her face tightly drawn. She closed her eyes. Then she leaned her weight on my arm, almost as if she wanted to collect other memories, or throw some away. All around, you could hear the rustling of leaves and birds singing. That spot was made for relaxing and meditating. It encourages you to analyze, to reflect on the past and to look peacefully ahead to the future. I understand how people like Fiorina could spend a week or so in those woods, far away from the chaos of city life. Although there were few conveniences, no amount of money in the world can buy that kind of the peace and tranquillity.

Fiorina started talking: "Pietro, you need to know that when you lose someone or – as in my case, when the people who gave you life and taught you how to live die, your soul, your heart feels strangled and you try to hold on to anything, even the thread of a spider web, just to keep going. My uncle was that thread. If only you knew how many times those thoughts had crossed my mind, especially during my trip from Cori to Rome, and then all the way here."

Hearing these words made my soul tremble. Seeing Fiorina's boutique, her house and her cottage on the lake in this little piece of paradise, it was easy to think that a woman like her had always had everything and that her life was a grand ball. Instead, as I listened to her tell her story, I realized that her soul seemed to be crying even though everything around her was marvellous. It was a beautiful day. It was calm and peaceful, full of beauty and wonder. At this hour, the lake's surface was quickly changing from a bluish-green hue with reddish lines to a dull lead colour. The sun played hide-and-seek among the tall trees. It was another world, which seemed perfectly suited to absorb the powerful mix of emotions that Fiorina was sharing with me. In the silence and in between Fiorina's sighs, I could not help but think that deep inside each one of us is a hole where we store the memories that we just can't forget, painful as well as pleasant.

"While my mind was still trying to bind itself to that spidery thread," Fiorina continued, "I tried not to lose myself in that mob of frantic people desperately searching for one another. I managed as best I could, juggling Flav and my luggage, when I heard someone calling me. 'Fiorina!, Fiorina!' My heart was beating like a drum. It was my uncle...

"He came towards me, making his way through all that confusion of men, women and children. A real disaster! My eyes started to shed so many tears that they must have looked like fountains. We hugged. I don't even know how long we stayed that way, maybe it was only for a few seconds. But it was long enough for me to see my whole life flash before my eyes. I came back to the present as soon as I heard Flavio cry. He pressed tightly against my leg, as if he were glued to me and cried. His uncle lifted him up in his arms and I did the same right after, but we couldn't calm him down, try as we might. During the whole trip he had never cried. He hadn't even fussed. Despite our presence, with all that commotion and uproar, combined with his fatigue, his hunger and the strangeness of it all, he exploded like a bomb that had been waiting to go off for years. Maybe he had felt abandoned, seeing me hugging my uncle. Eventually, he started to calm down.

"My uncle had gone to find a buggy for the luggage. Then we headed out of the station which, by the way, must have been a thousand times bigger than the train station in Cori. I followed my uncle toward the exit, with Flavio cuddled in my arms, while his little arms clung tightly around my neck. He was calmer by now but still confused. We were in the middle of a river of people, all walking as if they were in trance. My mind and my heart were burning with all of the thoughts and emotions I was experiencing.

"Outside the station people dispersed in all different directions, most heading towards taxi stands. Right in front of the station there was a huge building that was wider and taller than the others. I learned that it was the Royal York Hotel and that it was the tallest building in all of the British Commonwealth. My uncle ushered us towards a red car that was long and wide, something that I had never seen before. Once he had packed the trunk with our luggage, he gave Flav something to drink. He had calmed down enough to look at the car with curiosity. My uncle suggested that we best go home to eat something and rest up.

"It seemed that my uncle would never tire of talking. He said that he was happy that we were there and that it was the right decision to move to Canada. Toronto was a new city and there was room for everybody. Of course, one had to work hard just like everywhere else, but we were certain that eventually we would find our way. After his wife died, he remained alone. He said that our arrival had brought him company, but most all it gave him a reason to start living again. We both had to learn to speak English, and Flav would start school soon. I didn't have to worry because he would have other Italian kids in his class and he'd adapt quickly. My uncle's house was in an Italian neighbourhood, with stores close by that were owned by Italians. I wouldn't have any problems. But for us to fit in we would have to learn English well. He told me that for Flavio it wouldn't be a problem because it's a known fact that a child of five can learn and comprehend four or five languages.

"We were at his house in no time, or at least that's how it seemed. It was a white, wood frame house with a sizeable lawn. All the other houses were constructed of wood too, up and down the street, even on the other side of the street, and almost all of them were either white or brown, as if they had been made with the same stamp. A few hundred metres away, over the rooftops, a huge church towered above red brick houses.

"A woman roughly in her fifties emerged from my uncle's house with together with a young man. They walked towards us, happy to see us, like distant relatives that haven't seen each other for years. I later learned that the mother and son were Russian, Natasha and Nicolaj, and they lived a few kilometres from my uncle. Nicolaj worked at the same company as my uncle. Natasha cleaned and kept my uncle's house organized and she cooked for him. The house was big after all. Just on the first floor there was a kitchen, a living room and a bathroom and on the upper floor there were four bedrooms and a bathroom. My uncle gave us two of those rooms, the other two being his bedroom and a guest room. Natasha and Nicolaj unloaded the luggage and took them up to our rooms. My uncle in the meantime showed us the whole house. Behind the house there was a vegetable garden and a wide driveway for the car, and a garage, which was a separate structure from the house.

"My uncle told us that from now on this was our house. We had lunch, then he told us to wash up, see to our luggage and get some rest. We were obviously tired. There would be plenty of time to unpack what little we had managed to bring with us. After years of misery and tragedies, things seemed to be finally turning around.

"First, I gave Flav a bath and then I tried to put him to sleep in his room, but it was impossible. He wouldn't let go of me, even when I tried to push him away. I myself felt as if I was reborn. Even Flav seemed refreshed. When it was getting late, we said goodnight to my uncle and he told us that we wouldn't see him in the morning, as he had to leave for work and he couldn't reschedule. He told me not to worry though because, come morning, Natasha would be there with breakfast ready. We would see each other in the evening when he returned from work. We would have all the time we needed to unpack and get accustomed to the house.

"Obviously, it was impossible to convince Flav to sleep by himself in his own bed. I was dead tired, and so we held each other and we both fell asleep like sacks of potatoes. I didn't even think about the fact that in the morning I would have to talk to Natasha, who spoke only English and very few words in Italian. Flav and I slept through the whole night and woke up around eight o'clock. At first when I opened my eyes I thought that I was still dreaming. The windows didn't have wooden shutters like we had back home, and there were only white curtains made out of lace. I looked out the window and realized that it looked out on the backyard. It was raining a bit. We washed up and went downstairs, where Natasha was waiting for us.

At first it was difficult to communicate, but then everything went smoothly because I could tell that she was a good-hearted woman.

"That day went by fast. I unpacked my luggage methodically as I chatted freely, my mind racing. Gradually, too, I got to know the house. Before I finished putting everything away, I put the dirt that I had brought with me from Cori in a glass vase and placed the vase on the nightstand next to my bed. That way, somehow, I would be able to keep a piece of the world that I had left behind near me always – Cori, Rome, my grandparents, my father and mother and even Cencia, the notary, Costina and Mimma.

"To this day I still have that vase on top of the cupboard near the shelf and, if I happen to look at it, I smile. Now it doesn't bring back what I felt the first few times I looked at it, but it will always remind me that I came from another place. The vase with dirt explains that some of my dreams come from faraway days or things that somehow still live at the bottom of my soul and, thanks to you, I am able to remember other facts and people that I believed to have forgotten and lost forever.

"Natasha didn't leave the house at all until my uncle came back. She didn't want any help, not even to cook. Through signs and gestures she made us feel at home. Flav started to feel secure and quietly wandered all over the house. My uncle tried to bond with Flavio right away. He talked to him and tried to get him to play with anything he wanted. The next morning it was drizzling. My uncle stayed home and we talked the day away without stopping. He told me the whole story of his life. How he had felt when he suddenly lost his wife and how only Natasha and Nicolaj had been by his side, just as good relatives would have done, to help him get through the bad days and move on. However, from this moment on, he had me and Flavio to think about.

"I needed to get back to studying and Flavio had to go to school. I wanted to continue my studies because I liked it, but I also realized that I had a son. I had to work so that I could provide him with some security, because I didn't know what life had in store for me. I managed to convince my uncle to find me a job. It was better that I try to learn English sooner than later, and that's what I did. After a few weeks, I found a job as a cashier in a fabric and dress store right on College Street. I worked there for a year and I went to night school for English. After a year, I had learned it well and I was capable of carrying on a conversation without having to think first in Italian. The words came to me right away in English. My uncle helped by trying to make it so that I met people who spoke only English. And I spoke to Flav almost always in English. After all, it was even more important that he become fluent. He would look at me grudgingly those first few times that I spoke to him entirely in English, but later he didn't mind at all, and he literally forgot Italian.

"Then it happened that the Royal York Hotel, which was organizing a cocktail party for my uncle's company, was looking for a young woman who was competent in both Italian and English to work at reception. My uncle spoke with the manager of the company, who spoke to the director of the hotel. Three days later they called me. They asked me a lot of questions and my answers must have satisfied them because fifteen days later I received a letter confirming that they wanted to hire me. Thus, after a little more than a year, I left my job as a cashier at the store on College Street and I started working at the Royal York Hotel, one of the biggest and most recognized hotels in Toronto. I did feel bad about leaving my job at the fabric store because I knew the owners cared for me and I cared for them; however, I was leaving for something better.

"The only big problem was that I had to send Flavio to boarding school. The boarding school was close to home. We saw each other often, but slowly Flav started to have and live a life of his own. His personality changed and he started to close up. At first it had been difficult for me to get him to accept the situation. He had never been away from me. It had also been difficult to get him to go to school and study, but he got used to it. Now he spoke English fluently. He came home on Sundays, but often he liked to stay on at school with his friends instead of coming home. Only my uncle was able to convince him to come home once in a while. They were really close. Anyone who saw them could tell that they went together like peanut butter and jelly. When Flav was a little older, my uncle started to take him out and about, fishing and hunting. They would drive two or three hundred kilometres north of Toronto. Sometimes they were gone for two or three days. Those days kept him calm and relaxed. He and my uncle would both come back happy.

"As far as my job was concerned, I soon got the hang of it and I was also happy there. I started to think that I had made the right decision. My son got the chance to study in peace, which would pave the way for his future. Six peaceful years went by and I even managed to go to university and get a degree. However, one day, again the sky seemed to have come crashing down on my head. It was a sunny and hot July morning. I was calmly chatting with a client who had just arrived at the hotel, when suddenly Nicolaj arrived. As soon as I saw his serious face and his puffy eyes, I felt like I was going to faint. My first thought was that something had happened to Flav."

Fiorina pronounced the last few words with different tone in her voice, a sadder and softer one. It was as if the words didn't want to come out of her mouth. She stopped. She looked at me with watery red eyes. She seemed to be reliving those moments, as if time had stopped. She squeezed my arm with her hand, as if she needed to lean on me. I also felt my heart tighten. Nothing serious could have happened to Flav, seeing that he had grown into a good- looking man who was now waiting with Jadwiga to take us to the airport. Fiorina, her mind full of all those painful memories which still hurt, radiated a rare beauty. Life's hard shots must have turned her into steel, because a sad, rusty yet strong smile parted her lips and she started taling again.

"My uncle started feeling sick while he was at work. They had taken him quickly to the hospital. Nicolaj told me that he couldn't talk. The hotel started to spin around me. I was about to faint. Then I gathered some strength. I quickly explained the situation to the director and hurried to the hospital with Nicolaj. My uncle's condition eventually improved, but unfortunately he just wasn't the same. Twenty days later, we brought him home and it really seemed that he was getting better. It seemed to do him good being around us, especially Flav, who refused to go far from the house so that he could be by his side. My uncle decided to issue a will. He left me everything, the house, his savings and an empty 40,000-square-metre piece of commercial land. Flav was happy to keep his uncle company, but sometimes he fell silent. He would sit by himself and he didn't want to talk to anyone. It reminded me of the way in which his grandfather had died.

"Five months later, one December evening before Christmas 1959, my uncle had another attack. We took him straight to the hospital, but after six months of agony he died. We held the funeral service at Saint Mary of the Angels. There were so many people that day, all the Italians who lived around College Street were there. Everyone was talkative, but I was absolutely speechless, cold as a stone. My brain had shut down. My thoughts were in chaos. Flav was like a little child again; he wouldn't let go of me. No one could pry him from my side, it seemed. Once again we were alone, in a place that was totally different from where we were born and to which we could never return. I finally realized it that day."

Fiorina stopped talking. We walked in silence. I was unable to utter the words that would prompt her to resume her story. Luckily for me, Fiorina had been inspired by our chance meeting and so continued her story, to reveal her past, to bring it to life, and to pass it on to me. This made her feel lighter and calmer inside. She herself seemed convinced that I would, somehow, find a way to bring her story of pain and suffering – and flash of joy – to life, so that it would never die, that it would live forever!

XIX

Fiorina and Her Son Alone Again, Vahan the Armenian

The moment of my departure had arrived. I couldn't hide the fact that I was emotional. Jadwiga and Flav were buzzing around the car. They were loading our luggage into the trunk, and in an hour we would be leaving. The sun was already starting its descent. The place seemed enchanted, perfect for some peace and quiet and a bit of rest. Fiorina and I were linked arm in arm, under a sort of spell, just like a couple in love. Now we walked slowly and silently. Every now and then we stopped to admire the lake and the trees around it. A light breeze moved the leaves and changed their colours. One could see and hear the birds calling to one another and flitting through the trees. I squeezed Fiorina tight to me. She gave me a sense of strength. I told her so. And I wanted it to continue.

"Fiorì, at that age and alone again with a son in a world that still didn't feel like it was yours, it must have been very difficult."

"No! It had never been easy for me, and not because of the need for money. At least in that sector I had been lucky, and I had always had enough to not have to worry. Life was still hard for me however, because of everything that had happened. One after another my dear ones had passed away, and only in dreams would I have the chance to talk to them or see them again. I realized that I was lucky enough that Natasha and Nicolaj always came to visit me. Natasha always helped me clean and tidy the house. Then, the company that my uncle and Nicolaj worked for offered Nicolaj a good job with a better salary in Vancouver. Mother and son left us, on a river of tears. For a while we wrote to each other. However, as time passed our friendship faded. A few years later Natasha happily told me by way of a letter how Nicolaj had made her the grandmother of a beautiful baby.

"After my uncle's funeral, Natasha and Nicolaj brought us home and they stayed with us until late that night. Once everything was over, Flavio and I were alone. It was the first time since we had come to live in that house. The house had appeared big to me the first day that I had walked in it, but now it seemed huge, so big that I felt completely lost, body and soul. Flavio fell asleep right away. I remained awake, in the company of various ghosts, as if they were all there beside me – my mother and father, my grandparents, the war, Fontana Mannarina, the Moroccan soldier who pulled up his pants and fixed his shirt as if nothing had happened after he had ripped me in two, Cencia, and the notary.

"Flav slept in the room next to mine, I could hear him breathing heavily, as if he was also dreaming about how he had come into the world, and all the pain and suffering that he had endured from his first day of life until now. Poor child! And yet that same night after Natasha and Nicolaj left, it seemed that the house wanted to swallow me up, close in around me, protect me. Then, day by day, I started to deal with what needed to be done. I had to move on, I had to help Flav grow up and study.

"I had the house, a job and enough money that I didn't have to worry. Time passed and, long after my uncle's death, I realized that the piece of land that my uncle had left me was worth a whole lot of money. The company that my uncle had worked for started offering me a lot of money for it. In the middle of all those problems in my life, I found myself luckier than a lot of people who had to work hard from morning until night every day just to get by. Many of them also had to save some money to send to their loved ones that they had left behind in Italy.

"My biggest concern was Flav. I rarely saw him. You could say that I saw him only on Sundays. Often he would slink around the house. He was no longer a small boy. He wasn't calm like before. He was a teenager, a good-looking fifteen-year-old who could draw more than one girl's attention. His black eyes shone on that tanned face of his, just like the faces of the farmers in Cori when they came home from a long day spent under the sun trimming the vineyard or the olive grove, or after picking tobacco, or other outdoor activity. He started to ask questions about his father, and I used all kinds of excuses to hide the truth from him. He wanted to know why he didn't have anything that had belonged to his father to remember him by and why I had light skin and his was so dark.

"He knew that I was hiding something from him. Eventually, he stopped asking me questions. But the more time passed, the more he closed up inside a shell, just like shellfish do. I just didn't have the heart to tell him how I got pregnant, not to mention that I still felt ashamed. He went out with many boys his age, but I never heard him talk about girls. He also spent a lot of time by himself. Happily, he spent his time listening to music, reading or playing a few notes on his guitar. Fortunately, he did well in school; however, as time went on, I had a sinking feeling that something would go wrong as it always had in the past. I kept working at the Royal York and, at this time in my life, one could say that I was a good-looking woman. You can imagine."

At this point I couldn't help it and added: "You look pretty good even now."

"Don't lie, even if I like hearing you say that. There were a lot of men of all ages who buzzed around me, and most of them were Italian – not to mention all the male clients who passed through the hotel. Since that day of hell and everything that had happened with those soldiers at the Fontana Mannarina, I had never been touched by any male. Sixteen long years had gone by! Now I was thirty-one years old. Not only was my mind full of all kinds of worries, but just the thought of being touched by someone made me panic. The gentleman who owned the restaurant in the hotel buzzed around me as if he were a bee that wanted to make its way into the beehive. Yet he had a beautiful wife and two kids. He would do anything to be near me, and he found thousands of excuses just to come and say a few words to me. Apart from my own fears, it seemed that my destiny was to occupy myself thinking only about Flav and his life.

"Then on a beautiful October day, a man who must have been in his sixties came to the hotel. I remember it as if it happened only a few hours ago. He was Armenian, and later I learned that he was part Russian and a mix of several other races as well. He was calm, kind, and he always had a smile on his face. He stayed at the hotel for fifteen days. During this brief period he showered me with attention. He found many ways to compliment me, not on my looks, but for my work. I sensed right away that he liked me. I found him nice and I became interested in him. He happened to check in at the hotel a few months later and he remained for a longer period of time. We got to know each other, and the mornings that I didn't see him I had a strange feeling, as if something was missing. Then one evening when I got off work and I was about to go home, he was waiting for me. He insisted on giving me a gift and told me to open it when I got home. At first I didn't want to take it. I also didn't want to be rude and not accept it, after all, I do have some good manners. But my heart beat faster as I accepted it. It was a small book containing Shakespeare's tragedies. I had never read Shakespeare. With some embarrassment, I put the book in my purse and I walked out of the hotel.

"Outside it was raining lightly, and the people were hurrying along without even stopping to look in the store windows. I couldn't wait to get home, and I knew Flav would be home from school. The bus dropped me off a couple of hundred metres from the house. Now it was no longer raining lightly but pouring. I started to run, in part because of the rain, but also because I was eager to get home. As soon as I got closer to the house I saw that the lights were on, which meant that Flav was already home. My heart jumped. I didn't even remove my jacket when I entered, but went straight towards Flav as he came towards me. I was soaking wet but I squeezed him tightly to my chest.

"Flavio saw that I was drenched and out of breath. He thought that something was up and started asking questions. I told him that it was nothing, that I had run home from the bus stop because it was raining and that I was happy to see him. Then I told him that I had to go and change quickly because I was literally soaked to the bones. When I had changed and cleaned up a bit, without wasting time I went straight to the kitchen and started preparing dinner. Flav came and started asking questions again, but I easily managed to ask him questions instead. I got him to tell me about school, his friends and teachers. That particular night Flav was more talkative than usual, and he started telling me what he wanted to do when he grew up. He told me that he wanted to go to university and become an engineer like his uncle. Listening to him talk like that, suddenly he seemed older than his age and I was comforted by this.

"Later that night when I went to lie down I felt calm, having seen Flav so excited about his future. But I was anxious to start reading the Shakespeare book. The book contained *Romeo and Juliet, Hamlet, Othello and Macbeth*. It was a pocket-sized edition published by Collins. On the first page I found a note written in ink: London, 25 July 1951. The words were written in Italian. In the middle of the book I found two sheets of papers folded into four. He had written me a letter.

"He referred to me as "Miss," and he wrote that he had been impressed by how gracefully I moved and by the few words I said. He wrote that he came from Manitoba, where ten years ago his wife had died. She was also Armenian, and it was there that he had earned and put away quite a bit of money. Then he had decided to sell everything and move to Toronto to open a jewellery store. This is what he had been doing with his wife when he lived in Winnipeg. And now he hoped to find a woman who was willing to help him continue the project that he had started, instead of losing his life's work. He insisted that I seemed perfect for him. He asked me if he could invite me to dinner one evening, to the restaurant at the hotel, just to talk for a bit. He concluded his letter saying that he wanted to leave me with a kiss.

"Those words brought all the chaos and disaster of the war back to mind. They literally shook me up. I spent the night tossing and turning without sleeping. Fortunately, the next morning I didn't have to go to work because it was my day off. In the morning, while I cleaned and tidied up the house, I couldn't help but think about the Armenian and what he had written in his letter. Flavio spent the morning out and about with his friends.

"Once home, he saw that I was silent and caught up in my thoughts, and so he started asking questions again. I had no choice but to tell him what was happening to me. He was big enough to understand that it was perfectly natural that a young woman would draw a man's attention and may eventually get married. All his friends had a father and a mother. At one point he told me that he had been scared and worried that he was going to end up alone. He wanted to know if his father was alive or dead. He also asked me why I was the youngest of all the mothers he knew."

We had almost reached the cottage, where Jadwiga and Flav had finished loading all our luggage into the car and were now calmly chatting away on the veranda. Fiorina stopped. She gazed deeply into my eyes. I saw an immense field that led straight into her soul. She had arrived at another fork in the road in the story her life. The look on her face made me understand that she wanted to finish telling me her story before we got to the cottage. She squeezed my arm as a sign of trust, that she appreciated and was grateful for the bond that she had found with me. Then she went on.

"I hugged Flavio tightly. I felt a sense of calm inside that I never knew I possessed. I told him that I had been raped by four soldiers with dark skin when I was fifteen, and only God knows where they came from, these same soldiers who had come to free us from the Germans. They didn't worry about the pain and suffering that they left behind them. Now only God knows what happened to them. My heart tells me that the war swallowed them up and that they couldn't brag or tell anyone about what they had done to me, maybe because they were sorry. Or maybe it gave them a sense of pleasure. Who knows?

"I told him about everything that I went through when I realized that I was pregnant, and all the worries, suffering and misfortune that I had brought to my family. I told him that after a few days, I had felt my body and soul change. While he held me tightly, I explained that my family and I were ashamed, especially back then, as if we were responsible for their act of cruelty. I resisted the advice to have an abortion and, together with my mother and father, we decided that what grew inside me was my child and that I would give birth to you regardless of the cost. I told him that he was to thank for his grandparents' happiness, that he was the cutest baby, and that I would live only for him, giving up my own future.

"Flavio had fallen silent. He was stuck to me like a shirt, as if he were a part of me. He didn't speak. Then I felt my neck wet with tears, as Flavio silently wept. I don't know how long we held each other. I was finally free. I felt lighter now that I was rid of the heavy burden of that secret. Flav finally knew the truth. I felt as light and as free as a butterfly. I could talk openly with Flavio. Maybe he too could find some peace from all those unanswered questions that floated around in his mind. Now he would have the complete picture of the puzzle and be able to put together the pieces of those five years spent in Rome, our departure, the trip here, his uncle and the life we found in Toronto. That is indeed what happened. He was once again sweet and gentle with me, just like he was when he was a small child. Yet, there was still so much more we would have to face.

"The Armenian with his tactful approach and his attention to detail was slowly entering my heart. He would always stop and say hello at the reception desk and would hint that maybe we could go out for dinner, always in a delicate and polite way, before leaving the hotel or before going up to his room. After six months of coaxing and convincing, hinting and beating around the bush, I decided to make him happy and accept his dinner invitation. It was the first time in my life that I went to dinner in a restaurant with a man. Deep in my soul all kinds of different emotions that I had never felt before were brewing. Even if Flav was sleeping at the boarding school, I promised myself that I wasn't going to go home late. The Armenian's name was Vahan, and he took me to a nice restaurant on Bay Street near the hotel.

"He behaved like a perfect gentleman. He insisted on wanting to know more about me, and he was surprised when I told him that I had a sixteen-year-old son. Then he told me his life story. He also brought up what he had written in the letter. He wanted me to know that after all the time that had gone by, I was worth the wait. He said that I seemed to be made for him. His eyes looked so deeply into my soul that they seemed to penetrate me. He said that I had a strange glimmer of hope in my eyes, and that we could take everything that had happened to me and everything that had happened to him and put it behind us. He insisted on the fact that Flav wasn't a child anymore and that he would understand, and to think about it without giving him a quick reply." Fiorina stopped abruptly. "I'll have to tell you some other time how it ended, because it's better if we get going."

I saw that Flav and Jad were ready. As we reached them, they told us that they had already put everything in the car, but that we should check to see if they had forgotten anything inside. They would prepare coffee for us in the meantime. Everything was in order. Once we finished our coffees, we locked up the cottage, got into the car and left.

XX

Fiorina's Wedding, Armenia, an Unusual Relationship

Together with Fiorina, Jad and Flav I sadly left Awenda Park where I had spent a couple of days that would be difficult to forget –not only because it was a place so full of beauty that it would uplift even the saddest heart, but mostly because of the time I had spent with Fiorina, a Corese, whom I had never thought to meet so far away from Cori, with a story full of pain, as well as a few shimmers of glory. Often, as I listened to Fiorina tell her story, my own soul felt the same emotions, as if our two souls were interconnected. But Fiorina's story wasn't finished. What she had related foreshadowed more episodes that could twist your heart in pain, yet at other times widen it in the joy.

We had already driven all the way down Highway 93, and we were almost at the 400. The sun was slowly setting behind the various trees that lined the highway, many of them maple trees. Green, gold, brown, red and orange, all the brightly coloured leaves seemed to be sadly waving us goodbye as we flew past. One would need to be a poet or a great artist to truly capture all the colours. Flav had turned on the radio and Frank Sinatra's voice flowed around us as smooth as silk, like a caress of desire, lulling us into a communal silence that bound all of us. It didn't take us long to get on the 400, a virtually straight road that would take us right to the Toronto airport, where, a few hours later, I would be boarding a plane for Italy.

After covering a good stretch of road, Fiorina took my hand and squeezed it tightly. She moved closer to me, so close that I could feel her warmth. Then, with a voice that sounded as sweet as honey, she said, "Pietro, thank you so much for coming to spend the weekend with us, for your company, and for knowing how to untie all the knots that were tangled in my soul."

"Fiorì, my heart's buzzing and it doesn't know how to thank *you*. I never, ever would have believed I would have an experience like this. I am the luckiest person ever, lucky that you told me the story of your life with such truth that it cut straight to the bone. You revealed to me even the darkest secrets locked inside of you. I haven't given you anything important in return, whereas you have offered me all of your trust."

"Pietro, I'm shocked that you really felt all this, but you'll never understand the grounding that you were able to give me. You were able to get me to tell you everything I'd been through, and you can't imagine how good I feel. I feel lighter and cleaner inside and you don't know how happy I am, even if some skeletons are left in my soul, which only you can bring out. I'm sure that you could if you come back to Canada and you'd spend a day or two with me."

Meanwhile, Frank Sinatra sang: "*I left my heart in San Francisco,*" right when I felt like I was leaving my heart attached to hers. I would bring her whole life story with me. I knew that it would never leave me. As usual, Flav and Jadwiga were chatting away in English, but they spoke so fast and so fluently that it was difficult for me to catch even just a few words.

"Fiorì, if the devil doesn't mess up my plans, in a few months I will come back to Toronto. I'm sure that at least for a day or two I can meet up with all of you and we can spend some time together. But if you don't mind, I'd like to leave knowing what happened between you and the Armenian."

"I already told you that it was the first time in my whole life that I went out with a man on a date, not to mention that this man buzzed around me like a hummingbird around a flower. It was a really nice evening. I will never forget that night. It had started off with me hiding my soul behind a wall, but slowly as the words came out of Vahan's mouth, I started to look over my wall and slowly I came out into the open. First, I was impressed when I learned that *Vahan* in Armenian means 'shield.' As the dinner continued, the stories of what I had been through, but mostly the stories of what he had been through, caused me to feel safer just sitting beside him. After my uncle had died, I didn't have anybody but that dear son of mine. My mind started to tell me that I finally had an older person in front of me to talk to and to communicate with, and a person to escape from everyday worries with. It could only do me good, maybe even for Flav I thought.

"That night Vahan told me quite a few things about his life. He was born in Armenia in 1899. He was the son of a doctor and an owner of quite a bit of land. His life when he was a boy was uneventful. His father was severe and authoritarian even with his family, but he was often sweet and tender with the children. Vahan had two older sisters, Gayané and Ahktamar. He described them with a glimmer in his eyes, as if they were in front of him. He told me that they were both beautiful, just like his mother, who seemed like a queen to him. He

213

told me that his mother used to sing all the time, and when his father sat and listened to his wife sing his face became softer and sweeter and his light-coloured eyes seemed to bloom like the almond flowers that grew all around the house. Then came the worst part, and it was literally hell on earth. Vahan was fifteen years old. The Turks came and attacked and killed the Armenians.

"They started with the men, then the women, and lastly the children. It was a real massacre. His father tried to hide in the mountains, but the night he left the house was the last time they saw him. Like many others he was probably captured and then killed. They caught his mother, his sisters and then him. They put them with many other people, all of whom were to be sent to Aleppo. There were thousands of people; however, those who finally made it to Aleppo were very few. His mother and sisters were among those who didn't make it. They died for different reasons. One died from hunger, one from thirst and one from too much hard work. It was a frightening experience that still caused his heart to bleed a half century later. He managed to arrive at Aleppo with a few other people. A few years later he managed to escape and fled to Egypt.

"Once in Cairo, he and a few other Armenians who had been living there for some time felt that they were still in danger o being wiped out. So they emigrated to Canada, their 'Holy Land.' Once in Canada, his luck started to change. He married an Armenian woman who had also come from Egypt. Together they amassed a small fortune. But they couldn't have children. His wife died well before her time, leaving him alone and desperate. Slowly, he started to put the pieces of his life back together. After all, he didn't want to give up. He decided that he wanted to marry again, pass his knowledge and the story of his life on to a younger woman. That way his story and everything that had happened to his mother, his sisters and his father wouldn't be forgotten. More importantly, he wanted his story to be told to other people, to make them think and to help them build a better world for future generations. Now you know what happened to Vahan's family and you can pass it on to others.

"That night he asked me if I wanted to marry him. I gazed at him in silence for a long time. I wasn't able to say a word. I could see in Vahan's eyes all his pain and suffering as well as his worldly hopes and expectations. He also managed to intuit all my problems and worries as well. I decided to cast him a bittersweet smile, but I didn't know what to say. Inside my mind, my heart and my soul different words and feelings raged. But unfortunately none of the emotions and words seemed to win over the others. I felt as if my tongue was tied. Then the whole storm that was going on inside of me must have reached my eyes. Vahan silently took a long, comprehensive look at me. He told me to stay calm and think it over.

"We chatted away and our desire to know more about each other made time pass quickly. It was later than I thought. He called a taxi for me. Once we were in front of my house he had a look on his face that made him appear like a lost sheep. He asked me again if I wanted to be his wife. Once again I didn't know what to answer. I thanked him for the lovely evening and I replied 'see you tomorrow.'

The next day when he saw me at the hotel he came over to say hello. He looked deep into my eyes, as if he wanted to read my heart and soul. It was easy to see that the bee wanted in the beehive. I had many fears and I wondered how Flavio would react. Vahan continued to be a perfect gentleman. He also convinced me to go to dinner again. Thus, drop by drop, the water wears down the stone, just like the bee that hovers around the beehive to find its way in. Some nights I spent chatting away with Flav, who was eighteen years old at the time, as if we were brother and sister. I told him all about Vahan. He took it well. Even he thought that the time had come for me to marry.

"To make a long story short, in the month of May in the year 1963 I left the single's prison in which I had lived for thirteen years and I married Vahan. He had already transferred the interests that he had in Manitoba to Toronto. He had opened a new jewellery store in Richmond Hill, where he was having a house built. His store was prospering every day. After we were married, Vahan left his room at the hotel and came to stay with me at my house. Flavio, who understood that it was time for me to get married, didn't realize that it meant that Vahan would come to live with me. Flav didn't quite know how to react. It was like a thorn in his side. It was clear that the situation bothered him. One thing that seemed strange was that Vahan was always at home. So Flavio tried to stay away as much as possible. This, however, caused me to feel terrible. I tried to be sweet and understanding with Flavio, more than I had been before. But everyone knows time is the best healer, and so slowly time solved our problem. Even Flavio started to get used to it.

"In the meantime he had been accepted at university and he was happy to go. He spent most of his day there. We saw each other a bit in the mornings, but we managed to spend some time together in the evenings. Some nights he didn't come home at all. Slowly he started to get along with Vahan, enough to accompany him to the shop or to see how the work on the new house was coming along when he didn't have to go to class. I realized that Flavio liked the shop. He told me that he would watch Vahan mesmerized, as he restocked the shop with merchandise, caressing the items as he placed them in their glass cases. When it was time to close, Vahan would carefully put the most expensive pieces in the safe. He liked the clients that came to shop, the way Vahan seemed to satisfy them. And he was struck by the fact that these different people with different intentions and different tastes ended up buying the same things in the end. Flavio, who had been intent on becoming an engineer, came to me one day and told me that he wanted to open a jewellery shop just like Vahan's.

"As I mentioned earlier, Vahan had come to stay with me while they finished building the new house. He didn't sleep with me in my room but in the room that had had belonged to my uncle. Right after the wedding we left for our five-day honeymoon in Vancouver. I don't know if you've ever been there, but Vancouver really is a beautiful place, all spread out around the bay and looking out toward the Pacific Ocean. It leaves you breathless. The centre of the city is full of places to pass the time. Shops of all different kinds and for all different sizes of wallets – restaurants, cafés, cinemas, theatres, and with streets full of young people of many different races. And besides, I hadn't seen a beach since I had crossed the ocean. I was impressed as I recall. I liked eating at the restaurants that looked out over the water, morning and night. Once, the sky was full of ash- and charcoal-coloured clouds, as the sun set below the horizon, turning everything from black to red and leaving me awestruck as I watched the play of light and shadow. North Vancouver was surrounded by very tall mountains, tall enough that in May their peaks were still covered with white snow.

"Those five days passed by in a flash. I had never been on vacation and I had never experienced such worry-free days. I had insisted on sleeping in another room from Vahan's. I still had thousands of fears and worries. He wanted to sleep with me, but I wasn't ready, even if we walked up and down Robson Street holding hands, or along the shore of the bay, down the streets surrounded by skyscrapers or under the tall trees of Stanley Park. And I must say that I really liked it when he would take my hand or when his arm would circle my waist and he would squeeze me to his side. Sometimes we even walked along calmly for more than half an hour without saying a word. A few times he caressed my lips with his and I felt myself tremble and shake like a leaf hanging on a branch caught in a strong wind. But I just couldn't go any further. And so we left and went back to Toronto as if we were just good friends who had gone on vacation together. In Vancouver I had tried to contact Nicolaj. I found out, however, that he had moved to Calgary for an important job."

Fiorina was telling me not only a story, but some of the most intimate moments of her life, as if we had been good friends forever. As if we were one person and everything that was in her soul was in mine. In the meantime, the car continued to eat up kilometre after kilometre. Flav and Jad continued talking, and Fiorina and I seemed like two vases connected by a tube, an amazing bond, as if what was too much for Fiorina to handle slowly seeped into me until it evened out the levels between us, making them the same.

"And wanting to stay away from him, didn't it make him lose his patience?" I end up blurting out to Fiorina. I just couldn't help it.

"Vahan waited, maybe because he was older, or maybe because everything he had been through had made him more patient than Job. He understood that I was his wife and that we lived together under the same roof and he slowly won me over. As soon as he could, he would caress me or brush my lips with a kiss. He would touch me here and there and I would barely notice. Slowly, however, all those knots inside began to unravel. And the new house was almost finished. My husband was busy at the shop and with his other interests. So after we had spent some time mulling it over, we decided that it was time for me to leave my job at the hotel, even if I liked working there. It was time to concentrate on the house and concern myself with furnishing it. And so, to the displeasure of the owners, I left my job, having worked there for quite a few years. I, too, was sad. After all, I was attached to my job because it had given me a sense of peace, comfort and a lot of help.

"When Vahan came home at night I would greet him and give him a chaste kiss. I remember one night in particular as if it were yesterday. As we were kissing goodnight before going to bed, I remained practically glued to him. And I kissed him again. He squeezed me tightly to him, I let myself go and then suddenly he let go. We went into his bedroom and I stayed pressed to him. Then Vahan started to undress me while he touched me everywhere. I was a bit scared of what would happen, but I also felt myself start to burn as if I were on fire. I'm sure you know what happened next. After I overcame my initial fear, I was the one who wanted him to come to bed so that we could spend some intimate time together, to play in bed together. That day I seemed to become someone else. I liked being caressed. I myself was never tired of caressing Vahan and keeping the flame of his desire alive. After five or six months I still didn't feel tired. I never, ever would have imagined it. To tell you the whole truth, I felt happy, and when I looked in the mirror I seemed a bit prettier.

"A few months later, I started to notice wrinkles under and around Vahan's eyes. I asked him a few questions. His answers, however, didn't seem honest and were vague. On one hand anyone could see that he was happy. The shop and his business in general were going well enough to buy some apartment buildings, which he put in my name. We had also decided to move into the new house and to sell the one that my uncle left me. Even Flavio no longer thought of him as an outsider or someone who didn't have anything to do with us. Actually, Flav got used to spending time with Vahan and they were often together at the shop and at meetings, for business as well as pleasure. And yet something was wrong.

"Then one evening Vahan finally blurted out the problem. He was glued tightly to my side. He squeezed my arms and after a silence that lasted an eternity and somewhat confused me he finally spoke. He told me that he really hoped to have a child with me. But after almost a year of lovemaking and nothing, he felt discouraged and he had lost all hope. Only after Vahan's confession did I realize that I wasn't pregnant, and we had made love practically every day. He told me that he was sad for two reasons, because I wasn't pregnant and because he had also thought badly of his first wife. He had thought that it was her fault that they didn't have any children, and now he realized that wasn't the case and he could no longer blame her. That night he actually cried. And then after comforting him, we started to kiss and caress one another. One thing led to another and after we made love we both managed to calm down. That night was the first time that we slept in the same bed.

"From that night on I developed a tender feeling for Vahan that, until then, I had never felt. I tried to stay by his side as much as I could, especially after I had sold my uncle's house and we moved into the new one. I also started to spend my days at the shop. Very slowly I started to become the heart and soul of the place, with the clients as well as the suppliers. I liked it. Every day I tried to invent something new. I'm the one who moved the shop to where it is now, and I rearranged the glass cases, the counter and the office. Meanwhile, Vahan started to become attached to Flav as if he were his son, believing that he would live on through Flav by leaving him his legacy.

"As soon as Flav got his degree, he didn't even think twice about helping out even more at the shop. Then, bit by bit, he also started to manage what was mine and even what Vahan had. We had apartments, land, and we had more stocks than some companies. Flav had a lot of things to do and he did them with skill and patience. Even if he was still very young, he knew what he was doing and we often left him on his own because Vahan felt the need to travel. He had started to take me with him when he went to meet or locate other suppliers. Little by little, month after month, he took me to the major cities in America and Canada. I also used our trips to visit shops like ours so that I could learn all the different tricks of the trade and things that I needed to know regarding our business. I became interested in valuable objects that were for sale, and I started to visit the best art galleries in the big cities. That's when I bought my painting of Frida Kahlo that you saw at my shop.

"One beautiful day, after having spent it entirely with one of Vahan's Armenian friends who lived in Chicago, we got back to our hotel room when all of a sudden he blurted out that he really wanted to go to Armenia and that we both had to go. He couldn't wait to see the place where he was born and where he came from. It didn't matter that he didn't have any relatives left, nor the fact that he could only visit the Armenia that was part of the Soviet Union. To us, it seemed harder trying to find the small town where he was born because it was located in Turkish territory. He was worried that it would bring back all the hell that he had seen with his own eyes as a youngster. He was scared that his heart wouldn't hold out. It wasn't easy getting our papers and to organize the ten days that we were going to spend in Armenia. Out of all the trips that we went on together, that trip is the one that I will remember as long as I live.

"It was April. First we went to Moscow, and then we went all the way to Yerevan. When we left Moscow it was minus 10 degrees Celsius, and when we got to Yerevan that night the temperature was 18 degrees. We spent the first three days in Yerevan. There were many ruined houses and it was easy to see that the people didn't have much. The city was beautiful, interesting, and full of amazing theatres, concert halls and museums, such as Matenadaran, where they conserved thousands of scrolls and books that were centuries old.

"The ruins that had been dug up at Eribuni particularly struck me, as they revealed that Yerevan is one of the oldest inhabited places on earth. The monument and the museum that was built on top of a hill beside Yerevan in memory of the massacre carried out by the Turks in 1915 made my stomach turn. In front of the flame, which was in the middle of the monument, Vahan burst out in tears just like a lost child.

221

I couldn't calm him down, maybe because seeing everything made me realize that my heart was broken as well. Unfortunately, for Vahan all those days of hell on earth when he had lived there as a young boy flooded back into his mind, along with the memories of his father, mother and sisters. I guess it was fortunate that we started moving from one city to another, from one little town to another, and so on.

"Armenia is like one big museum. You can see churches and ruins that are thousands of years old basically everywhere. The thousands and thousands of ancient stone crosses embroidering the landscape reveal how early and how deeply Christianity had settled there. Then there are the mountains, which seem to touch the sky. There is one called Ararat, where only now I understand why Noah's ark ended up there during the great flood. The mountain known as Ararat is more than five thousands metres high. It is in Armenia, and all the Armenians in the world know that the mountain is theirs, even if it's considered to be in Turkish territory. It's so beloved that the most famous Armenian painter, Martiros Sarian, paints Mount Ararat into some of his paintings where it shouldn't be in the landscape, in front of him even if it's really behind him, for example.

"Wandering around Armenia you come across valleys and high cliffs that leave you breathless, flowers in the fields, fruit trees, vineyards and the sweetest people you could ever hope to meet anywhere. Almost all the land is located thousands of metres above sea level. Lake Sevan is located almost two thousands metres above sea level. It is absolutely marvellous, many kilometres squared with beautiful beaches. People go there to swim and to sunbathe in the summer. You can even find many beautiful ancient churches near and around the lake.

"We arrived at a place where there was a statue of a beautiful girl named *Akhtamar*. Her arms were extended, and in one hand she was holding a lantern. In front of that statue I heard Vahan recite an

Armenian poem. While he repeated it for a second time tears started to stream down his cheeks. Then he told me that it was a poem titled Akhtamar, written by Hovhannes Tumanyan, one of the greatest Armenian poets. The poem tells the story of Tamar, who lived on an island located on Lake Van, another Armenian lake that is now part of Turkey. At night Tamar would hold out a lantern so that her lover could swim to her on the island in the middle of the lake. Then one windy, stormy night, the wind blew out the light. Her lover kept swimming until he grew extremely tired, unable to find his way to Tamar. When morning came they found him lying dead on the shore. He had drowned. The people say that they found two words frozen on his lips '*Ah, Tamar!*' which later became Akhtamar. Even now, Akhtamar in Turkish Armenia is a name of a place and the name of a famous church.

"Vahan's tears were those of all the Armenian people scattered and lost around the world, the memory of an ancient civilization, and all the pain and suffering that until now had oppressed Vahan's soul. The compassion he felt seemed to shake Vahan's soul and it must have affected him deeply. Once we got back to Toronto he was no longer the same.

A few months passed and Vahan took sick. At the end of 1969 he died, leaving me and Flav alone. I had been with Vahan for six years. With him you can say that I was reborn, that I had become another person. After that brutal experience as a young girl, I had managed to learn to live with a man. At times, I had even touched paradise in a way that can only happen to those who live on earth. I had learned with time to be a business woman, to enjoy life, and not to be scared of anything. Vahan was gone now. Sadly, he left me when he could have finally enjoyed his life with me and Flav, who by this time had become a man. Of course, he had left me a lot of money and ways for me to continue to make more, but his loss caused the world to come crushing down on me.

Fiorina stopped, she took my hand again and squeezed it as if she wanted to pass on to me all the problems that had happened to her, as if she wanted to be sure that I had been listening, and that everything she had told me had reached my heart and had seeped through. I had been so amazed by everything she said that I didn't feel like interrupting her in order to tell her that I knew Armenia quite well and that I had been there three times. As a young man I had been struck by Gayané, a beautiful girl with shiny black eyes like the obsidian that can be found on the slopes of the mountains of Armenia coming down from Lake Sevan. I didn't feel like telling her that the music of *Spartacus* was playing in my head, the ballet written by Aram Khachaturian that I had heard one faraway April in 1970 in Yerevan, and that I had sat right beside Gayané. There was nothing else I could do but hold Fiorina's hand, raise it to my lips and give it a soft and tender kiss so that she understood that I had indeed accepted her invitation.

XXI

A Pause in Cori

"You still haven't finished telling your story?" said Flav with a smile, as Frank Sinatra hit the notes of "Old Man River."

We reached Vaughan. In no more than a half hour we'd be at the airport. I would have liked to continue listening to Fiorina tell her story. I really wanted to know what happened and what Fiorina did when her husband died. Flav persuaded us to stop for gas and at the same time get a quick coffee. Once at the airport everything would be a big blur of urgency, between checking in the luggage, lining up to get my boarding pass, getting my passport checked. After all that running around there would hardly be enough time for goodbyes.

We stopped for twenty minutes, just enough time for us to drink our coffees. I talked briefly with Jadwiga; she told me that she liked living in Toronto, especially since she met Fiorina and had gone to live in her house and to work for her. Once again she asked me if it was true that I was familiar with Poland and if I really had friends in Krakow. When I answered her that I would probably be going there in a few months, she looked at me with sad eyes and said with a few tears in her eyes that every now and then she felt a bit homesick. She said that if I happened to be in Zakopane during the winter months – her voice seemed to crack as she told me this – to look at all the mountains, especially the Tatry, where her father used to take her skiing when she was a girl. She had been there a year before she left to find her fortune.

Then we were off again. The rest of the trip to the airport was mostly silent, and we got there an hour before I had to board my flight. Flav was right. I barely managed to get everything done before I had to leave. Before heading towards the door where they checked the passports and where they wouldn't be allowed beyond, we exchanged our goodbyes. First I hugged Jadwiga. Flav was next. He told me to say hello to Rome, where he was born, adding that it would be difficult for him to go there. For him Cori, where he had been conceived, meant nothing to him. He knew it only to be part of his mother's soul.

Before Fiorina threw her arms around my neck, she took a long look at me and gazed deeply into my eyes, as if she could enter them with hers and leave behind those watery tears that made her eyes beautiful. She hugged me so tightly that I could feel her heart beating, as well as the warmth of her soul.

Then she said sweetly: "Come back. I'll wait."

With a bittersweet expression, I finished saying goodbye to them and then I got in line to get my passport and ticket checked. I looked back to wave goodbye for the last time and then I almost ran all the way to the gate where I had to board my plane.

Sleeping during a plane trip had always been difficult for me, but that particular trip from Toronto to Rome it was impossible. Every now and then I felt a bit sleepy, but I couldn't manage to fall asleep. I had my eyes closed almost the whole time and I wanted to relive my meeting with Fiorina, the story that she had told me, and everything I had seen in the last days, as if it was a film that played in my mind.

In the months that followed when I happened to be in Rome, Latina or Cori, deluding myself that I could resolve or try to resolve things that were much bigger than me, I often thought about Fiorina. Sometimes I told myself that it couldn't be, she didn't exist and that maybe I had dreamed everything. The truth was that I had really met Fiorina, otherwise I wouldn't have thought about her all those times. On my free days I would go around Cori to the different places that Fiorina had mentioned to see if I could find any trace of her life there.

However, women who had Fiorina's charm or who were tall and beautiful like her, in the streets or squares, were nonexistent. No one seemed to have had a childhood like hers. Cori had always been full of beautiful women; however, she was the child of a Corese and a Piemontese and maybe the misfortunes in her life and her living in another world had refined her more than the other Coresi, who had to work hard, picking olives for a landowner, trimming vineyards, baking under the hot sun, surrounded by tobacco plants, or having babies one after another and needing to feed them. Certainly, in the last few years Cori has made progress, and there are plenty of pretty girls that could fill both eyes with their beauty. Fiorina, however, had been kneaded from another type of flour.

More than once, when I was walking alone along the streets of Cori and thought of her, it was almost as if I saw her. However, they were only images of dear ghosts that danced inside my head. It helped me to understand that she really had impressed me. I even started to cautiously investigate to see if I could find someone who remembered her or her family. But half a century had gone by since the last time she had been to Cori. There weren't even people that made or fixed butts like her grandfather had done. It was difficult for me to find the slightest trace of Mimma's family, a family that had always lived in

Cori. Only some of them had left the town to go to Australia. There were a few nephews of Mimma's brother. The older one was the only one who hadn't moved elsewhere, but he didn't know Fiorina. After half a century, no one knew anything about Mimma either. All this made me think that our lives are short and fleeting. Just like a breeze that you barely hear coming and going, after a couple of generations no one remembers anything about those who had lived before them.

Only very few are lucky enough to be remembered because they are talked about in books. In books there is only one Saint Tommaso Placidi, one Sante Laurienti, poet, or a famous engineer like Alessandro Marchetti. People like these are born only rarely. Most people are born only to toil, to eat and then to vanish after living a life of hard work that devours them before they disappear forever.

I like going to the cemetery every now and then to visit my parents. While there, I like to take a long walk around to visit all the people I have known and who are now resting under the trees. The first time that I went to the cemetery after I got back from Toronto I searched amongst those who had been buried to see if I could find Fiorina's relatives. But unfortunately nothing was the same as it was before. Very few had been buried in the ground, and so I didn't find anything. In the middle of the chapels, wandering as far as possible, I started to silently commend them, one by one, to the one and only creator of the earth, the sky, the darkness and the light. One hopes that it's true, that everything comes to an end and He gently gathers all of us in his arms. I didn't even try to look for Cencia or the notary from Rome. Fiorina had told me that for fifteen years or so they had kept in touch by writing each other letters every now and then. But thirty years and more had gone by and she hadn't heard from her.

Six months went by in a flash. I thought about Fiorina, but in all that time I had never written to her and I didn't have any news about her, and so everything seemed like a dream that I had dreamt a long time ago and every now and then it came back to mind. Time passed and soon it was summer and I happened to have an opportunity to go back to Canada with a few people who were interested in attending an exhibition to try and sell wine, cheese from sheep's milk, and olive oil in Montreal. I had to cross the ocean again and so I decided to go to Toronto by myself and stay there for a few days of vacation.

Montreal is one of the most beautiful cities in all of North America. I had good friends there, many places to have fun, but I didn't let myself fall under its spell. Even in Toronto I had many friends, but Fiorina drew me to her as if I were a magnet and she was a piece of steel. The fact that in her veins flowed Corese blood, and a piece of Cori's history in her soul, drew me to her. That elegant charm and a beauty of hers made of fortune and security, where she had walked and fought her way through life, and done well, all this seemed to magnetize me. I was attracted by the desire, perhaps a little morbid, to hear her tell her story, a Calvary of a life, rarely recounted by a living person and therefore rarely heard. A Calvary to cry on, and sometimes to envy. In a word, an experience of life to feel like my own.

Thus overcome by the fatigue of those days in Montreal without sleep, one Friday afternoon in the month of July 2000 I arrived in Toronto. From the airport I took a taxi and asked to be taken to the Holiday Inn in Yorkdale, where I could easily take the subway to downtown Toronto, to find or be picked up by friends who lived scattered around the same area, in Woodbridge, north of Toronto, just in case I didn't find Fiorina. Yup, it could happen. After all, I hadn't let her know that I had arrived. I hadn't contacted her either when I left Italy, nor when I was in Montreal. I chuckled when I thought how this would be such a surprise for her. I was sure that as soon as I could, I would be able to call her. The fact is that I arrived at the hotel thinking about Fiorina. But as soon as I got there, I was barely able to freshen up because I was dead tired. I managed to throw myself on the bed without even putting myself under the covers. I was out like a light.

XXII

Fiorina's Hospitality

When I finally woke up it was seven p.m. I must have dropped like a sack of potatoes. I felt lightheaded, light as a feather. Before washing up, I thought that I should call Fiorina if I wanted to see her, always hoping that she was in Toronto. And yet I had a strange feeling that in some way I would see her, either that night, or maybe the next morning. I called her house and listened anxiously to the many rings, but no one answered. Not even Jadwiga picked up, and she was usually there. If I didn't find Fiorina, I would be so upset and my heart would be filled with regret.

Without hesitating, I thought about trying the store. At that hour I was sure that I would find someone there. After the first few rings I started to worry, and I must say that even only a few moments for me seemed to last forever. Suddenly, I heard a "hello" in my ear and I hoped that it was a good sign. It wasn't Fiorina, nor Flav. But at least someone had answered. I answered in English and asked to speak with Fiorina or Flav. The voice on the phone told me that neither one of them was there and to try at home, or on Monday.

I felt as if the roof had come crashing down on my head. But I found some courage and with a bit of anxiety I explained that on Monday I'd be leaving for Italy. I tried to explain the best that I could with my poor English skills that I wanted to meet with Fiorina. The man told me that he would do everything he could to get a hold of Fiorina or Flav, but that at this hour it would be difficult to find them. I felt a bit of sadness, and I almost wanted to cry. I hung up and I started thinking about what I could do. There was no solution, other than to sit in my hotel room and cry, even if that meant not going to dinner, just in case the person from the store was able to get a hold of Fiorina. It was important that I didn't move from there if I wanted to be contacted.

I didn't know what to do to avoid crying or feeling sad, so I turned on the TV. I started channel surfing. There were many channels, but they seemed all the same, until I got to a French channel that was showing *Questi fantasmi (These Ghosts)* with Vittorio Gasmann and Sofia Loren. In Italy I had never seen it. Of course, the movie wasn't *Questi fantasmi* by De Filippo, but it was good enough to pass some time. The actors were alright and Sofia as always was quite a sight to see. I had almost lost all hope as far as hearing from Fiorina. I was about to get undressed and to sadly slip under the covers, when suddenly the phone rang. I lifted up the receiver, my heart pounding loudly.

"Hello?"

"Pietro! What a joy to hear from you, how are you?"

It was Fiorina's voice that I heard in my ear, warm and sweet just like the music of a violin playing one of Mozart's sonatas. My happiness suddenly returned. We continued talking in English, then in Italian, and last of all in Corese. She told me that she was happy to hear from me. Then, with many reproaches, she told me that I should have called her to let her know that I was coming so that she could have picked me up at the airport. By this time it was 9:15 p.m. She wanted to know if I'd had dinner. As soon as I said no, she told me that she was wrapping up a dinner meeting with some suppliers at the restaurant in the Four Seasons Hotel, and they were almost done. If I wanted to meet up with them there I could order anything I wanted. But I would never make it down there in time from the Holiday Inn. I would be too late. She said that since she was with Flav I could get a bite to eat at the hotel where I was staying and they would come up and meet me for a coffee.

I don't know why, but suddenly I felt like I was no longer in my body. Not even a lovesick teenager knowing his girlfriend is on her way to visit him would have felt the same way. But it's the truth. I felt a bit tipsy, as if I'd been drinking. It was quite some time that I felt tied to Fiorina. I washed up and changed, and went down to eat. It was almost ten o'clock. At the restaurant there were still some people. This comforted me a little; I don't like eating alone, especially in a restaurant. The people there ate and spoke really softly, so softly that I felt as if I were in the middle of a public confession. I ordered a fresh salmon filet and a beer. I ate really slowly to let as much time pass as possible so that Fiorina would find me there. I even ordered an American coffee. It was half a litre of liquid. The waitress, a cute young girl with Asiatic features came to ask me every now and then if everything was alright. But time passed, and mother and son were nowhere to be seen.

It was almost eleven o'clock when I saw them appear, first Flav, then Fiorina. They both seemed younger than the last time I had seen them. Flav, always elegant, was calmly smiling and extending his hand to shake mine, but then came closer so that we could kiss each other cheek to cheek in a warm, classic Italian hello. Fiorina, with her shiny eyes and black hair, which was also shiny and straight as if she had just walked out of a salon, literally threw her arms around

233

my neck and in English said, "Welcome, and benvenuto!" I called the waitress and told her to add my dinner to my bill for the room. Then I proposed that we go and sit at the bar. All three of us ordered red Bordeaux to celebrate and to chat for a while.

Fiorina told me that as soon as they let her know that I was in Toronto, her heart seemed to buzz and she couldn't wait to see me. Then she told me that since she met me, everything that she had gone through in Italy and in Cori half a century ago seemed and felt a lot more recent, as if it had happened all just the other day. Even all the bad and negative things that had happened to her had come to mind. Some were bitter, some really bitter, but they were always a part of her. It made her feel complete, more so than she had ever felt up until then. For years and years she had found a way to keep everything that had happened to her far away, but now she understood that she still carried everything inside of her. She felt that she was the way she was thanks to everything that she had lived through until then. She had left Cori and Rome with her son to live with her uncle in Canada after she had lost all her dear ones in Italy. She told me that talking with me helped her to recall her story and made her feel good. It revived a sense of happiness in her soul, even if sometimes she felt a twinge of pain and tears fell.

It was almost midnight when she suddenly she asked me if I wanted to leave the hotel and spend the two days at her house. That way we would have more time to spend together and talk. It was the weekend and the next day Flav had to go and get Jadwiga, who had spent a week with one of her Polish friends, a lady named Roza, also from Wadowice. At first I put up a bit of resistance because it looked bad cancelling the room that I booked for three days only a few hours after I had arrived and, worse, at midnight. I didn't have the courage to go and tell the receptionist. Fiorina told me not to be silly and not to worry because it was easy. Then she said that if I didn't do it she would.

That's what happened. Half an hour later, after paying the hotel bill, we jumped into Flav's car and headed for Fiorina's house. While we were on the road they told me that Jadwiga had gone to spend a week with her friend Roza, who lived a few kilometres away from Niagara-on-the-Lake, the falls and the Niagara River. They told me that almost all the tourists who came from far away usually only visited the falls. Obviously, they're magnificent – one of the most beautiful things that nature has created in this world. However, the entire region around the falls should be seen as well. If one has some time to spend, it's worth a few days of vacation.

I would have my own opportunity to judge, even if we would only be spending a day there.

XXIII

Vacation at Niagara-on-the-Lake

We got to Fiorina's house at 1:30 a.m. There was not even time for us to have a quick chat. Before getting to the house they had told me that we'd be leaving really early in the morning so that I would have a chance to see a few places that were worth seeing. In fact, once we were in the house, Fiorina told Flav to show me the room that I'd be in. Flav insisted on bringing my luggage for me. The room was on the second floor, where all the bedrooms were located. Fiorina followed us up to show me all the comforts that the room offered so that I could use what I needed without any problem, pointing out the towels and the washroom, complete with shower gels, soaps, deodorants and scents. After they showed me where I'd be sleeping, they ask if I wanted to go downstairs to have something warm to drink. I told them that I'd rather pass on the offer because it really was getting late. They also decided to pass, agreeing that I was right, that it was very late. They informed me that they had decided to change the original plan. Instead of leaving at eight o'clock, it was decided that it would be better to leave at ten.

Once alone, I took a look around. The room that they had given me wasn't particularly big, but it had everything. There was a double bed with four pillows, a TV, a radio and a dark wood bookshelf, which contained a few books. Almost all of them were novels and a few books of history. There was a little table with a couple of magazines on top, in front of a pinkish armchair. On one of the walls hung a reproduction of a famous masterpiece, *Les Demoiselles d'Avignon* by Picasso. One could see even from the room that I was staying in that money obviously wasn't a problem for Fiorina.

I was dead tired. I finished unpacking my luggage. I washed quickly, put my pyjamas on, set the alarm clock for nine o'clock and slipped under the sheets. I turned off the lights and I snuggled up, hoping to fall asleep right away, even if I was sleeping in a new bed and I was excited about spending a few days with Fiorina. It didn't take me long to fall asleep and once asleep, I slept through the whole night. In fact, come morning, I woke up as soon as the alarm started ringing and I quickly jumped out of bed. I felt well rested. I'd slept at least six hours straight. I had a warm shower, shaved and at twenty minutes to ten I was downstairs, where Fiorina was already ready and coming towards me with a smile and a "good morning" as sweet as honey. She was beautifully elegant, wearing a pair of white pants and a tight red shirt. No one would have ever thought that she was in her seventies.

"Come in the kitchen. Breakfast is already ready. Flav's preparing the coffee. Let's try to hurry. That way we can leave by ten o'clock."

Flav must have heard us coming, as he was placing a pot of hot coffee on the table.

"Good morning, Pietro, did you sleep well?" he said to me in Italian.

"Very well, thanks Flav."

On the table there was everything one could imagine for breakfast – coffee, milk, different flavours of jam, different kinds of soft cheeses, boiled eggs, many sweets, like croissants, slices of bread to toast and fruit. I asked for two slices of toast and ate them with some jam and cheese. Then I peeled myself a banana and drank my mug of caffé latte. Fiorina and Flav did the same. It was just after ten o'clock when we were in the car and on the road. Fiorina wanted me to sit up front beside Flav because that way I would be able to have a better view of the landscape. But I couldn't dream of accepting. It didn't seem fair.

In a flash we had gone from Fiorina's house to Yonge Street, and then we had to head down the street and cut across the centre of downtown Toronto all the way to the Gardiner Express. From there we had to head towards, or parallel to, Lake Ontario until we reached the Q.E.W. Expressway, named after Queen Elizabeth. If I'm not mistaken, that road was the first big highway built in America. It is the only one that isn't numbered. It is named, they say, not in honour of Elizabeth I, nor Elizabeth the II, the present queen, but rather in honour of the wife of George VI, also named Elizabeth. She was a queen because she had married a king. In fact this Elizabeth, who lived past her hundredth birthday, had been present, with her husband, at the opening of the road in 1939. Today, this special road runs along the lakeshore, and leads all the way to the falls and the Niagara River.

We drove down almost all of it, passing St. Catherine's and the Welland Canal. We passed Hamilton, Grimsby and St. Catherine's before getting to the Niagara River. A few kilometres past the Welland Canal, we turned onto the 405 that leads to the Lewiston Bridge. Crossing the Niagara River, you get to the border, where you can enter the United States of America. We had already driven more than a few hundred kilometres from Fiorina's house. Flav drove fast, but not too fast, because from my window I managed to see an amazing landscape that left me breathless. To the left there was the lake and to the right you could see gardens, small towns, factories, fields full of grapevines and fruit trees. We frequently came upon signs directing us to one wine cellar or another. Having come from a land where for thousands of years grapes had been cultivated for wine, I was surprised to see that they cultivated grapes in Canada too. And I noticed that the vineyards were extensive and precisely ordered in straight lines so long that a human eye couldn't see where they ended; they seemed to be custom sown clothes made for the earth. The whole area was full of different wineries where they produced high quality white and red wine. There were many signs along the route, precisely indicating to turn here or to turn there, to visit, to eat, to sleep, to have fun or to go for a bicycle ride.

Now I understood the brochures that I had seen and read many times in the hotels in Toronto, which were about the streets, the wine, the group tours that they organized to visit the vineyards and the cellars. Fiorina and Flav were telling me that many wineries seemed like museums, to draw tourists' attention and to encourage wine tasting so that they could then make purchases. These cellars or wineries also organized feasts, concerts and plays for their visitors. Many wineries also had restaurants and served up good cuisine. One could spend entire days just winery hopping, one after another. Italy may have invented wine, but in Canada they took it to a whole new level. They know how to produce it and how to sell it. But it was expensive and difficult in Canada, because only very few areas can be used for wine production, such as the beautiful Niagara region that Flav and Fiorina were showing me, an area where one could find good earth and a mild climate provided by the lake, which protected the vineyards from frost and cold temperatures. There were kilometres and kilometres of vineyards, but lucky for us Italians, it wasn't enough for everybody.

We drove almost all the way to the Niagara River. When we came to the fork in the path we took the one that was parallel to the river, the Niagara Parkway that leads to Lake Ontario and the historical district of Niagara-on-the-Lake.

Now Flav was driving at a snail's pace so that I could see the beautiful landscape near the river and the American side of the falls. Every now and then he would drive down a small side street so that I could take a better look at the vineyards, wineries, houses and hotels. It was quite a sweet treat. Then they brought me to the oldest neighbourhood and we drove all around it. The small town didn't contain more than 15,000 souls, and it was beautiful, one of the most beautiful of all the ones that I had seen in Canada.

It was starting to get late. It was close to 3:00 p.m., well past lunch, and I started to feel a gnawing hunger that seemed to be eating a hole in my stomach. The others must have been hungry too, as Fiorina told her son to hurry up. It was time to put something between our teeth. We wanted to get to Jadwiga before she would start to worry. Just after three we were in the countryside among the vineyards. We stopped in front of an entrance of one of the many estate wineries. We didn't get out of the car. Jadwiga was already waiting for us with her arms wide open. Right behind her stood her friend Roza with her husband Roger, a big man who looked like a gentle giant. After we had finished with the introductions, hugs and kisses, they took us to a nice spot where there were other people, tourists and visitors who had eaten lunch some time ago. They had a table reserved just for us. I must say that it was a perfect lunch – a first course of oysters, which came from only God knows where, followed by cheese, meat, vegetables, and fruit that came from the same fruit trees that the winery owned. Not to mention high quality wine.

Roger explained to us that he had been making wine for as long as he could remember. His ancestors, who had left France, from some

town in Burgundy, had also been winemakers. Then his father had
passed the art of winemaking down to him, as is often done from
father to son. His winery was part of the Vintners Quality Assurance,
or QVA. Such a label on a bottle is a guarantee of the quality of the
wine. We finished eating around five o'clock – what a snack! Then
Roger took us on a tour of the building, the cellar and the different
rooms where the wine was made and where it matured in wooden
butts. We saw where they bottled the wine, where they conserved it
and where it was sold. The building had two floors. On the first floor
or ground level, you could find a little museum and the offices. The
restaurant was a big hall, long and wide, where events could be held
for three hundred or four hundred people at a time. On the second
level were the rooms for the people who lived there, as well as the
rooms that were part of the bed & breakfast.

Roger told us that his winery was one of the few that had started
experimenting with ice wine, to try to bring it to super refined levels.
Canadian ice wine has made this particular area of Ontario famous
all over the world. Roger explained the process and the history to us.
The grapes are picked from the vineyard when the temperature is
below -8 C, which means that the grapes are picked often at night and
pressed immediately when they are still frozen. The story goes that ice
wine was first created by mistake at the end of 1700 in Franconia and
in Germany. Only half a century ago they started to perfect it and to
produce it in great quantity. Now Germany and Canada produce the
best and the most ice wine in the world. However, it is the Niagara
Peninsula that produces a lot of the high quality wine, thanks to
the perfect climate and the earth. Canada exports this fine wine all
over the world. The best grapes for making ice wine are Riesling and
Vidal, but they are also experimenting with other types of grapes to
make red ice wine.

Roger's ice wine is made of two thirds Riesling and one third
Vidal. The frozen grapes are picked during the winter months. And

sometimes even at the end of January. Since low temperatures don't last long, even in Canada, the grapes have to be picked right away when the temperature is right, and that means even at night. It's understandable that it's more expensive than regular wine. The frozen grapes are as hard as marbles; the water they contain freezes solid, while its other elements and sugars remain the same. As soon as they pick the grapes, most of the water is eliminated, that way the sugar and acid levels remain high. The two things balance each other. The wine that comes out of this whole process is marvellous and makes you want to lick your lips. It's mostly a dessert wine, but it's also common to drink it after a lunch or dinner. I tried not to drink a lot, but it was even a pleasure for one's eye, as it was beautiful to look at. It looks like liquid gold and has a dry champagne taste with a hint of cooked figs and other aromas. I had a few glasses and I felt a little tipsy.

Fiorina noticed this and proposed that we go to a hotel nearby to rest up and spend the night. For her, it didn't seem like a good idea to return to Toronto at night. And we were also tired. Besides, Fiorina wanted me to see the sun set over the Niagara River, as it slipped below the American border and went to sleep. But Roger and Roza insisted that we didn't need to go to a hotel. They had room for us there and it wasn't a problem for us to sleep there. That night we could listen to a jazz concert and relax together. We hadn't brought anything with us to stay overnight. No change of clothes and nothing to wash up with. Roger told us not to worry at all, especially me. It wasn't the first time that visitors were unprepared to stay. He assured us that he would take care of everything and that we would find everything that we needed in our rooms. Then he invited us to go for a walk in the vineyards, along the little creeks and lakes among the trees.

XXIV

Fiorina and Flavio, Claire and Flavio

It was a hot summer day at the end of June. It was past five p.m., the sun was still hot and the sky was blue, even if every now and then a few ash-white clouds floated around. Roger's vines were on top of a sloping piece of land, and at some points, the higher ones, you could see Lake Ontario not too far away. Once in a while, you could catch a glimpse of a white sailboat out in the middle of the lake, slowly gliding across the surface. In the midst of the grapevines, which were all in straight rows, Roger caught up to us and started to point out which was the Riesling and which was the Vidal. All of them bore big bunches of grapes that wouldn't be picked before the middle of December, if all went well. The leaves were still green and dazzled one's eyes with a calming yet colourful fantasy. After about forty minutes we went back in.

They showed us to our rooms, where Fiorina told me that at seven o'clock she would knock on my door so that we could see and enjoy the sunset. The room was great, and I must say that it wasn't lacking a thing. I threw myself on the bed hoping that I would be able to take a quick nap. And so, I set my alarm clock for five minutes before seven. The wine, the digestion and the fatigue took over altogether, and I fell asleep. Thanks to my alarm clock, which rang quite loudly, I managed to wake up. I had barely finished getting ready when I heard someone knocking at my door. It was Fiorina. Always ready, delicate, kind and thoughtful. The four of us, Fiorina, Flav, Jadwiga and I, left. Roger and Roza had to prepare everything for the evening. Not only for us, but for all the other people who would be stopping there to eat or to enjoy the concert.

We arrived after crossing what seemed to be a sea of vines, houses, shops and wineries. We walked across the whole area until we reached a spot where we could see Niagara Falls and a section of the river. The sun was starting to set. Flav and Jad had their arms linked together as they walked along the edge of the river. Fiorina and I decided to sit down on a bench. A few clouds rolled in from where the lake and the river met, and a light mist began to rise. The sky along the horizon changed colours as the sun went down. At first the sky was an ash-grey shade. Then it became lighter, before turning apricot-yellow, pink, and finally a blazing fiery red. In the middle of the river a shiny band made up of thousands of colours reflected the sun. It was quite an emotional sight. Fiorina remained silent.

Suddenly, she blurted out: "I had the pleasure of seeing the same show years ago, in Vahan's company the summer before he died. It was certainly one of our last good, calm and peaceful days, before he got sick and his disease started to eat away at him, and before he left me alone forever."

Fiorina was calm and her voice was full of peace. She seemed to affectionately invite me to prepare myself for the rest of the story that had been interrupted months earlier when I had to return to Italy.

I grabbed one of her hands and caressed it, bringing it to my lips. I looked deep into her shiny, calm and moist eyes. One could read her soul. She smiled at me. I was full of tenderness. My heart felt as if it were larger and ready to absorb everything that Fiorina would be able to tell me. I felt a strange hunger to know more and I asked her: "What did you do when Vahan left you? What else happened to you, how did you manage to take care of everything that you had, and with Flav, who was, after all, still a young man?"

"The first days were the worst. I wandered around the house and I felt lost. The house seemed so big. Often, I was all alone because Flav had to look after the shop, the banks and the houses. He was a man. He had finished his studies and, because he had been constantly at Vahan's side and had gone everywhere with him, he had learned everything that he needed to know about the business. Several days later, even if I had many things to do around the house looking after the workers that I called in to help me, it still seemed that the house wanted to hold me in a grip of loneliness and tears.

Sometimes, I thought that I heard his voice, or I'd hear a noise and I would jump. So, I started to spend the whole day at the shop. I made an effort to make the shop look nicer, to entice more clients. I started to seek out suppliers, even when it wasn't necessary, travelling here and there by myself without taking Flav along with me.

"Three or four months went by and I continued to keep myself occupied; however, what darkened my soul didn't want to let go. It was the one period of my life when my mother, my father and my grandparents came back into my head, and many nights I dampened the sheets with a river of tears before falling asleep."

Fiorina remained silent for a bit. Niagara's water reflected yellow and red and it seemed to be listening to Fiorina's words. A boat sailed by us, heading towards the middle of the lake. Fiorina took my hand and gripped it tightly, as never before. Then with a warm and strong voice, with words that contained kindness and emerged from the deepest part of her soul, slowly, with significant pauses, she continued to tell her story.

"One night I went to sleep earlier than usual. I didn't feel like sitting in front of the TV or reading. I felt emptier than usual, tired, and my head felt really heavy. I spent an hour tossing and turning between the sheets. In the end, I burst out into tears. In that moment everything that I had lived through, from when I was young, up until Vahan's death flashed before my eyes. My tears hadn't come out silently like many other times. Flav, who had come upstairs to get an early night because he had to leave at dawn for a few days in Montreal, must have heard me crying. He knocked on my door and asked me what was wrong. Instead of calming down, I began to sob hysterically, hiccupping sobs as well.

"Flav sat down beside me and tried to calm me down, caressing my cheeks and my hair, while whispering the sweetest words possible. I squeezed him to me tight. I started to calm down a bit, but every now and then I sobbed and hiccupped. I was in a sitting position and I squeezed Flav to my chest just like I used to when he was a child. Only that he wasn't the one crying, I stopped sobbing, but the tears continued to fall, and I was still convulsing from time to time. Flav gently passed his hands over my face to try my tears. I told Flav to stay with me, to undress and lie down beside me. Maybe I might calm down.

"After a while, as I calmed down, I was slowly dozing off. All of a sudden, some ugly ghost must have entered my mind and I gasped. Flav moved closer to me and gathered me up in his arms. I squeezed him to me; he caressed me, he spoke words of comfort, full of sweetness. We were glued like husband and wife. At some point, I felt that he was excited. For a moment my heart stopped beating, everything stopped. I felt myself turn to ice. Then I felt a strange calm come over me. I felt myself burn up and it was almost as if I looked at myself from outside. I remained glued to Flav. My mind started to run wild. I knew that Flav was no longer a child. He was almost twenty-five years old. Even if he seemed to have been made to be admired, he had never brought any girls home. I had never known him to go out with anyone or if he had ever had a girlfriend, even though many girls buzzed around him.

"I felt almost paralyzed. Instead of moving away for fear of putting thoughts in his head that maybe he didn't have, and possibly because I loved him so much, all I could do was hug him even tighter to me, as he kissed my cheeks and told me to calm down and to try to sleep. I started to kiss him on his forehead and then on his neck. And then suddenly I moved to his lips, not just a quick peck on his lips in a motherly jest. No, in that precise moment, without knowing or understanding, we were only man and woman. My lips stopped sweetly on his, then I broke the kiss with my lips, and then I kissed him again slowly. He let me continue.

"I'm sure you can imagine what happened next. The blood was boiling in me and in him. I asked him if he had ever made love with a girl. He said no. And then no more words. For a while he remained silent. Then he told me that, even if he had thought about it, he was always scared, recalling what I had told him regarding how he had been conceived. After, neither of us managed to say a single word. Not from me or from him. Only silence and caresses. I realized that he really didn't know anything.

"Slowly, very slowly I guided him through what he had to do. I didn't even think about the fact that he was my son, that between mother and son it was prohibited what we were doing. Flav was my soul. What was supposed to happen happened. At the end, without words, without moans, we clung tightly to one another and we fell asleep. That night I slept like a log without ever waking up. When I eventually woke up it was eight o'clock. I felt rested and fresh. To me it seemed like every other morning. What had happened the night before didn't even come to mind. I didn't even notice that he wasn't home. But within five minutes it all flooded back. Flav, I immediately realized, had probably left already for Montreal. His flight was at nine. As soon as I thought about what had happened, I felt myself burning up from head to toe.

"At first I imagined that I had dreamed it. Then I realized that it had really happened. It wasn't a dream at all. How on earth did an absurd thing like that happen if I couldn't even imagine it ? I sat back down on the bed because I didn't feel my legs. At first I thought that I was in the middle of another catastrophe. How would we look at each other, what would we say to each other when he got back from Montreal? Could we know how or would we know what to say to each other? I felt scared and weak. I started to think about how Flav felt at this moment. Alone, far away, and he had to meet with one of our difficult suppliers. I spent the whole morning thinking about it while keeping myself busy between one thing and another. Then I went to the shop. All the work, talking to the employees or with the clients pushed my thoughts about what had happened between me and Flav away.

"At night all alone at home, my thoughts drifted back to the same problem. I was astounded as I began to realize that of all the things passing through my mind remorse wasn't one of them. I didn't even feel shame for what we had done. I went to bed with a strange sense of calm inside of me. With my eyes closed I calmly thought about the previous night and about how everything had started – the storm of emotions that had shaken every little piece of my soul and caused my whole body to ache, Flav's comforting caresses, feeling him excited as he lay beside me and how I myself calmly and securely guided him inside of me as if it was the most natural thing in the world. I wanted to smile. Everything that had happened between me and Flav had calmed my nerves and it had suddenly pulled me out of my depression caused by Vahan's death, as well as all the other never-ending disasters. Actually, they seemed like they wanted to finish me slowly, one day after another, until the last drop of blood and the last piece of flesh was consumed.

"With some trepidation, I realized that everything had been natural, feeling a tender pleasure, not only physical, but also emotional. Not even the first few times with Vahan had been like this. It was sweet, only and absolutely sweet. I felt like smiling again. Then I started to feel sad. The thing that worried me was that Flav probably felt bad. Then slowly, bit by bit, I fell asleep."

At first Fiorina had difficulty getting her words out one after another. She was basically stuttering, and then slowly, as she continued, she started to speak clearly. She told her story warmly, quietly, as if she herself felt that she was putting her heart inside of me, in a safe place for ever. She sat closer to me and she leaned her head on my shoulder.

Then she took a nice long and deep breath, and almost whispering she said: "Thank you for coming to visit me, and for knowing how to listen with heart, affection, trust and tenderness. I don't think of you only as a friend. I feel more like a sister who is simply talking to her brother about things that are hidden deep in my soul, to feel comprehension and comfort. I haven't gone to confession since my communion. I have thought about everything I've lived through many times over, all the difficult days or the days of happiness that have gone by in seventy years. Sometimes when I'm with you it's almost like being in a confessional. I still haven't told you everything, but I feel good, I feel lighter than I've ever felt before."

I wrapped my arm around her shoulders and I hugged her tight to me and I kissed her on her forehead. She looked at me with two shining eyes full of gratitude, even though I hadn't given her anything.

The only thing I had done was really listen to her. The sun was almost hidden and the colours were warm and comforting. A light fresh breeze had begun to blow and it kept us company.

We remained silent. Fiorina's head rested on my shoulder. Inside of me thousands of thoughts ran wild, which caused the words to stop at my tongue. My heart was beating fast, thanks to what Fiorina was telling me. I never, ever could have imagined a story like Fiorina's, so bitter, so sweet, so human, and yet so fairytale-like, and in the world of the fairytale you encounter fun, excitement and at the same time things to frighten and terrorize you.

In front of us, the colours of the horizon were plentiful and marvellous; always different, minute after minute, many beautiful things mixed together. All these things must have given Fiorina the courage and the calm to tell me all those secrets that normally one would never share because they are too complicated and unexplainable. Things that one could shed a river of tears for, and cause one to build a labyrinth of mysteries in their mind and soul. To think that not even a year ago Fiorina was basically nothing to me. I didn't even know she existed. Now I brought a big piece of her inside me, made up of all her pain, happiness and mysteries.

I didn't know what to say; however, I realized that I had met her in a moment when she felt pressed by the need to relive everything that had brought her pleasure and everything that had brought her pain in the last seventy years. I came from Cori, from her parents' world, the same world where she herself had lived a definitive part of her life. She must have imagined me as a mirror that she could look at and see herself reflected, the mirror that she had been looking for, for some time now and which she had finally found.

After a period of silence, which for me seemed to last a century, the only stupid, lame thing that I slowly managed to say was this: "Fiorina, you've earned a place in my heart and nothing could push you out. Something puzzling keeps floating in my mind, however, regarding the first night that I slept next to your room at your cottage in Awenda Park. That night I heard some noises that sounded like moans of pleasure, almost as if a couple were making love."

"Oh, you heard us! I didn't think it was possible. I guess I might as well finish telling the whole story. After two days Flav came back from Montreal. I was both happy and worried. I went to the airport full of fear, with my heart beating as loudly as a drum. As soon as Flav saw me, he greeted me with a strange smile on his lips. It was almost as if his lips barely opened, forming an enigmatic grin. He told me that his trip had gone well. We spent hours together but we hardly spoke, deprived of words as we were, except for the occasional question about what he was doing and what he still had to do. He gave me only quick and fast answers, which contained no more than a few words and then followed by a lot of silence, as if it were a luggage or a weight to tug a long. Two or three days passed by like this. Both Flav and I tried to stay busy doing anything that we could so that we wouldn't spend any time together. We only had time to say good morning and good night to one another.

"A strange sensation of anxiety came over me that made my heart cry, even though since that bizarre night with Flav all the suffering and all the worries that I had locked away after Vahan's death had passed through my mind. The weird way I acted caused Flav to clam up even more. At night when I went to sleep, the night seemed to last forever. Then, I finally told myself that I was the mother and that it was up to me to get us out of that mess of emotions and problems.

"And so one Sunday night, after we had spent the day doing different things in the house, I gathered up some courage and I started asking him how he was doing, how come he had become silent, trying to hint at what had happened between us. After a while he looked deep into my eyes and I stared right back into his. They looked like the eyes of a dog that had been hit and was waiting to hear a comforting word.

"Naturally, I told him that we hadn't robbed anything from anybody and even if what we had done could seem absurd it had happened naturally; we didn't have to hide our heads in the sand. We didn't owe anything to anybody. Maybe we should reflect on the fact that it hadn't happened only to us, there were the ancient myths. He told me that he felt awful. As soon as he started to think about it he felt his chest close up until he couldn't breathe and he felt strangled. Then he added that his first day in Montreal he hadn't been able to eat, not even a single bite of food. He was scared that he was or he could become a bad person. Then he confessed that he felt confused, and that during those moments of real suffering when he was alone, he thought about what had happened and sometimes he felt himself heat up, something pushed him to relive those moments and he felt a yearning that he couldn't stop. No matter how hard he tried, that feeling of desire continued and it scared him. He didn't know what to do to send it away.

"He had known and met pleasure that up until that night he had never imagined possible, and he didn't understand if it was simply physical or if it was something that came from his soul. With his mother, it was simply unbelievable! Suddenly a tear slid down his face as he told me what he felt inside: at the bottom of his heart there was a ball of bittersweet yarn and he was tangled in it, and he didn't know how to free himself. We remained silent for a while, then he said to me that, in all truth and honesty, after all the trouble that that experience had caused him, he didn't even know if he really wanted to be free of it. In a soft, shaky voice that was almost a whisper, he confessed that at certain moments he seemed to want to be caught up in that web again, to feel that sense of pleasure, which was a mix of flesh and soul. Then he added that he felt horrible.

"What would you have done in my position? I felt even more horrible than he did. It was as if my soul had been torn, ripped in two. Flav was my flesh and blood. I would give my life to see him happy. At that precise moment, I was a mother and a woman. I loved him more than my own eyes. This time I was the one who started to caress him, give him kisses while I whispered sweet words of comfort. How do you think it ended? We went to bed together and spent a long, calm, sweet night in a river of words. It was a beautiful night, which seemed like it was made out of honey. From then on, everything just seemed natural. For a few years, we lived together more like husband and wife than mother and son. For you it might seem strange.

"I've never had regrets. Even Flav became calmer, charming, he worked harder than ever and he was available and helpful with everyone who was in need. Most of all, I felt good because day after day I saw that he ignored other women in general, all those single and married women who buzzed around him. Flav, after all, had everything that a woman could desire, that was needed to draw a woman's attention. He was tall, he had a handsome face, two bright black eyes that looked like dark diamonds, he was relaxed and he was affluent. We often talked about this when it was just the two of us. It was time for him to find a girlfriend and eventually get married. And I started to feel the need to have some kids running around in the house. I was forty-five years old and in those years I had seen many things good and bad, bitter and sweet.

"Then one late Saturday night towards the end of January 1975, I went to wait for him at the airport. When I saw him walking toward me I noticed something different about him. It was as if he had consumed some alcohol and was a bit tipsy. He talked a lot more than usual. Once we were in the car heading home he suddenly blurted out that he had met a girl who seemed to be his other half. At home he told me everything that happened in one long breathe, without stopping. Covering his mouth with your hand wouldn't have even stopped him. He told me everything. How he met her and what she did. He also confessed that he had set aside some of the business that he had to attend to in order to spend more time with her. He couldn't wait to go back to Montreal to see her again. He wanted to invite her to our house so that I could meet her.

"Hearing him talk about her made me extremely happy. My heart seemed to expand. Maybe, finally it was going to happen. We weren't going to be alone just us two against the world, trapped in the routine that was the shop, the business, the money and everything else that seemed to have become a sort of cage. Now it seemed like the future could bring more emotions, passions, other people, a wife, a mother-in-law, maybe even some grandchildren to visit and watch grow day by day. I was really happy. Things finally seemed to go the right way for once.

"A year later, in the month of January, Flav got married. Once more, my life was turned upside down. It was the first time that it happened without a disaster or catastrophe. As you already know our house is very big. The truth is that three families could live in it. There was no need to build or buy another one. Claire and Flav decided to come live with me.

"They went to France for their honeymoon. First to Paris, and then they were going to visit the small village from which a century ago Claire's ancestors had emigrated to Canada. This small village, known as Pont-en-Royans, close to Grenoble, was home to no more than a thousand souls. Flav told me that the houses had been erected on the stone in the middle of the mouth of the river. Many were so close to the edge of the water that they appeared to be toppling into it. From there, one could also visit the Parc du Vercors, full of mountains, forests and animals. And there were caves that extended for kilometres, carved out of the rock over time through erosion. It was a must-see."

I burst out laughing, adding that the world really was a strange place. That small French village and the Parc du Vercors, I knew them both very well. I had been there, and I considered myself fortunate to have seen and visited those magnificent caves not too far from Pont-en-Royans. While I explained this to an astonished Fiorina, Flav and Jad appeared, completely out of breathe. They had been running. They urged us to take in the sunset on the lake. Fiorina seemed enthusiastic, and so we quickly ran to the car and jumped in.

We got to where the Niagara River meets Lake Ontario just a minute before the sun finished setting. There was a round wooden gazebo with wooden seats, but other people, who obviously had the same idea, were already occupying them. We stood next to the gazebo. You could see a bit of the American bridge at the other edge of the mouth of the river. The Niagara River brought a huge amount of water into the lake and it flowed at a great speed. The sun then hid from us strangers, and the fantastic shapes and the thousands of colours left even the coldest of hearts in jaw-dropping awe. The sun was going to bed. In the middle of the lake a few boats were buzzing around in the wind and water. There was a yellowish-red spot on the surface that looked like the shadow of some giant eagle. Fiorina squeezed my hand, as if with that touch she could transfer all the warmth and beauty that she felt inside and that we had in front of us, and to see if I had been equally moved by the amazing scene we had just witnessed.

It was already nine o'clock. Roger and Roza were waiting for us for dinner. We hopped back into the car and drove for about forty minutes. The jazz concert had started half an hour before. Outside in a big lot a couple of hundred people were seated. On one side there were five jazz musicians and a singer dressed in white and charcoal black, trying to liven up the night. In a little space they had reserved a table for us. All kinds of food and as much wine as you could drink started arriving. It was around midnight when we went to bed. I was still anxious to hear the end of Fiorina's story. But it really had gotten late and so we all said goodnight to each other. It didn't take me long to fall asleep, thanks to the wine and to the fact that I was exhausted.

The next morning I woke up at seven. The windows in my room weren't shuttered and, seeing how I like to sleep in the dark, the sunlight was my alarm clock. I looked out the window and the view of the lake, which was only a few kilometres away, was quite a wonder to behold. They call it a lake, even if one cannot see the other side. After I had shaved, washed up and dressed, I went downstairs where Fiorina was already sipping her usually large mug full of coffee while she sat with Jad and Roza. Flav still hadn't come down. Then they informed me that they wanted to go back to Toronto after lunch and so Fiorina asked me if I wanted to see Niagara Falls. I had seen them more than once before. I told Fiorina that I'd prefer taking a walk through the vineyards. That way we could chat and enjoy some peace and quiet since I had to leave on Monday, and God only knows when we'd be able to meet again.

Fiorina's shining eyes met mine and, from the glint of mischievousness, I understood that my proposal was to her liking. Even she needed some calm and peace to relax. In the meantime Flav had come down and so we had a nice breakfast together. After breakfast Jad and Flav decided to visit a family of friends who owned an antique shop in the heart of Niagara-on-the-Lake. Thus, I remained alone with Fiorina. Roger and Roza were busy preparing everything for the Sunday onslaught of tourists. Around ten o'clock Fiorina and I walked to a slightly uphill path that led from the cellar towards what looked like a forest of maples trees. We walked between the rows of vines for a few thousand metres. For a while, we walked side by side in silence.

XXV

Claire and Martine

When we got to the top of the hill where a wood of maples began, we stopped to catch our breath, since the hill was quite steep and what seemed to be a light walk had made us tired. We took a look around us. On top of the hill, under the cool shade of a tree that had branches so thick with foliage that they completely blocked the sky, there was a wooden bench with a table in front of it. We sat down and right in front of us you could see many high quality vineyards in the distance. Further off, the lake shone and sparkled, almost as if thousands of mirrors danced on its surface. From this marvellous vantage point we had a beautiful view. It wasn't hard to understand why someone had placed the wooden bench here! You could even see how big Roger and Roza's winery was: enough to see that with the vineyard and the rest of the land, it was a really nice property. It must earn them quite a lot of money.

Fiorina and I started talking about how generous, friendly, and nice Roger and Roza were. Afterwards slowly, very slowly, I brought Fiorina back to continue with her story. It was easy to see that she herself enjoyed telling her story. As soon as I asked if Flav felt bad having his wife and daughter far away, Fiorina's forehead wrinkled up. The light that I saw in her eyes seemed to come from a distant place.

"Even this is a complicated story that isn't easy to tell. Out of all the books and movies that I've seen up to now I must say that this kind of story has happened only to me and Flav. Then Claire arrived, and even she without wanting it, ended up tangled in the same ball of yarn as us. Claire isn't just a rare beauty, she is also gifted with a super fine intelligence. When Flav met her, she was working as a doctor at Saint Cabrini Hospital in Montreal. Flav met her when he had gone to the hospital to visit a supplier that had had a mild heart attack. She was tall, with copper red hair and green eyes that had little brown flecks, always full of a sweet warmth. She possessed a confidence that made her a magnet for men and women. Now she's over fifty and, if you happen to meet her, she's still able to leave you breathless.

"Claire came to Toronto without thinking twice. Seeing how money wasn't a problem for Flav, she could have had everything without working; however, she insisted in working, and quickly found a job at one of the hospitals. She was so busy that all three of us were only able to see each other on the weekend. She seemed satisfied. Not to mention that she was never tired. She managed to do all the housework while she continued studying, and at the same time she brought happiness to our family. She was not pregnant after a year and during this period I had started to wonder that maybe Claire wasn't interested in having kids because she was more focused on her career. Obviously, all these thoughts I kept them to myself. I've never talked about this with Flav. He was too happy. They were a great couple and I didn't want to disturb what they had with what was on my mind, not to mention the fact that I wanted to see a child arrive who had been conceived with love.

"But the things weren't the way I thought. It was in the spring of 1977, on a Sunday morning Claire approached me. As I looked at her, her eyes seemed to be made of pure light. She threw her arms around my shoulders. While she squeezed me tight to her chest she told me that she was pregnant and that she couldn't be happier. I shed a few tears of joy and remained speechless. I hugged her tight and I kissed her as if she was a daughter that I hadn't seen for years. As soon as Flav came back from his jog and found out, all three of us started to dance around like we were crazy. Martine arrived on Christmas Eve. You can't understand the amazing feeling of happiness that small child brought me, as if I had been transported to heaven. The years that followed couldn't have been any happier.

"Flav adored Martine and had eyes only for her. It seemed that he too had forgiven the world. Claire raised her daughter with ease, speaking both English and French fluently. The more she grew, the more beautiful she became. Her mother however didn't want to give up her career, and so I started to enjoy her a bit more, even if sometimes Flav and Martine left us to go away on vacation. Mother and daughter seemed to be glued to each other. When they were together it was as if they wanted to tell each other the whole story of their life. They seemed exactly the same in practically everything. They ate, laughed, sang, and moved exactly in the same way. By the time Martine was fifteen years old, she had already decided that she wanted to be like her mother, a doctor.

"In all this time how were things between you and Flav?" I couldn't help asking.

"We were back to being mother and son. What else could we be? His life, how he had been born, and everything that we had been through together would keep us forever tied to one another. He was crazy about Claire and Martine, and they deserved all his love and more. He seemed to be living in God's grace, seeing how he dealt with whatever came his way, whether it had to do with business or family: calm, faithful and always with a smile on his lips in the face of any problem. Very rarely did he think about where he came from, or why he had only me, his wife and his daughter around him and no one else. Here in Canada for many it was the same, although it happened that while talking to other students, clients or friends he realized that they weren't alone. They had relatives close by, or scattered about, or in other countries that their families had left in order to put bread on the table. Only we had remained truly solitary, without relatives – after all that had happened to us in life, to me and especially to Flav.

"Claire still had both her father and mother and other relatives scattered about. Martine had grandparents and a father who said yes to everything she wanted to do or have. Instead, the only person Flav had from his past was me. Those few times that he had had a storm in his head, it was to me that he blew off steam. On rare occasions when we happened to be alone and looked deep into each other's eyes, we became tender with one another, and that feeling of wanting made our hearts and legs tremble. But it rarely happened and it was completely natural – almost as if it were some type of coercion that we were used to repeating, to do the same things that we had already done, as some psychologists write, which is exactly what happened.

"Luckily, Claire didn't know anything about this whole story. I would have died, because she didn't deserve to be hurt or feel bad. She was a very intelligent woman who had poured all her energy into her career. She had a kind soul that only wanted to help others, and when she couldn't, she felt badly, mentally and physically. She had brought someone amazing, Martine, into this world, and she was giving everything to my son. Over the years plenty of men had swarmed around me, some maybe had deserved my honeyed responses, for their good manners, for their elegance, and even for the good looks. You have to believe me when I tell you that after my relationship with Vahan and with Flav, I just didn't have the heart to bring down the high wall around me for anyone else. The affection that I received from Martine, Claire and Flav was more than enough for me. Sometimes, it still happens to me now that a bee swarms around me trying to find a home in my beehive. But what I have is way too much for me. This is especially true since I met Jadwiga."

"Yes, I agree, Jadwiga is a pearl of a woman. Sometimes when you two talk to each other you seem like two sisters or two classmates who have known each other forever. Even when I see Flav with Jadwiga I have the impression that there's something between them and it's easy to see that they have a special bond."

"I've already told you that Jadwiga and I hit it off right away. From the first time I met her she was so agreeable. I had brought her to my house so that she could help me. Up until then I had never had anyone in the house. Every now and then I had called a few people, men and women, whom I paid by hour to help me, or Claire, to clean up the house or tidy up the garden. However, I was now sixty years old and Martine was a twelve-year-old who seemed more like four people. We all worked, and to be honest, a young, respectful and capable woman like Jad could help us out a lot. It didn't take long to see Jadwiga go from being a servant and an assistant to being a member of the house and a part of the family. She was simply too good, too available and too considerate. If you asked her to do something, she didn't even let you finish asking. It would already be done.

"She had won a place in all of our hearts and between us there was no difference; we were all equal members of the family. However, she and I spent more time together than the others. Thus, very slowly a very strong bond was created between us. She came to know everything about me and I came to know everything about her. Before she left Poland to come here in search of a better life she had lived with a man for a few years. Then, without any explanation he had left her to live with another woman. She felt as if she had been completely destroyed, and for this reason she decided to leave and to go as far away as possible. As she told me this, or whenever she talked about her family, her face would turn sad. That look of melancholy gave her a tender charm that made me feel close to her and it melted my heart. When we talked and confided in each other our different pains and suffering, she would look at me with those puppy-dog eyes moistened by tears and I would just want to hug her tightly to me to caress and cuddle her as if she was a small child.

"I was thirty years older than Jad, but we were exactly like two sisters. She was always at home or with me. Only during those few years when she was studying to become a nurse was she not always at home. She was happy that many young men swarmed around her. Sometimes she told me that she was tempted by some of the men, but then she was overcome by the fear that she would have to relive the same drama she had lived through in Poland. She was also fearful of losing the security that she had found with me, and so she didn't even bother. As a result, she became even more attached to me. Even if there was a big age difference like I said before, our being together and being present for each other produced a strong, caring bond between us. I must say that this fact helped me to keep those bees that swarmed around me and wanted to make their nest with me at bay. It also helped me loosen the bond between me and Flav. Even Claire got along well with Jadwiga, so much so that she even tried to convince her to go to work at the hospital where Claire worked. Worried, however, that she would lose her bond with me she refused,. But she was tempted on more than one occasion."

The more Fiorina told me her story, the more she seemed re-laxed, calm, rested, as if she had been freed from a heavy burden made up of the enormous pains that were crushing her. From the lake all the way up to the hill where we were sitting, a light breeze blew and caressed our faces. At the same time it made a sound like a sigh, as it moved through the leaves and branches of the trees all around. Here and there you could hear the singing of birds.

"To tell you the truth, seeing all the time that Jad and Flav spend together, the way their eyes meet, made me think that there might have been more than friendship between them. What you're telling me is making me a bit confused."

As I said my observation out loud, Fiorina smiled at me mischievously. She got up, took my hand and started pulling my arm to make me get up.

"Come on, let's walk a little more. Yesterday, Roger told me that there is a pond somewhere on the other side of the forest, under the slope of the hill, where he goes to fish for trout. He said that we could for there to fish for fun or to relax."

We went all the way down. We walked around the side of the pond for a bit, and then we started to head up and down the path that would take us back to the winery. As we started to walk along, we held each other's hand. Every now and then I had to help Fiorina climb over an obstacle or to cross some difficult spot on our path. We finally reached the flat terrain around the pond and headed toward the shore where we could see five or six people fishing. We sat down. After we had exchanged pleasantries about this calm and beautiful place, Fiorina continued telling her story.

"It isn't difficult to grasp that Jad and Flav understand each other as if they communicate using a language that only they know. They enjoy spending time together and could spend days talking and chatting away. When Claire moved to Montreal to be with her daughter, that sympathetic bond between them seemed to be stronger. I'd put my hand over fire if I'm wrong, but I'm sure that up until now there

265

isn't anything other than friendship between them. We're that close and we know each other so well, all three of us, that they would have told me straight up. As far as I know, Claire is and will forever be Flav's one and only love."

As she related her story, the intimacy between Fiorina and me was so intense that I didn't have to force myself as I expressed my thoughts: "Of course, having you, they can always let off steam and rest easy with each other. But if you get too close to the fire you can get burned. You have made this clear for me more than once."

Silence followed. Then I slowly found the heart to go over because I could read a mystery between the lines of Fiorina's final ambiguous words. "Why did Claire decide to go to Montreal seeing as how Martine wasn't by herself while studying in Montreal? Wasn't she with her grandparents?"

"You're a curious cat! You really want to pull out all the old skeletons that are hidden in my soul? It happened a few years after Martine went to Montreal to do everything that was necessary before starting university. While she was there, she called us every day. She told us that she was happy to be living with her grandparents, but she missed all of us, especially her mother. She also said that she was worried that she would have to study a lot, even if she had never had any problems before. As always, Claire continued working at the hospital, and even if she was worried that her daughter lived far away, she continued to be untroubled.

"One day in November she left to visit her daughter. She came back to Toronto late one night a lot sooner than we expected. It had been an awful day, the weather was horrible, and it rained buckets with lightning and thunder. That same night Flav had to come to my room to spend a bit of time with me. Claire went to sleep in her room and Flav wasn't there. She just thought that maybe he had gone somewhere. When she got home she had found the house calm and everyone was sleeping. It never crossed her mind that Flav could be with me. We hadn't realized that she was home. Claire was the first to wake up. As she didn't see anyone at breakfast, she came and knocked at my door.

"I thought that it was Jadwiga, and so I opened the door without hesitation, because Jad knew about Flav and me. You can imagine how embarrassing it was when Claire saw Flav peek his head out of the bathroom in my room. The whole sky fell on all our heads. Flav was already dressed, but it wasn't difficult to see that he had slept in my bed. Claire didn't even think about the biggest problem. We told her that I didn't feel well and the lightning and thunder had frightened me. But Claire was a doctor. It wasn't difficult for her to see that I was in good health. And besides, why hadn't Jad stayed with me during the night? Claire didn't actually think that Flav and I, a sixty-year-old mother, and her son could have gone to bed together as a man and a woman. But a doubt had lodged itself in her mind.

"That night when they were alone they continued the discussion. Claire was everything for Flav. Above all else, she was his ticket to normality, the way out of all the disasters from his childhood, the path for a life that was the same as everyone else's. We had reasoned together many times about whether there is such a thing as a normal life. I cannot tell how Flav saw it, but these are the facts.

"Flav decided to tell Claire everything. He didn't leave out a thing, starting from when and how he was born. The tone of the conversation was frank and straightforward, not at all bitter. Once again Claire demonstrated a rare and hard-to-come-by intelligence, and that she had a soul that was as big and vast as the sea. It was a really hard shot for her and now she was confused. But she had the strength to put her heart in her hands. Around midnight she came and knocked on my door. She was crying and sobbing as if she were a child. I hugged her tight. I trembled like a leaf caught in the wind, and I myself started to cry a river of tears. I felt ashamed and scared.

"My words were anchored at the bottom of my soul. Then, very slowly, they started to surface and we started to talk. We stayed up all night. Claire told us that she could understand what she had seen, especially after everything that she already knew. What had happened to me and Flav, starting from when I was a child. But at the moment, she didn't have the courage or the will to accept it. She wouldn't say anything to Martine, but she would go and stay with her daughter. She said that she would tell Martine that we had all agreed that she should have her mother by her side so that she could help her study as best she could. Claire told me that her heart hurt. She couldn't find a reason why everything suddenly hit her like a lightning bolt, and she just couldn't accept it. She would go to Montreal to think things over, to reflect and to try and reason things out. She cared way too much for Flav, for me and for Jadwiga. But her heart was bleeding and it ached."

XXVI

Fiorina and Claire

Fiorina had told her whole story. I guess you could say that she had finished her confession. It had been passed on to me, to my heart, to my soul, to my mind, and now I held her life story inside me. Sometimes, Fiorina's words made me feel bad. The curiosity, the needing to know, that feeling of wanting that no man can stop – it pushed her to tell her story. Sometimes, I had strong headaches, stronger than I'd ever had before. The only thing that made me continue was the understanding that Fiorina was freeing herself from weights that during her long life, one by one, had given her tears and pleasures, and it made me give her friendly jabs so she would let every single thing out.

The truth is that I was the one who suffered hearing Fiorina's last words. I saw that she was calm, more than she had been the first few times when she had told me all the things that had happened to her when she was a young girl. I thought to myself that she had told me everything because for some time she must have felt the need to talk. I had just happened along at the right moment. To top it off, I

came from the same town as her mother and grandparents. She talked
to me using the words that her own mother had used.

The sun was high in the sky, and it burned, as if it was on fire.
It started to feel like a hot day. In front of us, the people around the
lake were patiently waiting for the dumb fish to take the bait. Every
now and then a poor fish was hooked and pulled out of the water,
writhing hopelessly. Obviously, the fish couldn't do a thing. The
same way we are powerless to stop all the unwanted things that our
Heavenly Father gives us to deal with.

Fiorina was calm and seemed even more beautiful and mes-
merizing. I couldn't stop. Now that I had basically heard everything,
I might as well hear the end.

"Tell me how it ended. Even now, Martine still doesn't
know? Claire came back to Toronto? Did she and Flav see each
other? How do Flav and Martine see each other?"

"Claire's departure from our house was the exact opposite from
the day she had arrived. I was the one that felt desperate, scared, and
the heavy weight of the responsibility of her leaving. I had provoked
that disaster due to my pleasures and my weaknesses. I could have
done things differently. I wanted to rip my flesh apart with my own
hands because of that strong and sincere bond of love that I felt for
all three of them – Flav, Claire, and Martine, the grandchild I had
been waiting for since Flav and Claire were married. Flav wanted to
be the one to take Claire to Montreal.

"There was no way. Claire left by herself three weeks after that
morning, leaving us depressed and anxious. She left with a car full
of luggage, after shipping the bulk of her stuff. She quit her job at the
hospital, saying that it wouldn't be hard for her to find another job in
Montreal. In those three weeks we barely talked amongst us. Jadwiga
suffered silently by herself. She cleaned from morning until night so
that not even a particle of dust could cause a problem.

"The only thing that made the situation bearable was the strong love between Claire and Flav and her intelligence. Claire knew everything about my life and everything that I had gone through since I was born. She understood that we hadn't done anything to purposely hurt her or Martine. She wanted to, and needed to be alone to figure out how she felt about everything, to see which way she wanted to go; either she accepted her life the way it was or choose to stay away from us.

"No more than ten days after Claire's departure, Martine started calling her father and me. When she talked to us on the phone she simply told us what she did and asked how we were doing. We all talked as if nothing had happened. Often Martine told us that she missed her father and grandmother and she'd ask us to go visit. We'd hear from Claire once in a while when Martine, who didn't know anything about what had happened, would call in the presence of her mother. We'd exchange a few words and on special occasions we would exchange a quick greeting.

"The reciprocal caring, out of respect, out of devotion and for everyone's sake, helped to keep the promise that shielded Martine from the main issue. A few bitter words uttered by Claire unintentionally made me understand how she was suffering. She suffered not only for what had happened, but also for being far away from Flav. Flav tried to seem calm and peaceful, and tried burying himself in his work. He spent his days as if everything was normal. Between us there was the same love and tenderness as before, and it only took one good look into his eyes or an extended conversation with him to see that day after day the situation ate away at his mind, which wasn't peaceful at all, and piece by piece consumed even his soul. Even Jadwiga seemed to have become mute. She would only voice the necessary words to carry out her duties.

"The days ate away at us and no one was able to stop them. Despite the happiness, the excitement and the warmth of the last twenty years, the storm for us was unfortunately never- ending. But we couldn't continue living that way; it just wasn't life. It was up to me to do something. Flav seemed to deteriorate a bit every day. I felt bad thinking about how Claire must have felt. We knew that Claire had found a job at Santa Cabrini. One day I gathered all the strength that I could, I called and booked a hotel room and I went to Montreal. I wanted to talk to Claire alone. After that, I would and could hug Martine again.

"I arrived in Montreal one night in September of the last year. I had reserved a room at the Ritz Carlton Hotel on Sherbrooke Street. It was one of the best hotels. I knew it because I had always gone there with my husband. It was also centrally located. From there it was easy and pretty close to the best places in order to pass some time or lose the sense of time by going around from one boutique to another. Obviously, on that specific trip, these things weren't on my agenda.

"The next morning I had breakfast, and with my heart literally in my throat, I took a taxi to the hospital. I had never been there before. The first thing that left me completely dumbstruck was the signage. Instead of being in French and English, the signs were all in French and Italian. Claire had told me that the hospital had been built for the hundreds of thousands of Italian immigrants – so that they could be understood and able to explain what was wrong with them when they were ill. Even the maintenance employees needed to know Italian. At the information desk I asked where I could find Claire and if I would be able to talk to her. They indicated her office, but informed me that I would have to wait for her to finish her rounds on the floor. I decided to wait for her a few metres from her door. After about half an hour I saw her appear with two other doctors. They didn't notice me. All three of them went into her office. The two doctors left her office after roughly twenty minutes. Without waiting another second, I knocked and opened the door. Claire was startled to see me. After all, she wasn't expecting me. She looked at me with her beautiful eyes, which seemed to express both wonderment and worry. There was a trace of embarrassment on her face. Our conversation went like this:

'Claire…'

'What happened? What are you doing here!?'

'Claire… I can't take it anymore… I feel really bad… horrible. Flav's taking it worse than me… I don't know how you're doing… I would like to talk for a bit.'

'No, I haven't gotten over it, if that's what you're wondering… I'm certainly not in paradise… but I feel better if I remain distant. I can't talk right now because we have a patient in critical condition who has to be operated on in an hour. If you want, we can see each other in the evening. Does Martine know you are here? Are you going to be staying a while, or are you leaving right away?'

'Martine doesn't know anything. But I'd like to see her. If I can speak with you first and if you decide that I can see her, I won't leave right away. After all, it's the reason I'm here.'

'Tell me where I can find you, and as soon as I'm free I'll call you. It's better that Martine not know that you're here, at least for the moment. I would rather not lie to her and at the same time I don't want to disturb her.'

'You can call me at the Ritz Carlton. It's where I'm staying. I won't move from there until you call me.'

"Then her phone rang. She had to go. We said goodbye. She seemed calm enough. Too bad I couldn't say the same for myself. I headed towards the hotel feeling lighter because we had managed to break the ice. At lunch time I went to the restaurant in the hotel to try and put something in my stomach. At the Ritz they have a beautiful garden restaurant where I've always liked to eat. The plants are all real. It's almost as if you're really eating out in the open. However, it was the first time that I had eaten there alone. The restaurant was busy. A few men gazed at me curiously. I barely noticed, as my mind was buzzing with so many thoughts. Worried that I might miss a call from Claire, I hurried back to my room as soon as I finished eating. The afternoon dragged on. I even dozed off for a few hours. In the evening around six p.m., I started to worry and grew anxious. Time passed and no sign of Claire. I didn't know what to do.

"At seven p.m. I left my room. I couldn't keep thinking and being alone, so I went down to the reception. At the reception desk I told them that if anyone came or if anyone called, they would find me at the bar. At the bar I ordered a hot tea. There were other people who needed to pass an hour or two, and still others who were searching for a bit of company. A few tried to engage me in a conversation, but it didn't take them long to understand that I was somewhere else. I was scared that Claire wasn't going to show up and yet I knew that she was too polite and too intelligent to leave me hanging.

"My heart started to beat faster and louder as soon as I saw Claire. I felt reborn. Claire told me that she had had a difficult day. She hadn't called me because she had been really busy, and that she was also trying to figure out what to do, if she should tell Martine right away that her grandmother was here. And how to tell her that I knew that I was coming but hadn't said anything to anyone? How could she explain why I wasn't with them at their house but instead in a hotel? And why hadn't her father come as well?

"And so we had dinner together. Claire had explained to Martine that she would be out late because of work. Claire told me again that she really cared for us a lot. But at the same time, she still couldn't digest what she had learned. She was undecided. Either she forever cut the bond that we had or we maintain a good relationship despite everything that had happened. She was terrorized by her fear of having to tell Martine everything. She loved Flav too much, and me too in a way, which made her not want to throw everything away. However, the bigger problem was the fear of not being able to keep Martine out of this mess. After dinner we both went up to my room. We talked until midnight. My mind was full of so many fears. Claire was in pieces, stuck in between an anvil and a hammer. She didn't want Martine to have a broken family. On the other hand, it was difficult for her to pretend as if nothing had happened. She insisted that she had never once stopped caring for me. She said that she felt as if she were in my soul.

No matter how messed up or confused things were, we ended up with an understanding. We hugged and cried together until we started laughing. We had decided that it was better to not tell Martine anything, and that I shouldn't meet with her because she would become suspicious about the fact that I had come to Montreal without saying anything. In a few days Flav would visit and then we would meet all together afterwards. The next day wasn't a good one for Claire at the hospital and so we exchanged a calm goodbye.

From that night on things started to right themselves, thanks to Claire's great intelligence and to the strong bond between all of us. For all the heart and soul that I had put into it, things finally started to change. Every now and then Flav went to Montreal, and once in a while Martine came to visit us on her holidays. Claire remained at her daughter's side and would continue to work in Montreal until Martine finished her degree. All this happened fairly recently, maybe a bit more than a year or so before I met you. I wish nothing else bad comes to visit us, especially for Claire and Martine's sake."

Fiorina gazed at me. An affectionate but at the same embarrassed smile spread across her lips. She was beautiful. One could see that she had become lighter, and I began to think that maybe she had been waiting for a long time to tell the whole story of her life to someone – obviously to someone whom she could trust. It seemed to be medicine for her soul.

The sun was starting to turn and descend slowly on the other side. The original group of people fishing at the pond's edge had been replaced by three or four new couples, some of whom had arrived with picnic baskets full of food. Calmly and quietly they were already hard at work and each one was munching on a sandwich. As Fiorina finished saying her last words she stood up. It was time to go back. Lunch must be ready, and certainly Flav and Jad would have already come back. In fact, as soon as we got back to the cellar we found Flav and Jad waiting, sitting around a table with Roger and Roza.

At about five, after many jovial yet sad goodbyes, we left Roger and Roza's estate. They had given us the gift of an amazing first-class vacation, replete with friendship and thoughtfulness. We said farewell, but not without a new invitation from Roger and Roza to come back for a visit. They seemed to think favourably of me too, but then any friend of Jadwiga was a friend of theirs. Apart from all the emotions that Fiorina's story stirred up, I must say that it was an unforgettable experience to stand in the middle of all those grape vines, the air scented with the bouquet of wine, and to find it all unexpectedly in the Niagara Region of Ontario, so close to the falls.

XXVII

Somewhere Between Past and Future

The ride from Niagara-on-the-Lake to Fiorina's house was fast. Jadwiga was telling us that she had had a wonderful vacation with her girlfriend. She had been really happy to have the chance to speak some Polish again and to reminisce about the years when they were young girls and still lived with their families. They both hoped eventually one day to go to Poland for a vacation together, and I invited all three of them to come and visit me in Italy. I could tell that Jadwiga didn't seem to mind the idea, but Fiorina and Flav made me understand that it would be very difficult. Although half a century had gone by, the sweetness that surrounded the thought of seeing the land where she was born was still mixed with the bitterness of all the tragedies that she had lived through and that remained deep in her soul.

Flav, for the first time, spoke about his wife and daughter, saying that at the moment there were a few problems. His mind was completely caught up in trying to find a solution and he didn't think it would be possible to take an overseas vacation, even a short one. He was waiting for Martine to get her degree and then see if they could all be in Toronto or if he had to find another way so that they could all be happy. Fiorina uttered only a few words during the whole ride. You could feel the sincerity and strength in their bond, and you could see that they shared each other's problems, joys and happiness.

We arrived quite late. Fiorina asked if we want to go to a restaurant near the house to have something to eat. But we had eaten so much at Roger and Roza's place that it wasn't necessary to go and stuff our stomachs again. I stated that I would prefer some rest and if possible I wouldn't mind a cup of coffee. They all agreed. Jadwiga started preparing the coffee and putting out some sweets right away. Before going to sleep, I talked with Fiorina and I tried to convince her to find the courage to come to Cori. Meanwhile, Flav and Jad watched the news on television.

Suddenly, Fiorina grabbed one of my hands and pulled me towards the studio. On one of the shelves of the library there was an attractive vase made out of clear glass; it must have been about 20 centimetres wide and long, while the opening of the neck was no wider than 15 centimetres. Inside there was some sort of sediment. You could see something solid, dark and powdery. Fiorina took the vase delicately as if it were a relic. She moved the vase closer to me, her eyes moist.

"Inside this vase is the dirt that I brought with me from Cori. It's kept me company for half a century. Many times when I thought the world was against me, I would come here and hold the vase in my hands and bring it to my nose so that I could smell the scent of my motherland. I talked to this bit of dirt as if all the souls of those who had made me and who had left me were in it, and I prayed for their help. Our ancient ancestors would take urns that contained the ashes of their ancestors with them as they migrated from one land to another. I brought this bit of dirt with me, and believe me when I tell you that it has given me plenty of strength over the years. I even talked to the vase when everything was happening with Claire. I needed to find the strength to visit her in Montreal, to try and mend the strings that had been broken, to rewind the ball of yarn that had come undone – to try and put back together the people who had been torn apart.

"As you already know, something good did happen. Flav often goes to Montreal to be with his wife and daughter. Even if Flav and Claire still aren't completely back together, they manage to have some type of relationship. Martine is happy that she sees her father often. I hope that the years that I have left aren't just about money and all the problems that come with it, but rather to enjoy Martine's happiness.

"Tomorrow you leave to go back to Italy. Every time that you happen to come to Canada I want you to know that my house is always open. You are way more than just a friend. You're more like one of the family – you're the bright red thread that ties up all the pieces of my life. The red thread that represents my life: all the beauty of my childhood, suddenly becoming a woman in the hardest way possible, and everything that I've been and done in this new world, where the good things outweigh the bad.

"I have to ask if you don't mind doing me a favour. I don't know if the graves of my loved ones are still in the Cori cemetery, but if so, can you can take this dirt back to Cori for me and scatter it on top of their graves? If the graves have been dug up and they've taken the remains to the common ossuary, then scatter this bit of dirt underneath an olive tree that's right beside the cemetery. If it's true that souls exist, I'm sure that when I die my soul will somehow find my mother and father's. You are the only person who can do this favour for me."

A few tears slid down my cheek without me even crying. I hugged Fiorina. I took the glass vase that contained that bit of dirt that had been kept as a relic for half a century. After I had said goodnight to everyone I went to sleep, even though my heart was pounding so hard that it seemed like it was going to pop out of my chest. Before I fell asleep, all the things that Fiorina had said started to spin around in my head. Then the tiredness kicked in and I fell asleep, a sleep that was so deep that when I finally managed to wake up it was already nine o'clock.

I tried to get ready as fast as possible and to quickly finish packing my luggage. I left the glass vase that Fiorina had given me out. I thought that it would be better if I rolled it in cloth or put it in some kind of cloth sleeve to avoid the dirt being scattered if the vase happened to break. By the time I got downstairs it was almost ten o'clock. Fiorina was sitting on an armchair with a newspaper in her hands. She got up right away and came towards me. She was wearing white shorts with a red blouse and her hair was down. Every time she seemed more beautiful. No one would ever think she was older than fifty, even if they looked at her closely. Life had given her many hard shots, but certainly it had also given her things that many envied.

"You got a good night's sleep? I'm glad. It must mean that in my house you feel at ease. Come into the kitchen and have some breakfast."

"I slept like a rock. You gave me an overdose of emotions! But it's true; I feel calm and relaxed, as if I'm with family. It's almost as if I'm in my own house. You by yourself?"

"Flav and Jad went to buy something for lunch. We thought that it would be better to stop and eat something here before you leave. But we also have time to go downtown. Maybe you'd like to shop for a few gifts? With your coffee, do you prefer toast with bacon and eggs or toast with jam and butter?"

"To be honest, a bit of caffè latte with toast and a bit of jam is more than enough. If you don't mind, I'd also like to call up a few friends in Toronto. This is the first time I've come here and I haven't called or seen them."

"Yes, sir! I just want to know if you're planning on going out. I'll go get ready. I told Jad that we could have lunch around two o'clock and so we have enough time."

"Okay! Let's go for a spin, that way we can chat and maybe I can convince you to come visit me in Cori. I have a favour to ask. Could you give me a cloth or some kind of rag to put the dirt in, because the vase could easily break."

"No problem, it's probably better. I'll go look for a cloth or a cloth sack that you can use."

Fiorina went to get ready. I, on the other hand, after finishing my breakfast, made a few calls. It was the weekend and so I found few people home. The ones that I talked to were quite surprised to know that I was in Toronto and that I hadn't said anything to anybody. I was happy that I managed to talk and say hello to a few. It wasn't hard to explain that I had been in Montreal and I was only passing through Toronto.

Fiorina came back and brought me a nice-looking velvet pouch that had contained some sort of pearls or precious beads and together we put the dirt in it. We placed it carefully in the suitcase and then we went out. Fiorina had transformed herself once again. She was wearing jeans with a wool pullover and her hair was held back by a brown ribbon. The same colour as her sweater. I wore a tie and a jacket, as always, and I couldn't help feeling that I looked bad standing beside her. Once she had finished locking up the house we climbed into Fiorina's car. Then we slowly started to head towards downtown Toronto. In between a word or two I tried to insist with her that she should come to Italy for a vacation.

At a certain point she said: "In Italy there's no one left that I know. I'm well aware that it's there that everything started. And along with the horrible things, I spent a lot of good times and many worry-free days there as a young girl. My hopes and dreams, the sweet warmth of my grandparents, my mother and father, who seep into my heart, those are some of the best things that exist. Ever since I met you I've had a growing desire to go there. However, it's also true that it's here where I managed to put everything back in order; it's here where Flav and I put down roots, where through many difficulties we managed to find a sense of happiness that I didn't even know existed. It's where, as you already know, I've had many wrong experiences, which I'm still paying for. Every night, as I lay in my bed, I fall asleep praying to see them altogether again, Claire, Martine and Flav. The same way that I saw them a few years ago. Happy, united and playful.

"I know that if you have to move on, you can't be afraid of what you find up ahead. Whatever new change, the day before yesterday always leads to tomorrow. I know that the days to come hold the promise of choosing how we want to live, but we have to take what we get. However, I also know that men and women aren't like trees, birds, tigers or mountains, which do not know how to avoid getting wet when it rains. We can build a hut, or some kind of shelter, or we can invent an umbrella. If a terracotta pot breaks, only mankind is intelligent enough to fix it. I'd like to do something more to make all the people I care about happy. Then, after that, I can come to Cori for one last time, or die. As Socrates said, everything that I had to teach them has been taught and everything that I could give them has been given. As far as my life goes, I can consider it concluded."

I didn't know how to interrupt her. I didn't know what to say, or not to say, as she was right. We stopped beside the Eaton Centre, a microcosm of a town made up only of stores, big and small, reasonable and expensive, cafes and restaurants. People hurried about here and there just like in a crazy ant colony. I bought very few gifts to take back with me. Fiorina insisted on buying me a silk scarf as a gift. We sat down in a café to have something to cool off. It was 1:30 p.m. when we got back to her house. Flav and Jad were waiting for us. They had already prepared everything and, after a quick wash up, we sat down to eat.

After our coffee, Fiorina suggested that I go and rest up a bit. Jad and Flav really managed to surprise me. Each of them had prepared a gift for me. Jad gave me a wooden duck along with a small bottle of maple syrup. Flav's gift was a dark stone statue of a bison that weighed at least half a kilo. It was a work of art carved by an Inuit artist from the Canadian Arctic.

XXVIII

A Quick
Trip Home to Cori

It wasn't easy to find the right words to thank them. The only thing that I could say was that I would be waiting for a visit from them at my house in Italy. The invitation came from the bottom of my heart. I would never be able to forget the hours that we had spent together. The remaining hours before going to the airport went by in a flash. I insisted on calling a taxi, but it was completely out of question for them. They wanted to take me to the airport again, just like the last time.

When it came time to have my passport checked and to check in, Fiorina grabbed me and hugged me tightly to her chest.

"Don't forget me," she whispered in my ear in one long breath.

Then I headed towards the check-in counter without looking back. My heart was leaping about in my chest, and distress caused a few tears to escape from my eyes. All the physical and emotional tiredness made my head hurt, making it impossible for me to sleep even for just one minute the whole trip. I kept my eyes closed anyway. Actually, I wore one of those sleeping masks over my eyes so that the light didn't bother me. But my brain just didn't want to shut off. Fiorina's words, the things she had told me, the feelings and emotions that she made me live, they gnawed away in my head. It was sort of like a movie that played over and over again.

When I got home I was completely exhausted, as if I had been beaten to a pulp. I went to bed right away and I slept for fifteen hours straight. The emotions that I had brought back with me were so strong that it took me a week to get over my jet lag. A few days after my return, I took the cloth sack with the dirt that Fiorina had given me and I went to the cemetery. I walked everywhere. I searched inch by inch, but I didn't find any trace of Fiorina's relatives. I went to look for the grave digger and after an intense search of his memory he told me that they had dug them up many years ago. What little was left had been placed in the ossuary. I couldn't help but think that in the end we are no more than little dust particles blown about in the wind.

Fiorina had already foreseen it and she had told me to find an olive tree just outside the cemetery. I entered an olive grove and, under a lovely olive tree, I scattered two handfuls of the dirt that had crossed the ocean twice. After that day I immersed myself completely in all the things I had to do. Fiorina and the story she had told me grew distant and hidden among many other thoughts and memories at the bottom of my soul. Sometimes it would suddenly come to mind and then suddenly, as quick as lightening, it would disappear without a hint of thunder.

A whole year went by. Then one evening in July the phone rang while I was laying around on an improvised hay bed in my garden reading one of Elio Filippo Accrocca's poems. I had to write an article on it. The phone rang as soon as I started to read:

É tempo di tornare da mio padre
Non posso restare quassù,
dove tutto è intatto, bisogna
che torni alla contrada Mannarina
dove rami germogliano frutta
con foglie d'olivo.

It is time for me to return to my father
I can no longer stay up here
where everything is still intact, I need
to go back to the borough of Mannarina
where the branches sprout fruit
with olive leaves.

And suddenly Fiorina's story came to mind. I'm sure that no one would believe me if I tell them that as soon as I put the phone to my ear I heard Fiorina's voice. I almost had a heart attack.

"Hello, it's Fiorina! Pietro?"

"...Fiorina! How are you, it's a pleasure to hear you..."

"You're in Rome!? I can't believe it! When did you arrive? Where are you staying? Are you by yourself?"

"I arrived last night, and yes I'm by myself. I've got a room at the Hotel Quirinale."

"Why didn't you say anything? I would have come to pick you up at the airport."

"I came by train. I wanted to take that long-forgotten train all the way to Cori, but they told me that there isn't a train for Cori anymore."

"I'll come pick you up right away, and you can come and stay at my house."

"Come pick me up the day after tomorrow. I'd like to spend another day by myself to walk around Rome, and then I'd like to visit

Cori, just for a day. Unfortunately, I can't stay any longer because I have to be on a flight the morning after."

I tried to insist on visiting her right away, that way maybe I could convince her to come and stay at my house. But there was nothing that I could do. We ended up agreeing that I'd pick her up at nine o'clock.

The next day literally flew by. In the morning at a few minutes before nine I was already walking into the Hotel Quirinale. I saw Fiorina right away. She was seated, reading a newspaper. As soon as her eyes looked up, she saw me. She got up in a hurry and ran towards me with her arms wide open. We hugged each other. We were both so happy to see each other that we weren't even able to say good morning to one another. Then I insisted on her leaving the hotel to come and stay at my house, and that I would bring her to the airport when she was ready to leave.

"Even if it will be really late, I prefer that you take me back to Rome. I already feel my heart full of thousands of thoughts running in all directions. I prefer departing from Rome once I am alone, after my visit to Cori, because I'm sure that way I'll be calmer."

We headed for the car and I asked her why she had wanted to spend a whole day alone in Rome.

"You know that Cori's a big part of my heart, but Rome is where I grew up. I lived here with my mother and father. It's where I went to school. I spent many wonderful years here and, after all, we both know that the years that someone lives are exactly what makes them who they are. The many years of pain and suffering that I lived here – all of them also make up exactly who I am. I went to visit the places that I always used to visit; I went to my old school, to where I used to live, and where I used to go for walks with my parents.

"In the last half century I watched Toronto turn into a metropolis. Day by day, it changed until it was completely transformed, and I hardly noticed a thing. Instead, the one time that I come to

Rome, I find it completely different. Of course, St. Peter's Square is the same, and the Trevi Fountain is still the Trevi Fountain, and the Pincio is always the same, and even the colours and the surrounding atmosphere are the same. But the traffic, the stores and the people are different from when I lived here; I saw myself run across those distant years and I felt myself breathe the exact same air. In certain places I felt an internal 'something' snap and I felt as if a hidden cry and silence grew inside of me. I went to where my house was, and on the outside it still seemed the same; but some small details are changed. The colour and the signs indicate a whole different world. In my old house there's currently a dental office; and the house nearby where I used to take my son is now a lawyer's office. I didn't find any trace of Cencia and where the notary's office was. Now there's a Sicilian family that didn't know anything about who had lived there before.

"I sort of felt like a ghost, or as if I were sleepwalking. I pinched myself more than once to make sure that I was still alive or that I wasn't sleeping. It was sending a message straight to my soul and it was telling me that, sadly, a piece of my life had disappeared and whatever my mind had managed to remember after half a century, it was disappearing right before of my eyes. Even St. Peter's Square, the Trevi Fountain and the Pincio weren't *exactly* the same as they had been in my mind's eye. To me they appeared as beautiful places, more than any other place that I saw in America. But that was all. It was no longer my city, the city that I had left behind half a century ago as my heart shed a river of tears."

We were now out of the city of Rome, near the Capannelle. I wanted Fiorina to pass by Via Dei Laghi so that she could see Cori from the side of Faiola, part of the mountains down to Velletri. I was curious to know what had given her the strength to come back and visit Cori and Rome.

"How are Flav, Claire, Martine and Jadwiga doing? Why did you come to Rome by train? Where did you land? Why are you staying so little? Can't you stay a few more days? I could show you a lot of different things, beautiful towns around Cori that maybe you've never seen. Places that I'm sure you weren't able to visit when you were a girl, and show you how, for some, Italy has become just like North America in the half century that's gone by."

"I am here because finally Claire and Flav are back together, and more passionately than ever. Flav's decided to move to Montreal where we've opened another store. You should go and see it sometime. It's a lot better than the one we have in Toronto. It's right in the centre of the city. I decided to remain with Jadwiga in Toronto. I'm selling the shop because I don't have the strength and energy to continue running it, although I have one of the best and trusted store managers working for me.

"Martine got her degree and she's already working at the Santa Cabrini Hospital. I see that everyone's happy and I feel peaceful and calm. Claire and Flav wanted to visit France again. They were happier this time than when they got married. Martine also went with them and they insisted on bringing me. And so in the end I said yes. After we visited Pont-En-Royans, Grenoble and the whole of Vercors Park, I felt as if Italy was calling me. I wanted to see it again, to spend a few hours visiting Cori with you, to see my grandparents' world again. I had them take me to Chambery, to take a train for Rome. Jadwiga went to Poland with Roza. So that's the story of how I arrived here by train. I have to leave tomorrow because I have an important appointment with a possible buyer for Fiorina's Boutique, while Flav and his family are staying another week in France."

Fiorina told me everything calmly, and just listening to the tone of her voice you could tell that she felt God's grace. Then for the greater part of the trip we travelled along in silence. Each of us must have had a million thoughts on our minds. We stopped so that we could enjoy the panoramic view of the Lake of Castel Gandolfo. Fiorina had never seen it, and she was enchanted by its beauty. As soon as we descended the mountainside that took us to Velletri, after a few kilometres, past the roundabout, you could see Cori sitting on the Lepini Mountains, which belong to the Anti-Apennines. I stopped the car and showed it to Fiorina.

She remained standing for a long time, silent. Then she looked at me, her eyes shiny with tears, and she managed to say: "The last time I saw my mother's home town I was at about the same distance, looking out the window of the train as I was leaving for Naples to get on the ship. Now it seems bigger to me than it did that day, which is strange."

We got back into the car. We both felt a bit shaken. Fiorina remained silent for a few kilometres. Maybe she wanted to touch the town of her childhood only emotionally, the town where she had been forced to become a woman through an act violence. After half a century, whatever she had buried inside of her couldn't just leave her as if nothing had happened. To me it seemed like a mirror, where the image of her soul and everything that it contained was reflected.

When we arrived in Cori it was already ten thirty. At the Buzzia[30], when Fiorina saw that the railway track was gone, she was dumbstruck. As I told her everything that had happened in the last years, she asked me to take her first to the cemetery. After half a century it was difficult to find the right spot, for many people had found their graves in that holy ground. She was not able to orientate herself. Then, as she walked slowly along the surrounding wall facing Cori, she found the place where her mother and father had been buried. There were no more graves. On that spot, other people had found their eternal rest. Now there was a chapel where people younger than

---

[30]Buzzia is a location along road between Velletri and Cori, four kilometres from Cori, which had a little train station.

her parents were buried. They were unknown to her. She sat down on the step of the chapel where a tombstone read "Husband and wife who always loved one another lie here." Today at the cemetery people are no longer buried underground – only some of the poorer people who have asked specifically to be buried in the ground instead of being placed in a hole in a cement wall.

Fiorina covered her eyes with her hands; she put her elbows on top of her knees and lowered her head as if she wanted to doze off. She remained like that for five or six minutes. I gazed at this beautiful old woman, with her long, shiny black hair, like a young girl's, sitting on a stone step in front of me. She had basically lived through everything, this woman who had Corese blood pumping through her veins from her mother's side. All that she had left from Cori were the dreams that she had kept in her mind. When she lifted her head, her eyes were all wet, but they seemed to smile and they were full of light. She got up and threw her arms around me and held me tightly.

"You're the only reason that I feel like I still have roots here in my mother's town. If it wasn't for you, I never would have come back to visit Cori. And yet inside this cemetery I feel like there's a part of me. Where did you scatter the dirt that I gave you?"

"I scattered it underneath an olive tree, exactly like you told me. I can show you the tree if you like."

"No, let's leave it a secret, that way it will be the secret that ties you to me. I'd like to try and find the tomb of a young child that was maybe six or seven years old when we were all evacuees in the mountains and who died in his mother's arms because he was sick. I know it's difficult but I'd like to try."

The cemetery had changed quite a bit, but Fiorina managed to find the tombstone. On the stone the suffering of the mother and child were engraved thus: "A.S. 1937-1944." Fiorina stopped in front of it for a moment in silence, lost in her thoughts, almost as if it were her child.

"I never told you that when this child died I was really upset about it and it has stayed with me all this time. One night, when I was anxious about so many things and thinking about that child, I told my mother that I had decided to keep mine, even if I was no more than a child myself when those evil soldiers raped me. And believe me when I say that I still carry this wound in my flesh. From now on, when you come and visit your dear ones, don't ever forget to come and visit this child. It's a way of remembering me and it's like visiting my dear ones."

I placed my arms around her waist and squeezed her to me as if I had said, yes, I promised to do what she wanted me to do. We started to head back very slowly, but first we stopped for a few minutes in front of my mother and father's grave.

"They were both good looking," said Fiorina as she gazed at the pictures of my parents. "You've got your father's eyes and your mother looks like Greta Garbo."

I didn't know what to say, but it was a real pleasure to hear her say it. A few minutes later and we are already at the Croce. I parked the car so that we could have a coffee and then we could make our way into town. Fiorina couldn't help but look around her. Everything was different from when she left. There was no bridge over the ditch that ran alongside the first houses in the town. Everything had been filled in by the ruins of the houses that had crumbled; and where they had been levelled, they'd built new houses, all around the old town. Even the ditch had been filled in and you could no longer go to the Pisciareglio, a little spring, and take the stairs that use to pass under the bridge. The cross, too, had been moved to a different place in the square of the Croce, so called for the cross that commemorated the mission of 1842. Fiorina told me that on the 8th of December 1937 she stood in front of that same cross with her mother and her grandparents, during the mission of the Passionist Friars, and now it was as if she didn't recognize it.

I started to think that it had been a bad idea, insisting that she come back and visit Cori. In half a century it had changed way too much. Little by little, as Fiorina walked she grew more silent, and sometimes she seemed tense, but most of the time she was happy. She recognized the places that she had walked by, the places where she had sat, the places that she had been to or visited with her mother or her grandmother. The shoe stores, food stores, the hairdresser and barber shops, carpenters, tailors, and the saddle makers no longer existed. Along the side streets one no longer saw animals, like donkeys and mules. One could no longer smell that awful odour of the droppings left behind when horses, donkeys and mules returned to town from the vineyards or orchards. There were few people, no children, but the walls were still the same. It didn't matter how many houses the war had destroyed or how the doors and barns had been modernized, those walls had stood for too many years, built when North America was populated only by native peoples.

Halfway down via Ninfina, Fiorina decided that she wanted to go back to Saint Maria in Cori Valley. She walked into the church. There was no one there. The Mass had ended and it seemed strange to Fiorina. She sat down on one of the benches and remained silent for a few minutes. When we left the church her eyes were shiny and moist with tears. She didn't even make the sign of the cross.

"No crossing yourself in church? Are you also a nonbeliever, like me?"

"I never go to church. I lost that custom and routine that had been given to me when I was a child, and which I had kept up until my father died. However, I often call upon God with my mind and heart. I talk to him, I ask for his help, and I ask that things not go the way they do; but he doesn't seem to hear me. Still, it gives me some comfort. I strongly believe that it doesn't end with our death. I don't know what is on the other side, or what we'll find when we close our eyes for the last time, but I am sure that I'll find my father, my mother and my grandparents. It just can't end with tears. And what about the bond that ties those who came before to those who will come after us? This is partly what convinced me to come back to visit and see these places, at least once more."

"To me it seems like we come from nothing, and I don't know why, maybe because after we're gone we go back to being just dust. But the things that you're saying are the same things that give me a lot to think about. Often I think about the time that passes and the fact that we don't know what it is, when and how it started and where it goes – if we are the ones who walk in and across time or if it's time that crushes us or seeps into us. Sometimes I think that in some mysterious way we are immortal in some Cosmic Being that's always existed and for some reason He holds us there and no one knows why – so that sometimes it makes us happy and sometimes it fills us with pain. But I'm with you."

"Let's go and see who's living at my house," Fiorina said.

Fiorina walked in the middle of all the old houses of Cori as calmly and securely as if she did it every day. At a certain point she stopped. She squeezed her hand on my arm. She remained lost in her thoughts as if she were trying to gather strength. Then she pointed to a door at the top of a little veranda whose stairs led down to the street.

"It's Mimma's house! I wonder if one of her relatives still lives there. Maybe a brother or a nephew. Maybe we should knock?"

"Let's knock; I'm sure that someone will open."

Instead of knocking, we rang the doorbell. There was a surname that was certainly not Corese. A man wearing a turban on his head and who barely spoke Italian opened the door. He was an Indian immigrant, and I must say that he treated us kindly. With a bit of difficulty, he finally understood that the house had once belonged to Fiorina's friends before she moved to Canada and that she just wanted to see it. Unfortunately, he wasn't able to tell us anything. The house was owned by a woman in her forties who lived near St. Francesco and he saw her only when she came to get the rent. We said goodbye. Fiorina didn't even hide the fact that she was clearly disturbed. She had had dinner in that house with Mimma's mother and brother half a century ago before leaving Cori.

A few steps later we came upon the home of Fiorina. The exterior was exactly the way she had left it. Only the door was different. Fiorina was really touched. She approached her old house. There was a foreign name on that doorbell as well. Maybe it was Dutch? We rang. A man in his forties with grey hair and ash-coloured eyes came to the door. He spoke using broken Italian as he asked us who we were looking for and what we wanted. Fiorina asked if he spoke English. When he said yes she continued talking in English and explained that half a century ago she had lived in that house, which had belonged to her family. She also explained that it was the first time that she was back to Italy and asked if we could take a quick look around what once was the kitchen.

The man, whose name was Kirk, let us in. He introduced us to a woman roughly in her thirties. Her face was pink toned, her eyes were the colour of ashes and her blond hair was tied at the back of her head in a braid. It was easy to see that she was setting the table for a meal. They invited us to join them. We certainly didn't want to bother them. They told us that they were just passing through because they were on vacation. They told us that the house was owned by some Danish friend who had gone to Denmark for a few weeks. Fiorina was full of emotions, especially when Kirk showed her the bedroom where she had slept that last night fifty years ago. Her eyes filled with tears. She went to the window and looked out. Then she took a deep long breath, almost as if she wanted to fill her lungs with that air that came from the sea.

After we left the house Fiorina told me that the breeze was exactly the same breeze that she used to breathe in as a little girl when she stayed at her grandparents' house. The house was completely different, but the cupboard and the big table in the kitchen were the same ones that she had left there years ago. The town wasn't what it was then, but the walls of the houses still retained the fatigue and the tears of life of thousands and thousands of souls who had taken refuge in those houses before. The town wasn't what it was back in the old days, and it wasn't just because of the foreigners living in her house and Mimma's. It was also in the silence that you could hear at that hour in Piazza Ninfina. There were no shops, no mules, and there were barely any people. Fiorina was even more disoriented when she spotted a steel door where her grandfather's shop had stood, where he sang opera arias, as he hammered away fixing butts. I told Fiorina that it was a parking garage. She was dismayed to see that the saddle makers were all gone and that no one hung olive branches on the doors of the wine cellar to advertise the retail sale of wine.

It had gotten late. We started to head back up Pizzidonico, then Piazza Pozzodorico, then Via delle Colonne, and then we headed down Via Pelasga, then the Caroccio and the Cacania to get to the Croce where we had left the car. In a flash we headed to Settecamini's Restaurant where I had a reservation for two, thanks to a quick phone call. Fiorina didn't know that there was a restaurant where, while you ate, you could see the whole town from San Rocco to San Pietro, all the way up to the Madonna del Soccorso, from the Ponte della Catena to San Francesco and the countryside all the way to Velletri and the sea. Fiorina didn't remember seeing all this. After we finished eating, we took the car to the Boccatora della Selova, the entrance to the woods of the Cori mountains, where she had fled to during the war.

"I never would have thought to come back to these places and to feel the breath of life that passed through my fingers. I walked these streets when I was just a girl and felt and lived many worries and pain, and now with you, and the mess that is going around in my memory! At least, I was able to free myself of everything that I went through. I think I should be happy with whatever my destiny gave me. I know far too well that for many others it wasn't like that."

"It's such a shame that you can't stay a little longer. I'd like to walk all over town with you, to show you the public library, take you to the museum, to the schools, to visit all the remaining churches; to bring you to Fontana Mannarina, to Vattiodro, to walk through the vineyards, and to let you get to know the people who live here now. I'd like for you to meet up again with everything that makes this town important and beautiful, but most of all what makes it *our* town."

"Up until I met you, I had forgotten everything, even if it was stored somewhere inside of me. It's like it came back little by little as I told you my story, until everything that was inside of me woke up. Believe me when I tell you that waking up the past is painful and a lot of hard work. Needless to say, I couldn't have done it without you and I'm grateful because at some point all of this gave me a sense of pleasure and peace – even now, albeit with some sadness and a bit of melancholy. I never would have thought to come back to Cori. Instead, here I am, and I must say that everything that I'm seeing is way more than enough for me. However, I would like to walk up to the Tempio d'Ercole, to see the train station, if it's still there. I'd also like to go to the Soccorso, but I don't think there's enough time."

"We can go and see the station and even the Soccorso. We can get there by car. When you left, to get to the Soccorso you could only go on foot, but now you can get there by car."

"Really?!"

"Of course. Now from Cori to Roccamassima there's a paved road that passes beside the sanctuary and a side road brings you basically in front of it. I'd like you to know that many of these things were done because I had made it a point of getting it done when I was councillor of the Province of Latina. Even the roads for Norma and Roccamassima were done."

"You made me tell you the story of my life, yet I don't know anything about you. When you come and visit me again, and I really hope you do, you have to tell me something about you."

"I promise!..."

Once we were in the car we went, first of all, to the Madonna del Soccorso. She was amazed to see that it was bigger than when she left. A new part of the structure had been added to the old one in the years after the war. Furthermore, it now offered rooms to tourists – men and women. The church was closed, but Fiorina wanted so badly to see the inside that I knocked on the friars' door. They were happy to open it and let us visit. Fiorina sat on one of the benches, and after a while she knelt down.

Outside the church we walked a few hundred metres down the long staircase that brought us all the way to the town. She wanted to go all the way to the Santamaria Penitence Chapel, which had been abandoned for some time. It was beside an olive grove, where Fiorina used to go with her family to eat fresh, warm ricotta and bread, before Cori became a disaster zone. Fiorina seemed to be really moved.

As we climbed up the stairs to get back to the car, I said: "I've never seen you make the sign of the cross or see you kneel in church, but in front of the Madonna you seemed to be praying..."

"While I sat there, suddenly in a flash everything came back to me, everything that I had been taught when I was a young child, the life I had lived. I can't tell you anything about God, or the Madonna and the saints. I haven't practiced at all the last years, even if I've always been a believer, just like I told you when we were at Santa Maria in Cori Valley, because I am convinced that an eternal light exists where we all go and where we all meet. It was as if a blade made out of flames had suddenly cut right through my flesh. In a flash I relived the whole Fontana Mannarina episode, where the whole tragedy began, and I felt an irresistible force that made me forgive those who had literally torn me apart.

"They remain bastards. I have cursed them for a whole lifetime; but they were just a bunch of unfortunate people too. Other wicked people, more powerful than they were, took them from their homes and sent them faraway, to kill other poor people who hadn't done a thing to them. They killed each other just to make few rich and power-ful people happy. Those who hurt me, only God knows if they ended up buried far away from their homes forever. Obviously, forgiving what has happened can't change it, but it changes the meaning and it makes you feel lighter and it's easier to look ahead. I had to return to Cori to put all these pieces together, to see the whole picture clearly."

I thought about Fiorina's life, and how hard, painful and difficult it had been in many ways. Yet, on the other hand, it was so full of energy that not even a big sea could contain it all, and her story was able to teach us to look at the world in all its details, good or bad. It had enriched me as a person and it was still enriching my soul.

Once we climbed down from the Madonna, we parked the car away from the Piazza San Pietro and we headed towards the piazza on foot. Almost all the people who we met said hello and often calling me by name. They looked at Fiorina curiously, tall and elegant, and they probably thought she was a foreigner. Everybody in Cori knew that often my friends from all over the world come to visit me. Instead, Fiorina was one of them, not only was she a half-blood Corese, but she had been forever marked by the air and the Corese dialect, and by the emotions that everyone keeps safe deep in their soul.

As we arrived in Piazza San Pietro, Fiorina was disappointed to see that they hadn't rebuilt the church. The town square was a lot bigger, but San Pietro Church wasn't there anymore. Only the steeple had been saved from the bombs. It was there, as if it kept the Tempio d'Ercole company, a reminder that there used to be a second church that had been reduced to dust and whose rubble had been used to fill up the lake that was on Cori Mount. It was also a reminder that the bombs had destroyed practically everything during high Mass one Sunday morning. On January 30, 1944, after the air raid, they found only one shoe belonging to the poor priest who had been saying the Mass. Fiorina remembered that Sunday quite well. I could still hear the sound of those bombs falling and exploding over and over again in my head.

Before Fiorina cast a last bitter look at the Tempio d'Ercole, she pointed to a group of young boys kicking around a soccer ball and said: "Even if we were to tell them a hundred times that where they were playing once stood a church and a piazza that was always full of people and animals, they would never believe us."

It was already five in the afternoon. We were walking under an arch that led from Piazza San Pietro to Via Marafini when suddenly Fiorina told me that she'd like to walk one last time alone from the Mount to the Valley. I understood from what she told me that she wanted to walk alone around the town streets, just as she had done the last day that she was in Cori before she left for Canada. I didn't know what to say or what to do. I tried to imagine what kind of thoughts were whirling around in Fiorina's head. We agreed to meet up at the Croce at six o'clock.

At Via Cavour we split up. Fiorina headed towards the Santa Anna Quarter, while I took a shortcut through where a woman named Ncicca once had her garden. I got to the Piazza Segnina quickly, where I stopped to chat with my usual friends for half an hour or so. Before six o'clock I went and waited for Fiorina at the Croce. I started to worry because at 6:30 I didn't see Fiorina anywhere. Another minute or so went by and suddenly she appeared. It was as if I suddenly got my sight back.

We stopped for a bit at Caffè Sterpetti. Fiorina drank an orange juice and I had a coffee. Fiorina felt quite flushed, partly due to the hot weather and partly because she had walked quickly all the way back for she had realized that she was late. She seemed calm and satisfied. She told me that she had wanted to go back and walk around the town, to breathe in all the scents and to better hear the sounds of the town. The stench of manure was long gone, as well as the aroma from the cellars. Silence had replaced the sounds from the carpenters and the shoemakers. The town, compared to how she left it, was completely different.

What had left her even more shocked was a place called Piglione. She remembered it being full of people. Some sat along the half-wall, or in front of the Celani Pharmacy or the other shops. She remembered the people who hurried about, those who went to work, those who were going home, and the men who were scattered about in the little square before and after work. Now, instead, there was no one. Only a barber shop with a few clients, which closed up early.

And yet, along these streets and in those different places she seemed to have found herself. She recognized the walls of the houses and the ones that were ruined or old, which seemed to want to fall on her with the weight of all the centuries. She also recognized what seemed like a singsong, hearing some people speak the dialect, which was hers, only a little stranger. Maybe because it wasn't only a dialect. Sometimes it was half Corese and half Italian. However, she heard the same speech pattern of her grandparents, which had stuck in her head.

At times it was as if she were dreaming. In the dream she saw herself as a young child and she seemed to see all those people she had never seen again. It was only when she saw me that she knew that she wasn't crazy and that she wasn't a ghost either, but really walking in those places that she hadn't seen for half a century, places that were making her feel nostalgic.

We went to the car and headed to Via della Madonnina. Reaching the chapel we turned on the road leading to the train station.

As we passed by the Madonnina, exclaimed with a bit of nostalgia: "*Mater Divini Amoris,* how many times did I pass in front of you with my grandparents and my mother, in front of this very chapel, to go to the vineyard that we had at the Vattiodro. I was taught to make the sign of the cross each time I passed by. I also passed in front of the chapel in that horrible month of May during the war. I remember it as if it were yesterday and my mother praying and saying to her, "Mother of God, Mother of God, my…what else is going to happen?"

We arrived at the railway bridge. As we started to turn right to go to the station, Fiorina saw the new buildings beside the arch and she exclaimed: "And what's this?"

"They are water towers that pump water to the whole town of Cori. Somewhere under there is a lake that gathers all the water from the mountains of Cori and some from even further off. As you already know, if you take away the Pisciareglio, Fontana Mannarina, all you have left is a lot of humid dirt or Capolemole, where you can barely have a drink. In Cori there isn't any other springwater. Then, thanks to all the tests here they found this holy water, which freed everyone from thirst.

In the meantime, we had arrived at the square in front of the station, which had now become a wide clearing full of craters. It looked like a dump. We got out of the car. Fiorina looked around her, somewhat wild-eyed. It also started to rain lightly. The last time she had been there the place was alive. The square hadn't been paved, but the gravel was really thin, as if it had been hammered by an artist. There was a bus that came by and turned here to head back to the town. After all, Cori was at least three kilometres away. The station no longer had a roof or windows, or doors for that matter, seeing how the doors were now only bricks. Around the station, on the side where the square was, there were thorns everywhere, debris, trash and the wall of the building in the direction of land called Carbonaro, already hidden by ivy. In a few more years most likely the ivy will consume it all. Even the railway warehouse was abandoned and had become the home of some poor soul. The tracks were gone.

Fiorina fell silent, speechless is a better term, and she grew sad. It was almost as if time, which had slowed for her, had suddenly sped up right before her eyes. I felt my heart grow smaller and smaller in front of all that abandonment. For eight years I myself had walked into that station almost every day to take the train to Velletri, where I went to middle school and high school, from September 1947 to July 1956. It was in that square at seven o'clock in the morning where I learned to play soccer with other boys just like me, using a tin can or a cloth ball that we all kicked around for half an hour while we waited for the train to arrive.

Fiorina and I looked at each other. There was no need for words to understand that half a century had gone by, to say that we were the same, and yet at the same time completely different. We had told each other once that we probably met here for the first time without knowing it, on the train that in those days linked the towns of the Lepini Mountains to Velletri and Rome. We could never have imagined that we would meet each other in front of that ruined building, which had once been the Cori train station, in front of that decay, in front of that disaster, having known each other really in another world. The drizzle turned to rain. In a few minutes we would have no choice but to go back inside the car. Fiorina hugged me and squeezed me tightly.

"Pietro, life's really gone by. All this being abandoned has made me clearly realize that we are only what we remember to be...we live only up until we remember it...or up until someone remembers us. When I die, after a while my dear grandparents, my father, and my mother will really be dead. But I also know now that I will continue to live as long as you remember me..."

Right in that precise instant, as if Jupiter himself wanted to tell us that she was pronouncing holy words, a lightning-bolt shot out of the sky as if it were noon, and the thunder that announced the arrival of a storm right over our heads made us both jump. I hugged Fiorina to my heart, to try and chase away those demons from the past that had seemed to grab hold of both of us, and to feel that bond that lately tied us together – a Corese half-blood who had come back to Cori for such little time after half a century and a full-blooded Corese who had left for ten years to earn a living but who had returned to Cori, just like a swallow returns to the nest. Every now and then he had left the nest to explore other worlds and other people, hungry to learn, unlike a bird that migrates to warmer climes.

The rain was already running down our faces and so we hopped back into the car. We headed quickly back to Cori. The tempest had officially arrived. The tiny drops had now turned into huge fat ones. It seemed as if they wanted to break the hood of the car. Before going to have dinner at the "Checchino" with Fiorina we went to say hello to my sisters, who lived on Via San Nicola, where my wife and kids were waiting after I made a phone call that afternoon. The weather had calmed down, even if there were heavy black clouds hanging over the marina still.

When Fiorina was just a girl on Via San Nicola there couldn't have been more than five or six houses, and from the Piazza Segnina further on there were only vegetable gardens and orchards. The street wasn't paved, and towards the marina there were long rows of elm trees as tall as a building. It was no longer that way. As soon as we reached the beginning of Via San Nicola, Fiorina seemed lost. But as soon as we were in my sisters' house, Fiorina realized where she was. When she was a child the street was known as Regina Elena and she knew it far too well, for she passed it to reach the shepherd's hut, or she had walked by the Cypress[31], or on her way to San Nicola Church. Maybe our paths had crossed as she went back and forth, because I was always there on the street playing with my friends.

As always, as soon as I get to my sisters' house it seems like there's a party greeting me. This time the party was also for the one who arrived with me. Fiorina was most impressed by the two little trees of rosemary. Beside the second one, there was a nice mint plant. Fiorina stuck her face in the plant to smell it.

"I haven't smelled this scent in a long time. A little piece of paradise. It is what was missing to complete the masterpiece. I need this fragrance to relieve all the anxiety and the emotion of my visit. My destiny was to live far away, in another city where people talk in a different way, and there I must return. My life is there now. I have my son, my granddaughter and the house that holds everything, where I've lived all my pleasures and pains. You have to believe me when I say that all the fragrances of this return home are all gathered in this bush of rosemary. This scent will remain in my head 'til the day I die, like a bittersweet cry. My grandmother and my mother couldn't live without mint or rosemary."

My sisters took a liking to Fiorina. They insisted that we stay to eat. My nephews also came down to the piazzetta, the little square in the garden adjacent to the house. They went and bought several

[31]Cypress, in Corese slang procésso, is a landmark along the road to San Nicola Church.

trays of pizza and they made the panzanella.[32] It really did turn into a feast. We didn't get to Fiorina's hotel room in Rome until one in the morning. We couldn't do anything else but say our goodbyes.

During the car ride back to Rome from Cori, she told me that after the dinner at the piazzetta of Via San Nicola and then being at my sisters' house with my sisters, my nephews, my wife and my kids she could leave feeling calm. But a piece of her soul remained attached to what she had seen around Cori – the scent of rosemary and mint, the raindrops that had bathed her face in front of the abandoned station swallowed up by ivy and without any trace of tracks, and that big and festive family that surrounded me with so much warmth. That taste she really did miss. She said good-bye with a kiss on my lips, as sweet as honey and as tender as the fresh soft white cheese that my mother used to give me when I was a young child.

"If you can, come visit me in Toronto. I don't think that I will have the strength or the occasion to come back to Cori ever again."

---

[32]Panzanella is a large slice of stale bread soaked in water and seasoned with salt, oil, tomato and basil.

XXIX

Epilogue

Once I had said goodbye to Fiorina, I was like a zombie on the trip back from Rome to my house. In my mind everything that Fiorina had told me seemed to replay. I also realized that that story would never ever leave me. Fiorina would remain forever inside my soul.

After that night, I saw Fiorina again on several occasions in Canada. The warmth between us was always the same. Flav had moved to Montreal to be with his wife and daughter. Fiorina had remained in Ontario, in the same house in Toronto. She had remained with Jadwiga in that big house where at least ten people could live comfortably. The last time I saw her she told me that she had made her will. She left everything that she had to her granddaughter, except for the house, which she left to Jadwiga. A certain sum of the remaining money she had left to companies that gave donations and assistance to orphans or to women in difficulty, sometimes young girls with kids, with no husbands, or to those who had been raped, or were without money, or to immigrants.

She told me that Flav, Martine and Claire visited her often. She was happy that Martine, although young, was already well known as a doctor. She was tall, beautiful, intelligent and stubborn. She said she took mostly after her mother, and if she put something that she wanted to do in her head, the whole world could crumble, but Martine would do it.

The last time we met she insisted on bringing me to her cottage near Midland for two days. After all, she was about to sell it and there wouldn't be another occasion to spend some peaceful, quiet hours in a place that was so beautiful. When I woke in the morning I would find her ready to have breakfast after her usual morning jog or brisk walk through the woods. She pampered me like royalty for two days. Yet, Fiorina wasn't the same. Sure she was still beautiful and elegant, but when I left I had to admit that she appeared a bit older, thinner and in discomfort. She was still considerate and good to me. But the last two years that had passed seemed more like ten.

Not even a year had passed when I received a package in the mail in the last days of July. It had been sent by Martine P. from Montreal. Inside I found the book containing Shakespeare's tragedies that Vahan had given to Fiorina, and a letter from Martine. All the times that I had been to Canada I had never met Martine, who instead seemed to know everything about me, as it was easy to gather from what she wrote in her letter. She wrote also on behalf of her father. Fiorina had died a month before in the Santa Cabrini Hospital in Montreal due to a pancreatic disease. She had been assisted up until the end by Claire. She had had her daughter-in-law, granddaughter, Flav and Jadwiga by her side until the day she died. In only five days that horrible disease had destroyed her. She left this world chatting calmly away with them.

The day before she died she had expressly told Martine to welcome me like family every time I was in Canada, to send me the book of Shakespeare's tragedies as a special souvenir so that I wouldn't forget her. She had also told Martine to write that every time that I went to visit my mother and my father in the cemetery, I had to think about her. They had buried her in the cemetery in Montreal. There was no sense in bringing her body back to Toronto because they all lived in Montreal. Jadwiga had decided to sell the house that Fiorina had left her and was moving back to Wadowice in Poland, with the intention of buying and opening a bar in the square of the town.

Martine concluded by saying that I was a special person for her, due to the strong and unique bond that I shared with her grandmother. She would be happy to meet me. Her house, along with Claire and Flavio's, was also my house every time that I wanted to go to Montreal.

I couldn't hold back the tears any longer. What a destiny, Fiorina! She was gone forever! What had prevailed, the can be or the cannot be, the truth or the false, the good or the bad, the sweet or the sour, it's the same for everybody. Only Fiorina had lived that life. Born in Cori, Corese blood and a Corese life, her childhood and school days in Rome, a violent destiny full of bitter pains and sweet joys, half a century spent in Toronto and buried in Montreal.

I dried the tears that had completely soaked my face. I sat down on a tree stump in my garden. The world had lost its colour.

Other Works by Pietro Vitelli

Il primo italiano in Canada, storia del missionario F.G.Bressani, 1992

Amori di carta e inchiostro, 1992

Acrostici consiliari, 1993

Jo munno itèrza sta ncóra mméso a nnu, 1994

Amore parola al plurale, 1994

Muta il colore del tempo, 1995

Libro dei limerick a Cori e Giulianello, 1997

Parole dduci e mmare, Primo dizionario corese-italiano, 1997

Poesie russe, 1998

Tra il sogno e la memoria, 2000

Addio dolce Abruzzo, 2002

Canto d'amore per Lilli, 2002

Haiku, viaggio della memoria da Maenza ad Auschwitz, 2004

Enrico Tonti – Gaeta, Italia 1647-Mobile, Alabama, USA, 1704, Padre dell'Illinois, dell'Arkansas e della Louisiana, signore per venti anni della Valle del Mississippi, 2004

Cori-Pefki, città gemelle, 2006

Uci e parole réntro mmine, Dizionario Corese-Italiano, 2006

Fiorina, storia di una donna nel vento – da Cori a Toronto, guerre, stupri, emigrazione, famiglie, amori, 2008

Il nuovo e l'antico, poesie e canzoni, 2009

Quadri Canadesi/Canadian Images, 2011

Canto d'amore per Lilli/Pieśń miłości do Lilli, 2013

Giovanni Caboto, Francesco Giuseppe Bressani, Enrico Tonti – Protagonisti della scoperta, dell'esplorazione e dell'insediamento europeo in nord America, 2014

Sommario d'appunti di cronaca corana (1878-1948), 2015